Becoming Americana

Becoming Americana

Lara Rios

BERKLEY BOOKS, NEW YORK

THE BERKLEY PUBLISHING GROUP
Published by the Penguin Group
Penguin Group (USA) Inc.
375 Hudson Street, New York, New York 10014, USA
Penguin Group (Canada), 90 Eglinton Avenue East, Suite 700, Toronto, Ontario, M4P 2Y3, Canada
(a division of Pearson Penguin Canada Inc.)
Penguin Books Ltd., 80 Strand, London WC2R 0RL, England
Penguin Group Ireland, 25 St. Stephen's Green, Dublin 2, Ireland (a division of Penguin Books Ltd.)
Penguin Group (Australia), 250 Camberwell Road, Camberwell, Victoria 3124, Australia
(a division of Pearson Australia Group Pty. Ltd.)
Penguin Books India Pvt. Ltd., 11 Community Centre, Panchsheel Park, New Delhi—110 017, India
Penguin Group (NZ), Cnr. Airborne and Rosedale Roads, Albany, Auckland 1310, New Zealand
(a division of Pearson New Zealand Ltd.)
Penguin Books (South Africa) (Pty.) Ltd., 24 Sturdee Avenue, Rosebank, Johannesburg 2196, South Africa

Penguin Books Ltd., Registered Offices: 80 Strand, London WC2R 0RL, England

This book is an original publication of The Berkley Publishing Group.

Cover illustration by Lisa Henderling.
Cover design by Rita Frangie.
Text design by Kristin del Rosario.

PRINTING HISTORY
Berkley trade paperback edition / November 2006

Library of Congress Cataloging-in-Publication Data
Rios, Lara.
Becoming Americana / Lara Rios.—Berkley trade pbk. ed.
p. cm
ISBN 0-425-21191-6 (alk. paper)
1. Women immigrants—Fiction. 2. Mexicans—United States—Fiction. 3. Women college students—Fiction. 4. Los Angeles (Calif.)—Fiction. I. Title.
PS3618.I567B4 2006
813'.54—dc22

2006020047

PRINTED IN THE UNITED STATES OF AMERICA

10 9 8 7 6 5 4 3 2 1

To all the young girls who are struggling
to rise above their life's challenges.

Remember that it's up to you
to create the future you want and deserve.

Acknowledgments

This book required that I do some research in a world with which I was not familiar. I have to thank:

Kathy Bennett at the L.A.P.D. for your online class and for answering specific questions. And my friend Theresa—thank you for your input, as difficult as it was for you to share. If I got anything wrong, I apologize.

Huge thank-you to my publishing team: my wonderful agent, Caren, and everyone at Berkley—from my terrific editors, Cindy and Leis, to my very thorough copy editor and awesome cover designer!

My mother and brother, who always buy the most books at my book signings, and then force everyone they know to read them (and no, for all who ask, I never base my characters on my family—especially this one!). Thank you for your never-ending support. I love you!

And lastly, my husband, who alters his life daily to support my career.

Thank you all!

Becoming Americana

One

For Mexican families, Americanization often means that family ends up taking a back seat to survival or success.

LUPE PEREZ

Occasionally, we say things we don't necessarily want printed. Especially in a university newspaper where twenty-five thousand of your not-so-close friends can read it and learn details of your life you wouldn't confess to your priest.

As I waited in line to pick up a financial aid check, I paged through UCLA's *Daily Bruin.* On the third page I saw my name, read the first paragraph, and nearly dropped my backpack, the newspaper, and my eyeballs.

> Lupe Perez is the American Dream come true. A poor immigrant, forced to live in the slums of East L.A. and to resort to violence and crime for survival, overcomes her tragic childhood and makes the grade.

"The line's moving, girl," said this chick behind me.

I stared at the article. It was *all* about *me.* About how some people can succeed no matter what obstacles they have to overcome. About The Vibe, the center where I volunteer to help at-risk kids. About how I saved Tracey's life a few weeks ago. "Shit," I said. "I'm going to kill her."

My new sort-of friend Tracey recently got jumped on the way to one of the UCLA parking lots, and I happened to be there to help her out. She's the one responsible for the humiliating article, I'm sure of it.

"Are you going or not?" The annoyed girl behind me crossed her arms and jutted out her hips.

"Sorry," I said. I got out of line and went in search of Tracey.

Not sure where to find her, I dialed her cell.

She picked up on the first ring.

"Where are you?" I asked, doing my best to keep my impatience in check.

"Lupe? I'm in a history lecture. Bored to death," she whispered. Cell phones weren't allowed during lectures.

"Where? What building?"

"Royce Hall. What's up?"

"I'll meet you outside by the fountain when your class is over."

"Okay. I've got about another forty-five minutes."

"Fine." I hung up and headed to Royce Hall. When I got there, I sat on the ledge of the half-circle fountain to read the article more thoroughly. I couldn't believe it. Why would she do something like this? I *trusted* her. Though why, I don't know.

We met only about eight weeks ago—that fateful day in the parking lot. After putting in a whole day at the university, I'd been exhausted and was going home, willing my legs to initiate the trek to the parking lot. As I was about to reach the structure, a guy on a bicycle zoomed past me, almost knocking me on my butt. But my heavy boots kept me upright. I felt like one of those heavy-bottomed, blow-up punching dolls that always bounce back up. "Hey, you jerk! Watch out," I yelled. But whomever it was didn't apologize. He headed straight toward Tracey, who was walking a few yards ahead, rode up close to her, and snagged her purse strap right off her shoulder.

She'd screamed and struggled to hold on to her purse, but the jerk kicked her in the stomach and pedaled away with her purse.

I'd hurried to help her to her feet, and let her use my cell phone to call for a ride, since her car keys had been in her purse. I'd hung out with her and made small talk until help arrived, because she'd been a basket case. Basically, I was just a Good Samaritan. But she's been trying to thank me ever since.

I snapped the newspaper in my hand. If this was her idea of gratitude, she was going to be set straight once and for all.

I glanced at the Royce Hall entrance when the door sprang open and students poured out. Tracey had a confident stride as she moved toward me with a bright, cheery smile. I held the paper up to her flawless, Barbie face.

"Oh, my God. It's out." She took the paper, thrilled, and sat by the fountain where I'd been waiting for her. She read the article then turned to me with a huge smile.

"What are you smiling about? Are you responsible for this?"

"I have a friend who writes for the paper. I told him the story and—"

"You had no right to do that."

"But Lupe, your story is—"

"Mine. And I didn't need it blasted all over the damn paper."

"But, I don't understand. Why don't you want to encourage others who have had a tough life?"

I do, but on my turf, my way. "How is my personal business going to help anyone else? You took information that was private, that I shared with you, and *published* it."

She stood, her face losing all its humor. "Look, I'm sorry. But you should be thanking me here."

"Are you kidding?"

"No, Lupe. Some appreciation for the article would be nice. We had to pull some strings to get that piece in the paper, you know? I'm trying to help you."

"Of all the arrogant, offensive, condescending things you've said and done, this one tops them all." The first stupid thing she'd done was offer to pay me for helping her that night in the parking lot, like I was a damn servant who deserved a tip. "Do me a favor. Stop helping me."

She crossed her arms and looked down her nose at me. "Fine."

Tracey is totally stuck up, but she also means well. She really does. She's one of these nice white people that think we "people of color" have been given a bad shake in life and need a hand up.

And I'm one of those "people of color" who wants to tell them to shove their charity up their . . . anyway, Tracey and I have done nothing but clash since the day we met.

Disgusted with the whole thing, I tossed the paper at her feet and stormed away to work the evening shift at the Mexican joint in Ackerman Union—my contribution for the financial aid I receive.

I almost made it to the food court without being stopped, but before I entered the building, an instructor called my name.

"Lupe, I read the article in the paper, and the part about becoming Americanized is very interesting. Have you got a minute?"

I never have any minutes, but I nodded. Dr. Reyes teaches sociology and for some unknown reason seems to like me. He's always suggesting scholarships I might qualify for or job opportunities I might be interested in when I graduate. Since I like him too, I stopped to listen to what he had to say.

But as soon as he says, "I enjoyed the article," I realize he has nothing to say that I care to listen to.

"Glad my pathetic life is entertaining so many people."

He grinned, and his grayish beard, which is cut nice and trim, stretched across his chin. "I'm curious about what you said in there regarding the Americanization of ethnic minorities."

"Actually, I didn't 'say' anything in the article. I wasn't interviewed."

"But you did tell your friends that Americanization is a nonterm?"

"I did. But I didn't realize Tracey was going to—"

"I found that statement a bit controversial. I wonder if you can explain what you mean."

Okay, one day while getting to know each other Tracey and Madison kept repeating how great it was that I was able to become Americanized so quickly. At the time I wondered if that was synonymous with civilized, the way they were talking. Rather than state the obvious, that I've been "American" since the day I was born, I'd said that "Americanized" was a nonterm because as the United States absorbs more and more immigrants, what is considered "American" changes.

But now Dr. Reyes was staring at me and expecting some great philosophical oral dissertation. Damn the pressure.

"Well," I said and shrugged, "for instance, it's not unusual for non-Mexicans to have piñatas at their parties. At least in California, it's become part of the American culture of parties. It's also not unusual for Anglos to eat tamales during Christmas. Not that I know many Anglos that well, but I used to see them buying tamales from a lady who would come to my high school and take orders from teachers."

"So, you're saying that the immigrants are not becoming Americanized, but that America is changing and adapting to the influx of immigrant groups?"

"A little of both, yes." I mean, what the heck is American? "It's always been that way in this country. It changes and adapts to incoming immigrants. It's what makes America so cool. We're always growing and changing. Where other countries might buckle under the added pressure and stress, we adapt and become stronger."

Dr. Reyes stared at me like he was way too impressed and I wanted to pull my tongue out of my mouth. *Shut up, shut up, shut up.*

We strolled across campus, toward his office but away from Ackerman. I was going to be late to work. "Lupe," he said, slipping sunglasses on a face deep in concentration, "I have a suggestion for you. I'd like you to expand on this idea and write a thesis for a book."

"You want *me* to write a book?" Was he serious? *Quick, say something stupid.*

"I'm a mentor and advisor for the academic honors program. I'd like you to join that program and complete the thesis."

Oh, man. I don't need anything else to do. "But why—?"

"I was a lot like you when I was young, Lupe. I worked hard during a time when there were few Latino minorities in colleges. Trust me when I tell you that you'll never regret doing this."

In his office, he gave me the information. All I had to do was expand upon an idea that I'd never really considered. Piece of cake, right? "Will this raise my grade point average?" I asked.

"No, but you'll graduate with honors."

Since I still feel I have to prove to the world that I'm good enough, grades and tags like "honors" mean a lot to me. I sat down and filled out the forms he gave me. What the heck, who needs sleep anyway.

El Sombrero Gordo sits between Pizza Hut and a salad bar in the campus food court. I get the most customers, even with a lame name like the Fat Hat. I swear, some white guy must have named this place. How stupid. But the college kids don't care. Every night, they load up on greasy tacos and fatty burritos.

I dish up canned refried beans and nasty rice. That's my job. I hate it, but I don't have a lot of options. I'm not rich and my parents wouldn't have given me money for college even if they'd had it. I was supposed to be working and contributing to the family. Instead, I was going to college and living off them.

So to make up for being such a disappointment, I usually hurry home when I get off work and bring my parents dinner. They let me take as much food as I want from here because, after all, what are they going to do with these nasty leftovers?

"Hey, Lupe."

As I stirred the tray of beans and wiped the counter clean, I heard my name and looked up to find a cute guy I've never met before smiling up at me.

I sized him up the way I do most people. I can't help it. The minute I see someone it's like my brain goes into scan mode and starts picking out details.

With him, I saw a clean-cut, very graceful, classy looking guy. You know how some people don't do anything in particular to appear a certain way, they just are? Well, he was just standing there, not doing anything out of the ordinary, but everything about him said class. The only thing that made him sort of approachable was that he had this shy, vulnerable thing going that reminded me of the actor Josh Hartnett.

"Hi. Mexican today?" I asked, pointing at the steaming food in metal trays.

He shook his head and stared at me like he was doing a scan of his own, only it was masculine and intimate and made me want to run to the back and change my boring clothes and definitely lose the hairnet.

"No. Thank you," he said.

"I don't blame you. I can't stand the smell of this food when I leave here."

He grinned. "And will that be anytime soon?"

"Will *what* be anytime soon?"

"When you get to go home for the night."

"Yes, thankfully, I'll be released from servitude in less than ten minutes."

"Great. I'll wait."

I frowned, not understanding.

"I'm Will, by the way."

Another guy, a football-type who towered over the handsome Will, walked up behind him, so I raised an eyebrow at the guy. "Ready?"

"Yeah, I'll take the taquito plate and a large Coke."

I scooped up the beans, the rice, and tossed three taquitos onto the plate. "Six forty nine."

He handed me a ten-dollar bill, and I gave him his change and food.

Will waited patiently for me to finish.

I wondered why.

"I'm Will *Preston*," he said when the guy with the taquitos walked away, stuffing one in his mouth before he'd even left the counter.

"You said that already," I said.

"Name doesn't mean anything to you, huh?"

I searched my memory and frowned. "Should it?"

"I wrote the article in the *Daily Bruin.*" He inched closer to the counter. "About you."

Ah. Okay. Got it.

"I'm Tracey and Madison's friend and—"

"You were the one who did them the *favor* and got the article in the paper."

He sank his hands into his pockets. "And I hear you weren't pleased."

"Your writing was good. It's the topic that sucked."

A corner of his lips quirked up. "When Tracey shared what happened in the parking lot and how you saved her—"

"I didn't save her. She wasn't in any danger."

"Not how she tells it."

If she only knew I identified with the thief much more than I did with the likes of her. I knew about desperation. A few years ago, I might have been the one to steal her purse and run. And now she wants to make me out to be a hero. What a crock. "So, what, do I get a chance to sue you or something for writing about me without my permission? Is there some kind of journalism law that says you can't do that?"

He appeared to be amused. "Only if I damaged your character in some way."

He did. He made me sound like a saint. "My shift is over. I need to wash up and get out of here."

"I'll wait. Walk you to your car."

"That's okay. I can manage on my own. I'm Wonder Woman, remember?"

"I can print a follow-up story. Interview you. Get your point of view in, if you feel I didn't do you justice."

I yawned. Damn, I was tired, and in no mood to deal with anyone or anything else tonight. "You want a follow-up? Here it is: My life isn't a fairy tale with a happy ending. I've gotten jumped about a dozen times. My nose was broken twice, left leg once. I've tried just about every drug out there, and spent four months in a juvenile detention camp." I pegged Will with a cool look, which I've totally mastered by the way. "And I still go home every night wondering if I'll get stabbed or shot. I don't need anyone romanticizing what it's like to grow up being me. It sucks."

I left before he had a chance to respond. Stupid *guero.*

I got about fifty feet across Bruin Plaza when Will caught up with me.

"Hey, I didn't mean to insult you. And neither did Tracey."

"What, I should be grateful that you both had nothing better to do than strip me naked and push me out for the world to see?" I kept walking.

Out of my peripheral vision I noticed him checking me out. Maybe I shouldn't have provided him the image of me being naked.

"You should have heard her talking about you. How great you were, how cool you were with the police when you gave the report, how safe and grateful *she* felt that you stopped to help her out."

I glared at him from the corner of my eye. "Stopped? I was walking right by her. What was I supposed to do?"

"Point is, she just wanted to say thank you and let everyone know how awesome you were."

"Great. She did. Now go find your girlfriend, celebrate your good deed, and leave me alone."

"If you're implying that Tracey is my girlfriend, she's not."

We passed Pauley Pavilion, where a sporting event had things jumping tonight. Wish I had the time to hang out and enjoy college life like other students. At least every once in a while.

"In fact, I don't have a girlfriend," he said, walking by my side. "I've been watching *you* for a long time. Gotta admit that I agreed to do the article for the chance to meet you."

I shook my head. "Spare me. Please."

"What?" He laughed. "You don't believe me? I sit a few rows back from you in Cultural Ethics. I've been watching you all quarter, and thought you were hot since day one."

"Right." I'm not the "hot" type, trust me. With two plump parents you'd think I'd have some curves, but I don't. I'm small, I'm thin, and my favorite fashion is jeans and comfortable cotton tops. Not exactly dripping sex appeal here, you know?

"I'm serious."

We made it to the parking lot, and I stopped and faced him. "Why didn't you introduce yourself earlier?"

"You seemed so tough and unapproachable, and I'm a chicken."

That did it. He got me to smile. "Look, tell Tracey everything's cool. Thank her for her . . . gesture. Okay? And don't worry. I won't sue you." I took the steps down into the parking structure and he followed me to my bike, a 1993 Yamaha TDM850.

"You ride this thing?" he asked, clearly surprised.

"Yeah." I'm not a biker chick or anything, I was just lucky enough to get this bike for a couple thousand dollars. It gets me around. It has a couple of side bags for my stuff. It's got good tires, and it's sort of cute with blue and purple trim. Someday I'll get a car, but for now this is all I can afford. Besides, since it's the first vehicle I've ever owned, it sort of holds a special place in my heart.

"How about a ride?" Will asked.

"I've got to get home. Besides, why would I give a ride to a guy who writes lies about me?"

He crossed his arms. "Lies? Maybe you're being a little modest."

"Maybe you should interview the person you're writing about and get their side of the story before you print it."

"I'd like to. Let's go out for coffee."

"Forget it."

"Why are you so upset? Really?"

"I don't know," I snapped. "Maybe because I'm finally in a place, at a university where I can be like the rest of American society, and I don't want to be singled out. I don't want to be reminded of all the garbage I've been through."

"I understand. Tell you what, let's burn the darn article."

"Okay. Whatever." I unlocked my helmet.

"Have you got a copy? Give it to me." He reached out a hand.

"Now?"

"Sure. Come on." He pulled out a lighter.

I was starting to think he was a little crazy, but I reached into my backpack and gave him a copy of the school paper.

He lit the newspaper, holding it out at arm's length. It went up in flames, and he let it go just as the fire started licking at his fingertips.

"Whoo," he said. "Done. Now, how about that ride?"

I shook my head, my mouth sort of hanging open.

"Come on. Drop me off in Sunset Village, I live in the residential buildings there. My roommate will give me a ride back in the morning," he added.

I really wasn't sure what to make of this guy. "Ever ride a bike before?"

He looked self-conscious. "No. But I'd like to."

"Mmm." I didn't have an extra helmet, so I handed him mine. "Put it on and climb up," I said.

"You should wear the helmet. You're driving."

"We both should, but I've only got one. Wear it."

He didn't argue. After he had the helmet strapped on, he got behind me and wrapped his arms around my waist. I didn't like the way his larger body draped over mine. I felt trapped, smothered, uncomfortable.

So I turned the key and shifted into gear. The bike started, rumbling to life, greeting me like a gruff old friend. I liked controlling all that power beneath me. I left the university grounds carefully. I've already gotten two tickets for speeding. Jerks—university police are the worst for harassing drivers.

But once we hit Sunset Boulevard, I took Will for a nice, fast ride. He held on tighter, but I was sure he wasn't thinking any thoughts of how "hot" I was. I slowed down when I circled back into university grounds.

He got off as soon as I parked in front of Sproul Hall, and pulled the helmet off. "Woo hoo," he said. "You know how to drive that thing."

"Didn't scare you, did I?" A small, evil part of me hoped I had.

"Shit, yeah."

I smiled. He was cute. "So how do you know Tracey?" I asked as he handed me back my helmet.

We stood on the sidewalk. He dropped his hands into his pockets and smirked. "I did a stint as an Internet sports broadcaster and used to go watch the women's water polo matches last year. Tracey was good, so I interviewed her a few times. Then we all started hanging out. In the meantime, I decided I sucked as a sports broadcaster." As he spoke, his hazel eyes sparkled.

We stared at each other for a few moments.

"Well, thanks for the ride," he said.

"No problem." I climbed back on my bike.

"And sorry about the article."

"I'll try and forgive you. See you around."

He nodded. "You bet."

The first chapter for the book Dr. Reyes wanted me to write could easily be titled "Disintegration of the Latino Family." For Mexican families, Americanization often means that family ends up taking a back seat to survival or success. And my family was a prime example.

When I got home, I had to step around my brother, Carlos, and his criminal friends sitting on the porch steps. Great. I reached for a stick of gum. Just what I needed after my long day, which still required hours of studying before it was over. My brother had been out of jail for about six months and had picked up right where he'd left off. Dealing.

One of the men sitting with Carlos, a guy with a bald head and who probably weighed about three hundred pounds, grabbed my ankle. His hand climbed provocatively up the inside of my jean-clad leg.

"Let go," I warned.

"Hey baby, come on, how 'bout a little fun?" He smelled strongly of cologne and had a look in his eyes that made my skin crawl.

After momentary panic that I've learned how to control, I pried his hand off me. "Don't make me have to break your fingers. Keep your paws off me."

As I tried to hurry toward the door, he stood and blocked my way. "Hey," he said, adding a sick smile. "*Qué pasa*? Stay out here. Sit with us, *Míja.*"

I glanced at my brother, not that I expected any help from him. But he knew there wasn't a chance in hell I'd sit outside with his druggie friends. Carlos lit a cigarette and eyed me through the cloud of smoke he exhaled. He leaned back on the wrought iron fence that led from the street up the walk to my porch. He wore jeans and a white sleeveless T-shirt that showed off all his tattoos and heavy muscles—not a bad-looking guy. Too bad that on the inside he was a corrupt, evil bastard.

And since I was his favorite victim, I popped the gum in my mouth and braced myself for a new battle scar.

Two

Becoming Americana means you must break away from family and cultural traditions that are not embraced by mainstream America.

LUPE PEREZ

I turned my attention back to Carlos's friend, figuring I'd have better luck reasoning with him than relying on my brother to stand up for me. "Look, I'm not interested, *Entiendes?*"

"I might convince you to get interested, *niña,*" he drawled, reaching across and pinching my nipple through my shirt and bra before I realized what he was doing.

"Ouch." I shoved him hard out of my way. "*Pendejo.*" I tried to escape inside, but he grabbed my arm, making me drop my backpack.

All three guys laughed, including Carlos.

I ignored them and began recovering my things. Then baldy bent down and reached for the books. "You're a smart girl, huh?"

"I like to think so." I met his gaze.

"I could make life very easy for you, *mi'ja.* Very easy."

I bet he could. When a girl has a needle in her arm, she doesn't care what goes on around her. "Can I have my books back, please?"

"Beautiful and polite and down on your knees. Mmm." He licked his filthy lips. "Carlos, you didn't tell me your sister was so tempting."

"Must have slipped my mind."

I glared at Carlos.

"She's off limits, though," he said as he looked down the V of my shirt. "*Déjala.*"

Baldy had a hard enough time lifting his own body, but he picked up my bag as well and handed it to me. "Nothing is off limits if you want it bad enough. Remember that, *Querída.*"

I escaped into the house as my brother said something filthy and they all laughed again.

My mother sat in front of the TV eating some cottage cheese. I felt guilty for not bringing any food tonight. She got home between eight and nine at night and was too tired to cook. My father was already in bed.

"You've got to get Carlos off the porch. He sits out there conducting business until three in the morning, *Mami.* The cops are going to bust him again."

"Where have you been?"

"Studying," I lied. Just like I lied when I came home late the day Tracey got jumped. Last thing I wanted to tell her that night was that I was giving a police report. In this house, that was cooperating with the enemy. And tonight, I didn't want to share that I went on a ride through campus with a *guero.* "So you're going to let his garbage start again?"

"He's your brother. What am I supposed to do?" She placed her bowl on the coffee table.

I picked up the bowl and headed to the kitchen. "Throw his ass out," I said over my shoulder.

"I won't do that."

My mother was hopeless and my father even more so. Women were not to question men. And I had already been disloyal because I had testified against Carlos the last time he beat the crap out of me when he was trippin' on some acid.

"Well, I've got more reading to do tonight so I better get to it," I said as I walked back into the living room after washing her dish.

She turned back to the TV with a sigh. She pretty much resents the hell out of me for going to college. All of my family does. To them, too much education is a waste of time and money. Like my mom says, if I spent the four years at Wal-Mart rather than UCLA, at the end of that time I could be a manager instead of a new graduate with no money and no job. Maybe she's right. Who knows?

"Anything you want me to do first?" I asked.

She waved her hand in the air as if to say, "don't bother."

"Well, okay. Good night then."

My mother doesn't react much. She never has. Working all day at a clothing factory drains her of most energy. I wish I could say that I know she loves me even though she's not affectionate, but I'm not so sure. I'm pretty much on my own, and maybe I need to start thinking of moving out.

As I lay in bed reading my biology textbook, I heard Carlos and his buddies talking outside. I remember when we were kids and played with our neighbors from across the street—eight-year-old twins, Christina and Freddy. I was about five and Carlos was about eleven. Carlos liked being the oldest, the ringleader, and he always wanted to show off. So whether we played tag or hide-and-seek or red-light, green-light, he always teamed up with the neighbors against me. I think he didn't like his little sister hanging around him. Most of the time, I'd end up running home, crying to Mom while he and his friends laughed. Sort of like tonight.

But one day, he and I were on the same team along with one of the neighbor kids. We were playing dodgeball, and poor little Freddy was getting beamed by my brother, Christina, and me. Freddy was about to start crying when Christina kicked the ball out of my brother's hands, and then sent a second flying kick to Carlos's back, startling him and knocking him down. The twins ran away together, holding hands.

Carlos was fuming, and he called after them that he would kick both their butts next time. I remember thinking how lucky Freddy was that his sister took his side in the end and stood up for him. Carlos would never do that for me.

I held out my hand to help him up, even though I was half his age. He stood on his own and shoved me away.

Things only got worse as we grew older.

I closed my book and looked out my window. I didn't trust him. He hated me, and I knew he was just waiting for the opportunity to get back at me for what I'd said in court. This weekend I'd start looking for a new place to live. But where, and I how could I afford my own place?

Sunday mornings I always attend the family gatherings at my friend Marcela's house. Her family has sort of become the family I've never had, wished I'd had, and definitely should have had, if life were even the slightest bit fair.

Usually I got to their adorable home in the valley early and helped Marta, my substitute mother, cook until Marcela got there with her husband, George. Then Marta would shoo me out of the kitchen and her other daughters would continue to help as they arrived.

Today was tamale day though, so everyone helped out. We made an assembly line in the small kitchen, which was decorated with sunflowers and bordered with vines. Last Christmas I bought Marta an Aztec sun clock that she placed right above the window over the sink. The room was cheery and bright and probably my favorite in the house.

For the tamales, I prepared the corn husks and gave them to Katie, Marcela's youngest sister. She spread the cornmeal on the corn husks and passed them to Anna, the middle child, who added some meat, then to Marcela, who was acting more spaced out than normal. So her mother tactfully moved her aside and rolled and wrapped the tamales herself.

Marcela was then given the job of cooking the rice. Though she's the oldest, she's the one who cooks the least. For a while, she'd taken cooking lessons because she had money to burn, but eventually she gave them up and conned her husband into cooking. So putting her in charge of making rice wasn't a bad idea in and of itself—only slightly risky if she wasn't concentrating, and today she wasn't.

We chatted about all sorts of girl things, from husbands and boyfriends to clothes to gossiping about their family members. With Halloween only three weeks away, the topic of the day centered around Marcela's grandmother, who swore that her first lover (who died twenty-five years ago) returned each anniversary of their "union" to make love to her again as she slept.

"If you ask me," Katie said, "I think she's losing it. She's eighty-four and senility has finally claimed her mind."

Marta shook her head. "Her mind is as clear as when she was your age, *mi'jita.*"

"So does she actually orgasm when these yearly visits happen?" Anna asked.

"Ew, yuck. Shut up," Katie said.

We all laughed except Marta. "Yes, show some respect," she said.

"She's the one who brings it up," Marcela defended her middle sister as she stirred the sauce into the rice.

"I think she's crazy or full of it," Katie said.

"You don't think it actually happens?" I asked.

Katie gave me an incredulous look. "Get real. An eighty-year-old ghost molests her once a year?"

I smiled. "I guess if you're going to imagine something happening to you, that's not a bad hallucination."

"I wouldn't want my first lover coming back to bother me," Anna said.

"Me neither," Katie agreed.

"Ditto," Marcela lifted a finger in the air.

"No, but I'd go for Elvis Presley." Marta smiled mischievously.

"How does her current husband, Rogelio, feel about this?" I asked.

"He says that when he goes to Heaven, he's going to beat the shit out of the SOB," Katie laughed.

"Come on, girls. Work faster." Marta pushed on Katie's shoulder.

"Bueno," Katie whined. "Don't rush me."

"We want to eat today, *mi'ja.* Hurry it up. You're holding us back."

We resumed our efficient assembly-line production, and I smiled inwardly. I loved Sundays. The best day of the week.

When we were finished with the tamales, Marta complained that she'd forgotten to buy whipped cream for the flan.

Marcela jumped out of her seat. "Lupe and I will go buy some."

"We can eat the flan without cream," I said, perfectly content to stay in the warm kitchen with all its tantalizing aromas.

"No," she pulled me out of my seat. "Let's go."

"What's the big deal about cream," I asked as we headed to her BMW.

"I've got to tell you something."

"What is it?"

She gazed at me from across the hood of the car, then shook her head and got inside.

Joining her, I put my seat belt on knowing she'd spit it out eventually. The woman has worked in Hollywood creating animated movies for too long, and she was into drama.

"Should I guess?" I asked as she drove out of the quiet, tree-lined suburb.

"No, no." She stopped at a street light. "I'm just not sure I can say the words."

I sighed and waited.

"I'm, ah, going to . . . I'm pregnant," she spit out and stepped on the gas, leaving skid marks as she peeled into the intersection.

I smiled. "Really? Well, that's great." But I didn't see the expected sheen of happiness reflected on her face. "Isn't it?" I looked over my shoulder and remembered the skid marks. *Maybe not.*

She pulled into a shopping center parking lot, found a parking spot in front of a Vons grocery store, and killed the engine. "I guess," she said and hugged the steering wheel as she lowered her forehead on it. "George is thrilled. But . . ."

"You're not."

"A baby?" She angled her head. "Hell, Lupe. I don't have time for a baby."

"You're not getting any younger, dude. It's now or never." She was thirty-three and she looked awesome, but, still, biological clocks tick whether we like them to or not.

"Thanks. I appreciate that."

I slid closer to her. "You'll be a great mother. You can do this."

"I hope so." She smiled and wrapped an arm around me.

I could feel she was frightened. I hugged her back. To me, Marcela was part friend, part older sister, part mother. When I was just a thirteen-year-old kid, I pulled a knife on her, tagged her car, and put her in a situation that almost got her raped. I was a real prize. But she saved my life. I loved her, and I didn't love many people.

When she pulled back, she wiped her eyes and her hands were shaky. "So, how are things at The Vibe? I haven't had time to stop by lately."

After getting me on the right track and enrolled in a private school that she paid for, she opened The Vibe, a youth empowerment center whose goal is basically to get kids off the street. We ask kids to sign a contract saying they're willing to turn their backs on gangs, drugs, and violence and instead reach toward a positive future. And in exchange for their word, they receive life management training and a cool place to hang out.

I say "we" because I work as a volunteer there every day. I even chose the name. Marcela had asked me to come up with something that would attract kids like me, and I'd thought The Vibe sounded like a cool nightclub-type name—a place I'd want to hang out at with friends. She loved it and the name stuck.

I eased back into my seat and opened my car door. "Ryan's got everything under control. You know how he is." Ryan Nash ran The Vibe. Marcela is basically The Vibe's mastermind and financier, but she doesn't involve herself in the day-to-day management.

We left the car and headed into the grocery store. The air outside was misty, a gentle reminder that winter was on its way.

"Good. And school?"

"Great."

We strolled side by side. We're basically the same height, Marcela a medium build, me super thin.

"How are things at home?"

Ah, the million-dollar question. "Now that Carlos is back, it's getting worse."

"Move out, Lupe." We entered the store and walked to the cool dairy section.

"Not that easy."

"It is easy, girl. You find a place to live and I write the check. I told you."

"And I told you, I'm not taking any more money from you. Besides, you've got a kid coming now. You'll need it."

She placed a hand on her hip and stared at me. "Lupe, I know he's your brother, but he can't be trusted, and sooner or later—"

"I know. I know." Marcela had witnessed the last beating Carlos had given me. She'd tried to stop him and failed. So, she knew what he was capable of. "Don't worry. I can take care of myself."

Marcela picked up a can of whipped cream. "But you don't have to."

Yes, I did. I was an adult now, and I had to be able to take care of myself. "If he ever touches me again, I'll kill him," I said simply, and meant it.

But Marcela frowned. "Wonderful. He'll be dead and you'll be in jail."

I didn't answer her, because I'd have said that I didn't care.

"Don't be stupid, Lupe. You have a future. Get out of there, finish college, and get on with your life."

Marcela, her family, and even Ryan have been saying this for so many years, I'm actually starting to accept it as my fate. Ingrained on the side of my head were the commandments—*finish college, get a great job, make lots of money, become a real American. Leave all this Mexican shit behind.*

I took the whipped cream from her hands. Life was always so much simpler for Marcela. Sometimes I wonder if people actually do you a favor by continually telling you how bright your future looks. The pressure, the expectations, can sometimes be too much. "Let's go, dude. I'm hungry. And you've got big news to share with your family."

"Oh yeah," she said, creases appearing on her forehead as she frowned. "Hey wait, let's check the labels. This might not be the best brand."

But I knew a stalling tactic when I heard one, so I ignored her and kept walking to the check-out stand.

When Marcela shared her news with family members, they were practically drunk with excitement. To them, Christmas had come before Halloween. The first grandchild would be born soon, and this baby would belong to them all.

I could tell she was overwhelmed. She joked away all their plans for baby showers and warned them not to start buying *any* baby items. But no one listened—they all planned among themselves as if Marcela weren't even in the room. George squeezed her shoulders in support and I sent her a hang-in-there wink.

I watched her *endure* all the attention, feeling for her because I knew she didn't want it, but also envying her luck at having a family who doted on her. I didn't know what it felt like to be smothered in family love.

Sometimes, I'd give anything to have what she had—though in a way, I did. This *was* my family.

I took off a while later sort of excited about the idea of being an aunt. I'd never admit this to Marcela, but I couldn't wait.

Not in the mood to go home, I drove to UCLA instead. In the library, I picked up a few books on Latino culture. Powell Library was practically empty. Everyone with a life was out having fun on Sunday night.

Choosing a cubicle, I pulled out a notebook and wrote the title—*Becoming Americana.*

I thought back over my not-so-long life and wondered if I'd indeed undergone an Americanization process. Yes and no: I was born American, but my parents weren't. When I got into the school system, I had to relearn everything—the English language, what to eat, what to wear, what was cool, what wasn't.

I sighed and leaned back in my chair and gazed around the mausoleum-like library. What I really learned was that everything outside my home was safe and good, and that if I was going to survive and be happy, I needed to flee my home and family.

I'm still in the process of fleeing.

As far as I've gotten, as close as I am to being what most of America considers acceptable—inside, I haven't changed at all.

And I wonder, will that be the vital detail that makes me fail in the end?

Three

Becoming Americana means you must grow a tough outer shell.

LUPE PEREZ

Okay, I admit it, I think I'm hot shit. Been like that all my life—what can I say? In my neighborhood it was be tough or be dead. I chose tough.

So as I pulled my switchblade knife out of my pocket and swung it around in front of a guy with low-slung jeans and a huge attitude, I was in my element.

The same way a magician might demonstrate his props to an audience, I arrogantly displayed the Grey Concord knife with its sleek design, gray enameled body, and stainless double-edged blade. Man, it was a beauty.

"Survival in America comes at a price," I said in my most intimidating and hard voice. "And everyone has to pay at one time or another. Ready to pay?"

I placed the gleaming blade right below his Adam's apple. The sharp tip created a dimple on his skin.

Full of bravado, he lifted his chin and puffed out his chest, challenging me.

"I won't cut you," I said. But for just a second, I felt this sick wave of power that the blade had given me many times in the past.

I challenged the group of teens watching my demonstration in the youth community center. "Some of us pay with the loss of our innocence, others the loss of our soul, and still others with something tangible, like our family." They didn't need to know that in some respects, I'd lost all three.

I pulled my knife back and sent my hostile volunteer a silent apology for scaring him. I'd chosen Diego as my pretend victim because he had been the most obnoxious in today's group. Bragging to his buddies how he'd jumped girls like me in the streets before, and had taken care of business. I wanted to show him that a twig of a girl could be just as dangerous as a muscled dude who weighed three hundred pounds.

"Those that don't survive pay the ultimate price—the loss of their lives. And I guarantee that if you resort to weapons like these," I held up my knife again so the eight or so kids draped in their chairs could take a good look, "you won't survive."

"Out there," Diego said, raising an eyebrow in defiance, "you would have never gotten that *fila* out of your pocket."

"Willing to bet your life on it?" I met his arrogant gaze with the confidence of my own.

He grinned, but I could tell he was reassessing my speed and skill, and the fact that he hadn't even seen the knife coming. "Naw, it's cool," he said and stepped back, offering me a *cholo* handshake.

I folded my blade and stuffed it back in my pocket then shook hands. "You see guys, one day, you'll be caught using your knife or your gun by the good guys at the L.A.P.D. and they'll put you away."

Making eye contact with those who looked the toughest, I continued. "Or you'll come up against someone who has a bigger weapon, someone who surprises you, like I just did with Diego." I paused. "And you'll die. Then it's over. Really over. Not like in a video game. Think about it."

The kids looked at me with distrust. Some of them with a superiority that said, *you don't know shit.* But I do. I've been where they are now. "Survival in America—power—comes from turning your back on the street and deciding you ain't playing that game no more. If that's what you want, you're in the right place."

Nash pointed at his wristwatch and I nodded, knowing I was out of time.

"All right guys, I've got to get out of here. See Nash and he'll take care of you."

Ryan Nash is totally amazing and deserves all the credit for The Vibe's continuing existence. I help out a few hours every morning, but he's the one who makes things happen. He works with the kids who show up looking for help, and keeps them motivated and challenged. Like a crazed evangelist, he walks the streets and storms the schools seeking out the "at-risk" kids—the ones that would be lost or dead if it weren't for him—and convinces them to choose life, to choose salvation. And this has nothing to do with the spirit. No. By salvation, I'm strictly talking making it to their eighteenth birthdays physically alive.

As I turned the group over to Nash, about half the kids walked out, hurling insults on their way out the door. We were used to that. Hey, you can't save everyone.

I hurried back to the small employee lounge—lockers on one wall, a mirror on the other, and a huge table in the center—and picked up my backpack. Shit, I'd be late for my classes at UCLA again. I never seemed to be able to leave on time, but if I didn't stop by the center in the morning, I'd never be able to return during the day. My schedule was too tight.

Nash peeked inside and smiled. Caught me staring at my skinny self in the mirror. I smiled back and pretended I was picking a hair out of my eye.

"Someday, I want to learn how to do that with a switchblade knife." He moved his hands and arms around, imitating me.

"No you don't," I said and looked away from the mirror.

He shrugged and smiled that cute smile of his.

I've had a crush on Ryan Nash since we opened up this place and Marcela hired him to run it. Of course, "a crush" is putting it mildly. I knew from the first moment I met him that he *was it.* Sort of like a pilot might know that he was always meant to fly or an astronaut might realize the first time he looked up at the sky that he just "had to" one day go up in space and walk on the moon. Well, I knew the day Marcela introduced me to Nash and he looked into my eyes that I loved him. Crazy, huh? It was like some tension inside me eased because I knew I'd found what I was meant to find in this world.

But to him, I've always been a kid. He's eight years older than me, which sounds like a lot, and I guess it was when I was thirteen. But now I'm not a kid anymore.

Problem is, I'm not a girly girl either. I run around in jeans and a T-shirt half the time. I have boring, straight black hair. And I don't know how to get his attention the way girls do with boys. As I walked past him, I paused for just a second. "Ryan?"

"What is it, cutie pie?"

Will you go out with me? Say it. Say it! The brave part of me encouraged, but the wimp part took over and instead I said, "Ah, be careful when you leave tonight."

He reached across and straightened the strap on my backpack that had gotten twisted against my shoulder blade. "Don't worry about me."

"I do."

He angled his head and gazed at me through warm, deep blue, sexy-as-hell eyes. "I can take care of myself, hot shot. Watch your own back."

"This is my neighborhood. I was born watching my back."

"One day soon, you're going to graduate and this will all be a bad dream." With a swipe of his hand across his forehead, his long strands of dirty blond hair cascaded back and out of his eyes. And I was mesmerized.

Even the way he wore his hair, cut in a shaggy, layered style that reached his shoulders, was a major turn-on for me. Wild and loose and free—his hair, like him, couldn't be held back. It had to hang down, long and uncontrolled. Though I know his intent was to look like some rock and roll musician from the oldie bands he liked so much, to me, he was my very own wise mystic in the flesh. All knowing. All good. As perfect as they came.

"You'll never have to set foot in this neighborhood again," he promised.

Pulling myself away from silently worshiping him, I took a physical step back and said, "My feet are firmly planted in this area." I'd never stop volunteering at The Vibe. This place reminds me daily of where I've been, how far I've come, and how far I still have to go.

"No. You're on your way out, Lupe. And when you get out, don't ever look back," Nash said.

That was his goal—to get me out. I suppose seeing me succeed, watching me pass that imaginary line from barrio chick to middle-class American woman would signify to him that *he'd* accomplished his goal, done his job. But if success meant leaving him behind, as well as the kids who might need me, did I want that?

"So get to class," he said, snapping me out of my thoughts.

I glanced at him. Again, he made me feel like a kid. I had this urge to do something, anything, to make him look at me as an adult, as a woman. Maybe plant a big kiss right on his sexy lips. Or pull my top off and show him that I had tits now, maybe not big ones, but I had them. But, unable to get up the nerve to do something like that, I nodded and left.

Around the side of our building was a run-down, smelly alley where people from the nearby apartments dumped their trash bags full of diapers, homeless guys urinated, and I . . . kept my bike. I strapped my backpack down and grabbed my helmet as I straddled the seat.

Then I went through my routine: placed a stick of gum in my mouth, wiped the seat, climbed on, and pulled my keys out of my pocket. Just as I was about to start the bike and get my helmet on, three guys suddenly appeared behind me out of nowhere, startling the crap out of me.

One took the helmet out of my hands. "Where you goin', bitch?"

I recognized them as three of the boys who had been in the group I'd just finished lecturing, but not my macho volunteer, Diego. These guys were probably about sixteen- or seventeen-year-old punks. (I call them punks in the most loving way. I understand where they're coming from and I understand the tough act.) Old enough to know better and way too close to my age for comfort.

"Give me back my helmet," I said, resisting a patronizing sigh. Didn't I just show them I could more than protect myself?

The other two guys got closer, crowding me and my bike. "Or what?" one of them asked. "You gonna use those fancy blade tricks on us?"

They all laughed.

Oh, I get it, this is a challenge. I blew a couple of little bubbles with my chewing gum and put the key in the ignition and started the bike. It roared to life, making them take a step back. "I told you. I don't use the blade anymore." Then I reached for the helmet, but the idiot wouldn't let go. *Pinche cabron.* Just because I understand them, doesn't mean I'm willing to take any shit from them.

I held on tight to the helmet and brought my left leg straight up between the guy's legs until I slammed up against his crotch. And this wasn't an easy thing to do with the heavy boots I wear. I bought these boots at a secondhand store. Probably meant for men, but I loved them as soon as I saw them because they look tough—like they can survive a military bombing or something—and when I ride my bike they keep my feet warm and safe. And no matter what hits them they still look great. Getting kicked by them is enough to change your attitude big time.

The guy let the helmet go and doubled over with a yelp, his hands covering his balls.

Before the other two could react, I placed the helmet over the gas tank, hit the kickstand, and turned the throttle. The bike screamed out of the alley. Glancing back, I saw one of the guys chase after me, but he gave up about half a block later when he realized I was too far ahead of him and he wouldn't catch me.

I rode about ten blocks away before stopping to dial the cops—my buddy, Captain Martinez.

"Hey, it's me," I said when he answered.

"Ms. Perez. What's up?" In the background, I heard the usual station noise along with an extra loud voice of someone who didn't sound particularly cooperative or happy to be there.

"Could be trouble outside of the center," I said. "These three punks. Can you send a patrol car, just in case?"

"You okay?" he sounded concerned. I appreciated having the cops on my side. Sure felt better than having them chasing me down.

"I'm fine. They circled me outside when I was leaving, but I took care of it. I just don't want them stirring trouble for Nash or, you know, when other kids leave."

"I'll send a car out right away."

"Thanks." I slipped the helmet over my head and raced to UCLA.

I slid into a seat in my cultural ethics class as quietly as I could and got a few stares from other students. For the first time ever I noticed the future *Enquirer* reporter, Will, about three rows above me. He discreetly waved a few fingers while holding his pen with his thumb. A warm smile touched his lips.

I faced the front, determined to pay attention. I managed to put everything else out of my mind for about ten or fifteen minutes. Education is all I've got, I reminded myself. Focus.

But before I realized it, my mind began to drift. I wondered who would come to The Vibe today. If any of the kids would get arrested. Can I work with Captain Martinez on creating a catalog of child abuse offenders and drug pushers in our neighborhood? We've talked about it, but nothing is simple when you have to follow the law and protect criminals' rights.

But to be perfectly honest, as proof that I haven't changed all that much, I firmly believe the law could go screw itself. Because to protect victims, I'd break any and all laws without even blinking.

I sighed and focused on the instructor again.

Soon the hour is up and I've missed the entire lecture, daydreaming. Damn. So I sit and make notes about things I'd like to discuss with Captain Martinez and Nash. Those things seem to matter more to me than a bunch of mumbo jumbo about personal responsibility and how conscience is the basis of human character anyway. Though I won't admit my feelings about college to anyone other than myself, I often find myself thinking "so what?" when an instructor is lecturing. But I chase away those thoughts. I'm supposed to like it here.

Will stopped beside me. Mr. Elegant in Dockers and a coffee-colored top. "Class is over."

"Hi, Will."

"I told Tracey that you've sort of forgiven us both, but you know, she won't believe me unless you agree to have lunch with us."

Cute. "You're having lunch with Tracey?"

"And Madison. In about three minutes. Join us?"

I rested back in my seat and examined Will. Clean-cut with supershort brown hair, dimples, and a perfect speech pattern. So different from the guys I was used to dealing with. The kicker was that though he had everything going for him, behind the outward confidence lurked a charming insecurity that seemed to draw me in.

I could use a lunch break, and a little social time with people outside The Vibe. I folded my notebook into my backpack. "Let's go."

Tracey apologized, and I apologized, what the heck. We both meant well. Besides, after being at UCLA for over a year and not getting to know anyone (not that unusual since I don't live on campus, don't participate in any student activities, and the university is the size of a small town), it was nice to start making some friends.

Seated outside on Ackerman Union's patio, Madison stretched back in her seat and tipped her face to the sun. "I'm tired. Screw food, I need caffeine."

"I'll get you girls drinks," Will said. He took orders for both food and drinks and took off, refusing to accept cash from any of us.

Tracey watched him walk inside. "He likes you, Lupe."

"Yeah, well, he'll get over it." Last thing I wanted to do was encourage their gossip now that I knew I couldn't trust them with much more than my grocery list.

"He's cute. Don't you like him?"

"Sure, he's nice enough. But I also thought the frog in biology lab was cute, and I still dissected him."

"Ouch." Madison cringed.

"Okaaay," Tracey said.

"So, what exactly upset you about the article, Lupe?" Madison changed the subject, though I wasn't sure it was a better one.

Neither did Tracey. She shifted uncomfortably. "I need a manicure."

I crossed my legs and studied these rich girls with nice clothes, perfect makeup, and yes, manicured fingernails, and knew they could never understand the world I came from. "First of all, you made me sound like gutter trash that managed to get washed into a better neighborhood by accident. Then a saint who goes around rescuing other losers. Losers who will infect society unless I am able to ride out on a white horse and save them."

Will was back in time to hear my nice little diatribe. He placed a coffee cup in front of each of us and tossed a handful of half-and-half cups and sugar packets in the center of the table. Then he gave me and Tracey our cheeseburgers and sat down with his own double cheeseburger and pile of fries. Ah, the mixture of scents from grease to strong coffee made my stomach growl.

"Actually," he said, "if I can butt into your conversation, making you sound like a saint was probably my fault. I sort of embellished a bit with dramatic adjectives."

"Bad writing," I said. "You should embellish with nouns, not adjectives." Could I attack my food now?

He grinned. "You told me my writing was good."

"I was being nice."

"Oooh, that hurts." His grin was sort of shy and teasing, and for a second, he looked so adorable that I simply stared.

Madison sipped her coffee and frowned, at the bitterness or

maybe the heat. Since she reached for a packet of sugar, I guessed it was the bitterness. "And no one made you sound like gutter trash, my dear. The piece was simply supposed to celebrate the greatness of our country where a girl like you can succeed despite the appalling upbringing you received."

Madison was a no-nonsense type of girl. Intelligent, came from money, and would one day take her place in the world of business. She was working toward some type of high finance career. Sure, she liked to party and to screw around with men (wonder if she'd like me to print some of the things she said *she'd* done), but that was the youthful spirit in her. Once she got out of college, she'd be the type that ruled the world.

"The piece was not about 'a girl like me.' It *was* about me. And if this country were really so great, maybe there wouldn't be ghettos to have to rise above."

Madison raised an imperious eyebrow. "Our country is not at fault for the ghettos."

"Of course not. Must be the fault of the lousy minorities who just love to live in broken-down houses, get second-rate educations, and dodge bullets from drive-bys every other night. Right?"

Tracey cut her cheeseburger in half and shoved part of it at Madison. "Here. Eat."

Madison slipped on some sunglasses and waved away the food. "No, thanks."

Tracey then leaned across and touched a small gang tattoo I had between my thumb and index finger. "Living downtown sounds exciting to me. You've really lived. Not like us."

Yeah, must be rough to grow up in a lily-white suburb with no gangs hanging out in the street, not fearing for your life, having parents home every night who care what you're doing and with whom. I eased back, trying not to make it seem obvious that I was moving my hand off the table.

Will placed an arm behind my chair and caressed my shoulder with his fingertips. He'd been listening and watching me with a pensive look in his eyes. "Man, I admire the hell out of you," he said.

"Admire?" I turned to him.

"Yeah, to thrive and be where you are now after the life you've had."

"Yeah," Tracey and Madison both agreed.

"That's all we were trying to say with the article," Madison said.

These people were insane. I wasn't thriving. I was surviving. Though if they didn't shut up and let me eat, I'd start wasting away for sure.

"Sure, you're an inspiration," Tracey continued. "But, don't worry." She held out a hand. "Now that we know how you feel, we won't do anything like that ever again."

I smiled. A small part of me actually liked that these rich girls were taking an interest in me. I was used to their type who, all through the private high school where Marcela sent me, walked by me like I was nothing more than a wad of gum on the sidewalk. Something you noticed but avoided. And now, all of a sudden, I was interesting because I was different from them.

"So how about some excitement?" I asked.

Both Tracey and Madison perked up.

I held up my hand with the tattoo Tracey had been fingering. "Let's go get one?"

Tracey's grin widened, but Madison shook her head. "No way."

Tracey leaned into Madison. "Come on. Let's do it."

"Hell no. I'm not permanently marking up my body. Forget it."

"Well, I'm in," Tracey said. "Will?"

"You girls go right ahead. I don't like pain."

I didn't really want him to come along anyway, so Tracey and I made a date to go and get tattoos the next week. Then finally, we ate.

Will walked me to my next class with his hands buried in his pockets and his thoughts seemingly elsewhere.

"Well, here we are," I said when we reached Knudsen Hall.

He moved close to me and hooked an arm around my waist. I don't know when he decided it was okay to share this type of familiarity with me, so I pulled back.

"Tell me something," he said.

I turned to him and looked him right in the eyes. "Anything as long as you don't print it, and by the way, I don't like guys touching me without my permission."

"You've got too many rules," he said. But he stepped back. "Better?"

I nodded.

"So, how much of what I wrote about in the article are you still living?"

"All of it."

With a disbelieving stare, he asked, "All of it?"

"I still live in East L.A. I'm still poor. I still make a choice every day whether I want to take the easy way out and do things I know are morally and legally wrong, or come here and work hard for the promise of a better future."

"Ethics," he said with a smile. "Tough."

"Not so tough. When you grow up in the barrio, and see some of the things I've seen, you don't want to stay there."

He reached up and pushed some of my hair back that came loose from its braid. "You've got more balls than I do."

"Sorry to hear that." I angled my head. "And hands to yourself, remember?"

He chuckled. "Sorry." Then he glanced at the building behind us. "So what are you majoring in?"

"Computer graphics. I hope to go into architecture."

"Cool."

"It's sort of fun and I'm pretty good at design. I can build a website in no time."

"Have dinner with me." He had a faraway look in his eyes that told me he was no longer listening to what I was saying.

"Thanks, but no," I said.

"Why not?" he asked.

Why not? I didn't have a great reason. I just didn't date. Men made me nervous. Granted, my experience with men has been with the losers from my neighborhood, and perhaps Will was different. Still . . . "Why do you want to go out with me?"

"I like you. You're cute."

"So are lots of other girls."

He shook his head. "You're real. You say what you feel. And you've got this attitude, this drive to become something better and greater and . . . it's inspiring."

"Don't *you* want to become something better and greater?"

He shrugged and leaned close to me and touched his lips softly to mine. The kiss wasn't pushy or arrogant and he wasn't taking anything from me. On the contrary, he was filling me up with something warm and beautiful.

As he ended the kiss, he smiled. "Yes, I do, Lupe. Now that I've met you, I want to be *everything* I can be. I'd be ashamed not to be."

I eased away from him and touched my lips with my fingertips. Can't believe he kissed me. Can't believe I let him. "What did you do that for?" I whispered.

"Sorry. I couldn't resist."

I glanced away. Students were walking past us, in and out of the building. No one seemed to notice that my world had frozen in place. I didn't know what to feel, what to say, what to do. No one had kissed me in—had a guy ever really kissed me? Or had there only been sex?

"Will you at least share a cup of coffee with me Wednesday after your biology class?"

I shook my head. "I've got lab."

"After lab?"

I had an hour before I had to be to work at the food court, so that was doable, but . . . But, oh my God, I couldn't see this guy again. He was too . . . nice.

"Come on," he teased. "Don't make me beg."

"Will, please, don't."

"Then have a lousy cup of coffee with me. No big deal. Just coffee. Uh-oh, I'm starting to beg."

"Okay." I nodded. "Okay."

His smile grew. "See? That wasn't so hard. See you then."

Though I walked into the building, found my class, and sat through lecture, I don't remember what it was about. After that kiss, I was too bothered to remember much of anything. Not that it was even a big deal, I mean, jeesh, it was nothing more than a peck. But given the fact that it was the first time in years that a guy touched me, that I actually liked it bothered me. Then there was the small detail that I was thinking of a guy who wasn't Nash "that way." . . .

Four

Becoming Americana means learning to fight your own battles.

LUPE PEREZ

I awoke with a start at the sound of creaking furniture and a weight on my chest, and found Carlos sitting on my bed staring down at me. He clasped a heavy hand over my mouth and my heart began a frantic beat. My fear was so intense that I couldn't move.

"Shh." He put a finger to his lips. "I need money."

I nodded in agreement so that he'd know I understood what he wanted and that I was willing to give it to him. Slowly, he took his hand off my mouth.

"How much do you need?"

"All you have."

"I have about fifteen dollars in my wallet."

"Don't play dumb. I need real money."

"I'm not giving you all I've managed to scrimp and save, Carlos." And if he saw where I hid my money, he would take it *all.* He wouldn't be content to take part of it.

He shot me a murderous, threatening look. But I was fully awake now and the momentary fear that had taken me back to my childhood disappeared. And he must have seen the change in my face.

"I need a couple hundred. I'll pay you back." He reached across and caressed my bare neck and down my shoulder. "One way or another."

I hit his hand away, disgusted by the feel of his fingers on my skin.

Without hesitating he returned the slap, only it was across my face, and hard enough to knock me across the bed. The blow brought tears to my eyes as I held my cheek with my hands. "You bastard! Get the hell out of my room."

"Give me the money now," he said, without much emotion. The terminator came to mind.

Through the strands of hair hanging in my face, I glared at him. Why? Why should I hand over my hard-earned savings to him? Because I was afraid? Not a good enough reason anymore.

"Fuck off," I said.

He lunged at me, but I rolled off the bed, grabbed the rickety old wooden chair I'd bought for three dollars at a thrift shop, and slammed it across his back, busting it into a dozen pieces.

As he cried out and attempted to recover from the blow, I ran out of my room. The noise woke up my parents and they ran out to the living room just in time to catch my brother grabbing hold of my hair and lifting his fist over my face.

My father hollered and pulled my brother back. "*Que haces?*"

"She broke her chair on my back. She's crazy. *Loca.*" He shoved me away from him like I was burning his hands.

"You did what?" My mother frowned, accusing eyes sentencing me before I could explain.

"He attacked me first. He came into my room."

"*Basta,*" she said. "You'll never change. He comes home and you start trouble already."

"*I'm* making trouble?" I shook my head, deciding it was hopeless to try to explain. "You always defend him. Always."

"That's because she knows I'm doing what's best for this family. What are you doing? Always thinking of yourself," Carlos accused.

My father shoved Carlos back and grabbed a hold of my chin. He examined my face, then scowled at Carlos. "Keep your hands off her. You're not her father or her husband, *entiendes?*"

Carlos nodded curtly, but his eyes promised that we'd finish this later.

I turned away and locked myself in my bedroom. Staring into my mirror, I examined my face. Shit. I'd have a bruise for sure. What the hell was I going to do? I rammed my fingers through my hair and plopped onto my bed. A splintered piece of wood poked my thigh. I threw it to the floor with more force than necessary. I heard my parents arguing in the living room, no doubt blaming each other for the lousy kids they'd raised. Carlos went out the front door. The screen door slammed after him. I glanced over my shoulder out the window. He strutted down the street, head held high and a huge chip on his shoulder.

As if suddenly kicked by an invisible alter ego, I sprang from my bed and got a screwdriver from under my mattress. I hurried to my light switch plate and took off the cover. From inside, I pulled out my cash. I counted the hundreds and twenties quickly. I had a little over three thousand dollars. Not enough to live on for long, but enough to get by for a few days with a little help from my friends.

I slipped on some jeans and stuffed the money in my pockets. Then without considering much what items I was taking, I packed some essentials into a large duffel bag. Running outside, I dropped my textbooks into my bike's side bags and tied the duffel onto the back with bungee cords. Then I drove to Nash's apartment, wanting to catch him before he left for the center.

It was about six in the morning when I rang his doorbell. When he opened the door, he caught Carlos's handprint on my bruised face immediately. He reached across and took my elbow and pulled me inside. "What happened?"

"My brother."

Nash swore. "Call the cops. Now."

"No. And tell them what, that he slapped me?"

"Tell them everything. I bet if they searched your place"—he pointed out the window as if my home were right outside—"they'd find enough drugs to put him back behind bars."

"Nash," I sighed. "Let it go." I pushed past him and placed my duffel bag on his couch.

"You're going to do nothing?" His lip curled into a snarl and he shook his head.

"I'm going to leave." I ran a hand through my hair, shaking loose the helmet head. Nash just didn't understand that it was pointless to involve the cops in family matters. The police wouldn't do anything, and snitching would only make matters worse for me. "This is hard for me to ask, but can I stay here? Just for a few weeks until—"

"Of course. I have an extra room. It's yours."

"I'm going to get my own place, but—"

Unexpectedly, he pulled me hard against his body and wrapped me in a fierce hug.

Oh my God. He was warm and practically naked and *holding me.* All of a sudden, I forgot all about my brother and being homeless. I wrapped my arms around Nash's bare waist and enjoyed the warmth of his arms around my shoulders and back.

"Stay as long as you want," he said, and planted a kiss on top of my head. "I mean it."

Oh, this was heaven. I tipped my head and looked up at him. Maybe he'd kiss me again. On the lips this time. I was becoming acquainted with my feminine power and it felt great. Though it probably wasn't completely fair of me, I decided to play up the fact that I needed him. He seemed to respond to this.

"I didn't know where else to go. Marcela would take me in," I said. She and George bought an awesome home a couple of years ago in the Palisades and she had tons of room. "But I hate to impose on her and George, especially now that she's pregnant."

"Pregnant?" Nash looked down at me, a stunned look on his face. We all knew how she felt about having kids, and all thought that her continual pleas to George that he wait until "next year" was her way of postponing kids indefinitely.

"Ah. I probably shouldn't have said anything yet."

He loosened his arms, which gave me this terrible feeling of loss. So I rested my head on his naked chest again, listening to his soothing heartbeat. "I hate to admit this, but I was so damned scared," I said. "When I woke up and Carlos was on my bed, I felt like I was thirteen. I thought it was going to start all over again." I was no longer just vying for his strong arms to stay around me, I was reliving a past I wanted to forget.

Nash held me tighter and caressed my back. "You're going to be fine, Lupe. That's all over."

"I know. I'm not a kid anymore, but . . . just for a moment . . ."

He walked me to the kitchen, keeping an arm wrapped around my shoulder, and poured me a cup of coffee. Then he sat across from me at the kitchen table. "You don't ever have to go back there. You understand? Did you bring all your stuff?"

"Not all, but I don't have much anyway." I took the coffee cup and began to feel silly for acting so weak.

"Whatever you need, we'll buy you."

"*I'll* buy whatever I need. All I want is a place to crash for a while. I'll help buy the groceries—"

"Don't be ridiculous."

"Nash, I won't be a burden to you. I've been a burden to everyone since the day I was born. I'm tired of it." The needy girl of a few moments ago was thankfully fading as renewed anger at my situation made me want to take control.

"You could never be a burden to me. Don't you realize how I feel about you?"

I swallowed and looked into those glorious blue eyes. They seemed to touch me softly and lovingly. Maybe losing my home would turn out to be a good thing. Maybe he was just waiting for the opportunity to get closer. Maybe all he had needed was a little encouragement from me.

"You're like a sister to me, Lupe. We're family. Right?"

I felt my heart deflate. A sister? What a horrible thing for him to say. But I smiled at him, just a little. "Thanks," I said.

"I don't have much, but you're welcome to all of it. Including my bank account if you need some money to buy more clothes or something. Okay?"

"I won't need that."

"If you do."

"Ryan, you're . . ." Sweet and considerate and wonderful and everything I've ever wanted. "I love you," I said with all the feeling and passion I'd stored up for him in the past six years.

His smile was instant and brilliant and happy. "I love you too, kid."

Kid. Kid? On second thought, maybe he wasn't so wonderful.

He released me and went into his room to get dressed, and I was left in the small living room feeling awkward and alone.

Nash went to work a short time later. "Relax. Make yourself at home," he said as he walked out.

I decided to skip everything today, even school, and curl up on the couch to catch up on my sleep. I called the cafeteria first and told my supervisor I wouldn't be able to make it tonight. The girl who's my manager wasn't very happy, but too bad. I couldn't go in today with this bruised face. By tomorrow, the ugly mark would fade enough for me to cover it up with makeup. That done, I closed my eyes and was out almost immediately.

I woke up about five in the afternoon and took a shower in Ryan's small bathroom. It felt great to get clean.

Naked—well, wrapped in a towel—I emptied my duffel bag on the bed Nash gave me. I didn't have much. I groaned and picked up a pair of panties, some jean shorts, and a simple white T-shirt. Then I pulled out a stick of gum from my backpack and began to roam through the tiny apartment as I chewed.

And I'm not kidding about his apartment being tiny. You couldn't open his front door all the way, because he'd positioned a bookcase on the wall directly in front of it. Then, once you got in, his living room looked like someone had set up a garage sale. His couch and TV and coffee table and more bookcases would have made the room crowded enough, but Nash had to cram in a weight bench, a half dozen potted plants, stacks of DVDs, a desk, and a filing cabinet. Even his kitchen had a table that needed to be folded to allow for food prep. But at least he had two bedrooms. And he was willing to let me use one.

The apartment was in the Olympic Park neighborhood of L.A., which wasn't much nicer than Boyle Heights where I grew up, and I wondered why he didn't choose to live elsewhere. He must be able to afford better—Marcela was a generous boss.

I looked out the dirty window at kids playing soccer on a patch of grass downstairs. They made me smile, just for a moment. I liked kids. Maybe because I was never able to be one myself. And every time I saw kids laughing and doing something innocent, my heart sort of swelled and I knew *that* was the way it was supposed to be.

Someday, I'd make sure my own kids never had to go through the things I have.

Realizing where my thoughts had strayed, I almost laughed. I took about a half step back and sat on the arm of the couch. My situation sucked—what was I thinking about kids for? If I didn't hurry up and make something of myself, my kids would grow up exactly like me. I looked around the room. In a place just like this.

I shuddered. What the hell was I going to do? I couldn't live off Nash. Just because he was being kind and offering help didn't mean he really meant it. And even if he did, I wouldn't impose on him long term.

I dropped back on the couch, my legs still dangling over the edge of the arm. For once in my life, I wanted to take control of my future. Part of me wanted to cry, and another part wished I had a picture of my brother on a punching bag or a ball so I could kick it around and slam it against the wall.

I considered my options, and none seemed thrilling. I could go find a job, quit college, and get my own place and pretty much kiss my future good-bye. Or I could live off Ryan or Marcela and keep going to college while I worked for spending money and remained dependent on others for the next few light-years. Or I could go back home and sleep with my knife under my pillow.

I rolled off the couch. "Why does life have to be so fucking hard?" I asked out loud in the empty room.

My mother believed in guardian angels and even though her life was shit, she felt she was being watched over. I wasn't sure I believed in anything. But for just a second, it seemed as if I received an answer to my question—and it said, "To make you stronger."

I blinked and shook my head. "Fucking great, now I'm hearing voices in my head."

I climbed over the couch and jumped over the coffee table trying to get away from myself. I went into the kitchen planning to prepare dinner for Nash and myself. But his fridge was empty. I changed into a pair of sweatpants and took off to go find some food.

With the sun setting, city lights beginning to glimmer, and the cool California evening making its stereotypical movielike appearance, how could my life be so messed up? I rode my bike up Western Boulevard willing myself to feel better. The Hollywood sign was somewhere up ahead of me. I couldn't see it, but knew it was up there, and it taunted me, like it did most people who lived here. This is Hollywood, it reminded, where anything can happen. Magic is everywhere.

What a crock. Nothing was real in this town—that was the problem. The ugly stuff was swept away and hidden and we were fed sound bites of what life was supposed to be like. And like suckers, we believed it.

I made a left on Wilshire Boulevard deciding to go to the Farmer's Market to pick up some fresh vegetables for dinner. I saw an unusual opening and sped between rows of cars, weaving in and out of congested lanes, making progress despite the traffic. All of a sudden, I heard a siren, and glanced over my shoulder to find a motorcycle cop signaling me to pull over. Great. Now what?

When I pulled my helmet off and he saw I was a girl, he seemed momentarily thrown off his mission. But he recovered fast enough to ask for my license, which I handed to him almost before he finished. I knew the drill.

"Something wrong with your turn signals?"

"No."

"Moving in and out of traffic like that without signaling is dangerous."

What? Motorcycles rode the lines all the time. "Did I break some traffic law or not?" I wasn't in the mood for this crap. Shouldn't he be out busting guys like my brother?

He raised an eyebrow. "You've committed a traffic violation according to vehicle code 22107, yes, which states that no person should move right or left upon a roadway until such movement can be made with reasonable safety and then only after giving an appropriate signal," he recited as if he were reading from his code book. Wow, photographic memory.

Still, I wasn't that impressed, and if he wanted a signal, I had the perfect signal for him. "I *was* getting around traffic, *safely.*"

"You didn't even see me when you made the turn on Wilshire, did you?"

"I'm sure you were in plain view." I couldn't help the sarcasm. Usually, I got a speeding ticket every other month from cops who hid behind a liquor store waiting to trap an unsuspecting, hardworking rider like me. Didn't these guys have anything better to do?

"I was sitting off to the side watching traffic when you screamed past me."

"Off to the side," I said with a laugh. "Right. You must be very proud of yourself."

He wrote me a ticket and handed it to me. "If that was your idea of trying to sweet talk yourself out of a ticket, you failed. Drive *safely.*"

Shit. I leaned on my bike and stared at the ticket. Back to traffic school, if I qualified to go again. After your second ticket in a year you lost the privilege to reduce your fine by attending school and had to pay the full fine.

He paused and turned to look at me. "You okay?"

I glared at him. "Aside from being currently homeless, jobless, and getting a huge ticket? Just perfect."

He pointed at my face. "If you need one, I can recommend a women's shelter or—"

"I'm fine." I met his gaze and saw the questions in his eyes. "Thanks." I meant that, by the way.

He nodded and got back on his own bike.

I did the same and crept along with the rest of the Angelenos stuck on Wilshire Boulevard, until I made it to my destination. Though I've got to admit, fresh vegetables no longer seemed that appealing.

Afterward I dropped by The Vibe, even though I hadn't planned on it today. Still, it was only eight o'clock and Nash wouldn't be home until after eleven, so why not go help out for a couple of hours before making dinner?

When I strolled through our glass doors, I was greeted with high fives and cool hellos from lots of the kids I hadn't seen since I started working mornings.

They had the GED prep class in the evenings and a group of about nine kids were enrolled. Others milled around doing their own things. I recognized Diego, my tough volunteer from a few days ago.

"Hi," I said.

He eyed me up and down in a way that would be totally intimidating to outsiders. "Finally pissed someone off enough that they taught you a lesson?" he asked, pointing at the bruise on my face.

I smiled. "You should see the other guy."

With a knowing nod, he dismissed me and went back to his video game.

"Glad you're here," I said.

Diego grunted, which was probably all I was going to get from him. So I headed to the office to visit with Nash. But when I opened the door his voice boomed.

"I don't care if you have to rewrite the damn grant ten times," Nash barked at Valerie, who was currently being treated to one of Nash's passionate flare-ups. "It has to be right. We need the money." He gazed at the door. "Lupe. What are you doing here?"

"Sorry to interrupt."

"No. We're finished. Rewrite it." He flipped the papers back to our secretary and grant writer.

I sent her a sympathetic glance.

Thank you for interrupting, she mouthed, and I had to laugh as she disappeared.

"I see you're being your charming self again today." Nash *was* a charmer, but most of it was reserved for the kids. Those that worked for him were expected to share his intensity for The Vibe, and give 110 percent.

"I hate half-assed jobs. If she doesn't want to write the damned thing correctly, then she should say so and I'll find someone else to do it."

I rolled my eyes. "Right. Because, people are beating down the door to work here. Calm down and be nice."

His sharp gaze rested on me, then he blew air out of his nostrils like a bull and the corners of his lips curved up. "I'll apologize to her later."

"Good. Did I miss anything interesting today?" I walked farther into the room.

"Same old thing. Why are you here?"

"I'm bored."

"Very funny. You should be resting."

"I rested. What was I going to do in your apartment by myself?"

"Whatever you wanted."

I wanted to be here. "I noticed Diego out there. Glad I got through to him."

"Don't know if you did, actually. He came in with a knife wound on his arm, but says he was just goofing off with his friends."

"Mmm, probably lying."

"Probably. But at least he logged in about four hours today. That's four hours he wasn't on the street."

Logging in hours meant the kids were rewarded with things like books, music, or tickets to movies and concerts.

I picked up the calendar of events that I was responsible for keeping up-to-date. "There you go. Success."

He grinned. "See why you're so wonderful? The eternal optimist."

"Yeah, right." Next month I was planning a rape crisis prevention workshop, and I could use a couple of quiet hours to put it together. So I took my day planner and calendar and headed to the front desk. "I'm making dinner tonight, so don't pick up any junk food."

"Really?"

I liked the happy look of surprise on his face. "Really. Can you make it out of here by eleven?"

"If *you* are making me dinner, I'll be there whenever you say." He winked and made my night.

I still couldn't get over the fact that Nash and I would be spending the night together. So to speak.

Five

Becoming Americana means major makeover time.

LUPE PEREZ

With all my love and adoration, I made Nash a vegetable stew. As that was cooking, I called Marcela to tell her what had happened.

"I'm glad you left. We'll find you a place this weekend. You sure you want to stay with Ryan? You can come stay with me or with my parents."

"I'm fine here." I stretched across the couch. "Your parents live too far and you need your time alone with George. You don't get enough of it as it is."

"I know. I'm working on cutting back a bit at work. Actually a lot of our CGI work is going overseas. I've got less people to manage these days."

"Good."

Nash walked through the door and my heart skipped a beat. He smiled and held up a hand in hello.

"Listen, I've gotta go," I said, sitting up. "Don't worry about helping me find a place. I'll look for something on my own."

Nash frowned. "Who you talking to?"

"Marcela," I whispered.

He made a motion for me to hand him the phone.

"Hold on, Marcela. Nash just walked in and wants to talk to you."

"Hey," he said. "We've got it covered. She's going to stay here for a while. Yep. I know. I know. I will." He tensed and his jaw tightened. "You know me better than that."

I watched him curiously, wondering what she'd said to annoy him. Nash wasn't easily upset. Especially by Marcela, whom he considered the best boss in the world, because she left most major decisions to him.

Then he listened while Marcela spoke, and he seemed to relax again. "I know you do. I'll tell her. Bye." He hung up. "She said she'll call you on Friday. What smells so good?"

As he hung up and refused to meet my eyes, I wondered what they'd discussed. "Vegetables."

He strolled into the kitchen and opened the pot, taking a huge whiff of the steam that circled his face. "Mmm, smells great. Is it done? I'm starving."

I peeled myself off the couch and sighed as I went into the kitchen. "Nash, I'm not going to stay for long. You and Marcela don't need to worry about me."

"No one's worried. Stay as long as you want. I've got plenty of room." He washed his hands in the sink, then snatched a towel, dried off, and tossed me a sexy grin.

He had plenty of room? I glanced around the kitchen that could barely accommodate the two of us. If I wanted to walk past him, I'd actually have to squeeze against his long body. The image made my face warm. "I just want to make it clear that this is my problem, and even though I appreciate your letting me stay for a short while until I get on my feet, I don't expect you or Marcela to solve it for me."

Placing a hand on the counter, he leaned forward. "Listen to me. You were the first official member of The Vibe. From the day

Marcela introduced us and I saw how brilliant and special you were, I promised myself that I wouldn't fail you."

If I accomplished anything by staying, it would be to make him stop treating me like a child. "But it's my responsibility not to fail myself, not yours, and besides, I've always been perfectly capable of taking care of myself."

He grinned again. I amused him one heck of a lot.

"Oh, I know, hot shot, and I would never dream of implying you're not, but do me a favor."

"What?" I asked.

"Humor me. I want you to have the spare bedroom and stay with me until you graduate."

Unable to hide my surprise at his very kind but insane offer, I stared at him openmouthed. "You want me to stay with you for three years?"

"Sure."

I laughed. "Set the table. Let's eat. You're obviously suffering from low blood sugar."

He smiled and did as I asked. Apparently, he wasn't going to argue about eating. He handed me two bowls. I scooped up the stew and filled the bowls. He took them and set them on the table with a huge satisfied grin. "There's bread in the cabinet above the toaster. Can you bring some?"

"Sure."

We sat down to eat, without further conversation. He inhaled his first bowl and asked for seconds.

As we were finishing, he reached across and patted my hand. "That was great. Thanks."

I glanced at his hand and wrapped mine around it. "You're welcome."

He tried to pull his hand back, but I held on.

"I'm going to go change into some shorts," he said.

"Wait, Nash I . . ."

"What?"

I gazed into his warm eyes and caressed his hand, trying to make it seem like an absent gesture. "Can I ask you something personal?"

"That depends. How personal?"

"Why do you stay at The Vibe? You have a degree in psychology." He'd gotten his degree a few years ago. When the center opened, he worked during the day and took night classes. "You're always telling me I've got to move on—well, what about you?"

He shrugged. "I'm happy where I'm at for now."

"But you live in this dump. Sorry, but it is. And drive an old clunker car and—"

"Hey, it's a classic."

He drove a Buick Skylark from the mideighties, hardly a classic. But I ignored the comment because I was trying to make a point. "And put up with problem kids all day long."

His hand flipped and he now held mine. His thumb rubbed at the soft inside of my wrist. "They're not problems to me. They simply need a break."

"I know, but—"

"And I like being there and helping. That's why I got the psych degree. I don't want to work with rich old women who are depressed and bored with their pampered lives. I want to help kids with potential. Kids like you."

"I'm not a kid."

"You know what I mean."

"No, I don't know what you mean. Listen to me, I'm grown now. I'm not a kid. Look at me."

As if forced to do something that made him uneasy, he stared at me—mostly at my face, with a quick glance at what he could see of my upper body above the kitchen table. He nodded and swallowed. Then he pulled his hand away. "Okay."

"I've been through a lot of shit in my life and I've had to grow up fast. I was barely a kid when you met me."

"I know, Lupe."

"I may only be nineteen, but I'm not naive or innocent. I know what I want and I know how to get it." A bold-faced lie; I wasn't sure how to get what I wanted and sometimes I wasn't even sure *what* I wanted, except for one thing—for Nash to see me as a confident woman for once, instead of a girl. "I don't need you or Marcela to hold my hand anymore," I said.

He stood and leaned over me. He kissed the top of my head. "That may be true, but I can't stop wanting to protect you. I told you, you're like my kid sister, Lupe. Now that you're here, I want you to stay." He caressed the side of my bruised face. "Think about it."

I stretched to a standing position and my breasts rubbed up against his chest. It stopped him cold. All color appeared to drain from his face. I think I even heard him gulp.

"Your kitchen is small," I whispered as I gazed into his eyes.

He straightened, cleared his throat, and said, "Yeah, sorry. I'm going to go change, okay?" Then he practically ran out.

Ryan Nash was going to accept once and for all that I was *not* his kid sister. I'd move out, for sure, but not until I'd gotten Nash's attention and he'd noticed I was a woman. Besides, I needed to find a second job and start making some real money before I could think of leaving.

I cleaned the kitchen, and then went to the living room to stare absently at the TV while I daydreamed about my next move.

I tracked down Tracey and Madison at the outside tables of Ackerman Union on Wednesday to see if one of them would take notes for me in biology class. I planned to spend the day looking for a job.

They both spotted my bruised face right away, but happily didn't mention it.

"So you're going job hunting?"

"Yeah. I want to work for a while and get some money to get my own place."

Tracey slurped her Diet Coke. "Who have you been living with?"

"With my parents."

"Bummer."

If she only knew. "Yeah."

"What kind of job are you going to look for?" Madison asked.

I lifted a shoulder into a shrug. Best I could probably hope for would be waitressing. Tips could be good.

"How about something in the field you're going into?" Madison asked. "Assistant to some architect or something. Can you read blueprints and work the computer programs?"

"Sure. But those jobs are hard to get for . . ." I was going to say for someone like me, but changed my mind. "You know, on short notice."

Tracey raised up her sunglasses and leaned closer to me. "You helped me out in that parking lot, no matter what you may think. Let me return the favor."

"What are you thinking now?" I asked with admitted suspicion.

"My uncle owns an advertising agency in Westwood. I bet he'd hire you as an assistant if I asked him to."

I didn't know what to say. "Ah, doing what?"

"With your computer graphics experience, I bet he'd find something. If you're serious."

If I wanted to get my own place, I had to be. "Never been more serious."

"I'll talk to him," she said as if it were already done. "Call me at about three today and I'll tell you what he says."

"Thanks. I really appreciate this."

"Just watch yourself around him," she said and winked. "He married the last friend I introduced him to. She's twenty-two and he's forty-eight, but what the heck, if Tom Cruise can do it, why not my uncle?"

And on that note we parted and went our separate ways.

At three, I called Tracey. "What did he say?" Although thanks to her last comment, I now pictured a dirty old man and wasn't very enthused about meeting him.

"Meet me back in Ackerman Union," she said. "I need a smoothie."

Nervous and anxious and curious, I crossed campus and headed to the food court.

"I called and got you an interview. Best I could do. But at least he'll see you, right?" she said once we were face-to-face standing in front of the juice bar.

"Great. Thanks."

"Want one?" she asked as she took her fruit drink.

I shook my head.

Tracey performed a critical scrutiny of my body, reminding me of some girls in high school who used to make fun of the way I dressed. For the longest time, I never realized that my clothes were shabby. My mom shopped at secondhand stores and we didn't much care if things matched. As long as it was warm and not too worn, it worked. But when I got out of grade school, I realized there were cool clothes and dweeb clothes. Since I knew I'd never be able to afford the cool clothes, I decided to purposely dress as trashy as I could.

Now I stuck to jeans mostly.

"Ah, Lupe, you'll need to show up to the interview dressed . . . appropriately," she said, almost embarrassed.

I couldn't get offended or angry like I did in high school. She was right and she was trying to be helpful, not condescending.

I glanced down at my beloved boots, my worn jeans, and my light blue T-shirt that said *L.A.* in big letters and beneath it, *sexy, feisty, and captivating.* The insinuation was that the city *and* the woman wearing the shirt were all of these things. I bought the shirt for half off, figuring it would make a great college shirt. But definitely not appropriate for a job interview.

"I know. I need to do a little shopping," I admitted. "Would you mind helping me?"

Tracey acted thrilled to be asked. "Not at all. Let's go!"

"Now?"

"Have anything better to do?" She raised an eyebrow, challenging me to think of anything that could possibly be better than shopping.

I had classes clear up until six tonight then I had to work at the food court. But . . . what did any of this matter anymore? I needed a job more than I needed the classes. I'd just skip them. Looked like maybe my mother was right. People like us, we didn't have years to waste in college. We needed to survive. We needed to work. At least for this quarter, it looked like I'd be dropping my classes.

Tracey was a trip. She decided that I needed to dress professionally, but in a hip and sexy way. After all, I was young and would be working for an ad agency. I didn't necessarily need suits. But I needed to knock her uncle's socks off, meaning that a proper display of my body was important.

"Just for the record," I said. "I prefer not to be hired because of my looks."

Tracey flashed a lopsided grin. "Honey, it doesn't matter *why* he hires you as long as he does. So if we can make you look too delicious to resist . . . why not?"

I hedged. "Well, because—"

"Don't get me wrong. He's a perfect gentleman and he'll never lay a hand on you. But he likes to look. Hell, he's in advertising. Everything around him is beautiful. So let's make sure you are too."

What, I was going to argue with that? "Lead the way."

Tracey's huge grin was eclipsed only by her rush to get to the clothing racks.

I emphasized the need to spend as little as possible. I avoided the word *cheap*, but I'm sure she understood after I nearly passed out at a dress and jacket combination that cost $495 *a piece*!

I couldn't even afford to spend that much money on my *entire* wardrobe. So we attacked the clearance racks and found some great items. Bought a couple of skirts, including a tannish and black wool pencil skirt that Tracey called brunette and black. Whatever.

"We'll match it with a black jacket, then you'll sort of have a suit, maybe for the initial interview, and we'll get a couple of blouses for more casual days. Ooh, like this." She lifted a delicate silk blouse.

"Looks like something my grandmother would wear," I said. "No, I take it back. Looks like something *your* grandmother would wear. Mine was too poor to buy silk."

Tracy laughed and held it up against my chest. "It's vintage and feminine and it's in. You'll look fantastic."

"But I can see through it."

"You'll wear a black bra. Or we'll get a cami to go underneath."

Should I admit that I don't know what a cami is? "Okay," I said instead.

She continued to pick stuff out for me and I tried it all on. Because of my thin frame, she said, silk looked good on me. So I ended up with a lot of it. Even a crinkled silk chiffon dress that looked so good on me in the dressing room, all I could do was stare at myself.

"Do you like it?" Tracey asked.

Stupidly, tears moistened my eyes.

Tracey's smile withered. "Hey," she said. "What's wrong, Lupe?"

"Nothing." I started to take the dress off.

"Look, you're worried about money, right? Forget the cost. This will be on me."

I turned and stared at her with a frown that I didn't intend to have, but I couldn't help it.

"What?" she asked.

"Why would you volunteer to pay for my clothes?"

"Because it looks good on you and I want to."

Suddenly, I was pissed. I wasn't a fucking charity case. "I'll pay for my own clothes. Thanks." I started to take the dress off, trying not to rip it, but I wanted the damn thing off.

"Lupe, it's no big deal for me, okay?"

"It's a big deal for me," I said through clenched teeth. "You don't even know me. I'm supposed to walk around with clothes you bought me? Are you nuts?"

Taking a step back and staring at me like *I* was the nut, she shook her head. "Forget it." She began picking things up and re-hanging tops.

I counted to ten and told myself I was handling this all wrong, but it was hard for me to accept help. Always had been. "I'm so close to being homeless, it's not even funny, Tracey." I sat on the tiny bench in the dressing room. "I'm living with Nash, a friend from the youth center where I volunteer. I . . . I don't have money for new clothes. My friend Nash wants to help me. You want to help me. But I can't do shit for anyone. You know what I mean?"

Tracey stopped hanging tops but didn't speak. She just studied me with a funny look on her face—a mixture of pity and I don't know what else. I hate pity.

I picked up a hanger and twisted the clamp round and round.

"I've got to tell you something," Tracey said.

I gazed at her.

She met my gaze, then nodded as if to say, here goes. "I'm not rich. My parents are upper middle class and they have money, but they don't have a bottomless bank account. Most of 'my group' from high school was very wealthy and I had to pretend to fit in. That included staying far away from girls like you.

"There was a kid who used to ride her bicycle to school, and she was on the poor side. One day, some guy—I don't know if he was her boyfriend, but I think he was—was beating her up. I saw it after school. She saw me too. But I turned around and walked the other way." Tracey avoided my eyes as she remembered.

I stared at her, remembering all the times Carlos beat me up and no one helped—the neighbors all heard, sometimes even saw, and I wondered how come no one ever helped me.

"But you didn't hesitate when that idiot stole my purse. You ran right over. You did what you could to help. You stayed with me." Her eyes connected with mine now. "So maybe I don't know you that well, but I want to, because you had the conviction to do what I couldn't."

Great. She's helping me to ease her own guilt because she let some girl get beat up.

"Maybe I don't want to be a stuck-up bitch anymore," she added.

I smiled.

"There's no glory in being an elitist." She reached across and hesitantly touched my cheek. "Who hit you?"

I was so surprised and thrown by her question that I swatted her hand away.

"I'm sorry," she said immediately.

"No, I'm sor—" I looked away, gathering the courage to answer her question. "My brother hit me. He's an asshole. A druggie. He just got out of jail a few months ago. He's why I moved out."

Tracey nodded, then picked up the dress that had started all this. "You look amazing in this."

"Hey, Tracey."

She glanced at me.

"You couldn't have stopped that guy from hitting that girl. And you might have gotten hurt." I shrugged. "That's the truth."

"I didn't help her because I didn't want to get involved with her kind of people—white trash. I told myself she deserved it for picking that kind of guy to begin with. Wasn't my problem."

"You're right," I said. "You were a bitch."

We both burst out laughing.

"I guess I need some good clothes. I'll pay you back when I get my first check."

It looked like Tracey was going to wave away the need to repay her, but she nodded. "Pay me back one outfit at a time. Don't give me your entire first check. Please," she said in a tone that told me she'd feel ashamed to take all the money I worked an entire month to earn.

I decided I was pretty lucky. I kept finding people that were willing to help me. Only a complete idiot keeps turning her back on a helping hand. And I wasn't a *complete* idiot.

We left the mall with six bags full of clothes and shoes and other accessories. She drove me to Nash's place and we dropped the bags in the guest room, where there was evidence that he had been working to make room for me to move in indefinitely.

Yes, I was extremely lucky to have such great friends. "So," I said to Tracey. "Ready for that tattoo?"

She drew in a breath and cringed with a partial smile. "Let's do it."

We drove to Sunset Boulevard in Tracey's cute car, and after finding a lot to park in, decided to stroll until we found a tattoo studio that appealed to us. Sunset is full of bizarre people with purple hair and nose rings drilled into patterns. And now that we were approaching the Halloween season, that was even more true.

One such character bumped into Tracey, and when she apologized, he went off on her, cursing in a lunatic fashion typical of these guys who hung out on Hollywood streets.

"Hey, chill," I said, and with a growl he tromped off to hate someone else.

Tracey stared at him wide-eyed, but as soon as he cleared away, she burst out laughing. "What was that exactly?"

"Careful, that bitchy part of you is rearing its head again."

She made a gesture like she was erasing her last question. "Okay, okay, I'm being open."

We stopped at the window of a tattoo studio that was right in the center of Sunset Strip. "Try this one?" I asked.

"Looks clean." She pushed open the doors and Anna Nalick tunes greeted us. "I can't catch something like AIDS by doing this, can I?"

I shrugged. "You planning on getting a tattoo or taking one of these grunge guys to bed?"

She swatted my upper arm. "Smart-ass. When they puncture your skin, there's bound to be blood. And if they don't clean their equipment before going on to the next customer . . ."

"Let's check them out." I urged her all the way in. She was scared.

Tracey asked all her health questions, until she seemed satisfied that these people were professionals who took all necessary precautions. So we got started.

This was crazy. I didn't have the money to waste on a tattoo. But I got excited and really wanted to get one now that I was here. First we had to decide what design we wanted. There was an Aztec tribal design that caught my eye.

"Like this one?" my artist asked.

Though the tribal one interested me, I didn't want anything

that could be considered too Mexican. I was moving into the mainstream and my buddies Nash and Marcela would hang me if I branded myself with Raza icons.

"Great colors, huh?" he asked. "And it'll look great on your skin coloring with the golden sun and all."

"What else do you have?"

"In this style?"

"No."

"You want something feminine, dark, animals?"

"Ooh, look at this butterfly," Tracey said.

I glanced beside me at the design she was pointing out. "That would look cool on your hip."

My guy dragged my attention back to him. "How about angel wings?"

Angel wings? I smiled. What was it when you had two words that were opposites, and you put them together like "same difference"? An oxymoron? That's what me and angel wings would be. But the idea attracted me.

I was on my own, flying free for the first time in my life. Wings were perfect. "I think I'm going to go for this," I said to Tracey.

So Tracey sat to get her butterfly on her hip, and I got angel wings on my lower back.

Two hours later we left with our designs permanently etched into our skin, covered by large bandages, and both wondering if we were going to regret it later.

"I hope Brian likes it," she said. "He's the new guy I'm dating and he's *so* hot, Lupe. Wait until you meet him."

"Lucky you. I hope someone likes mine someday, because I can't see the damn thing and it hurt like hell."

Tracey hung her arm on my shoulder. "I know for a fact Will would like to take a peek right above your ass. And below too if you'd let him."

"Stop it," I said. I wasn't interested in Will and I didn't want her to encourage him. In fact, I was ready to make my move on Nash. Next weekend, I planned to make sure we spent some time alone.

We got back to campus in time for me to run to the cafeteria and do my nightly duty with the *frijoles* and greasy tacos. Four hours later, I took off my hairnet and apron, ready to go home after a busy night serving fast food, and Will walked up. "Leaving?"

Will. Handsome, sweet. The guy who kissed me. The kiss I liked. Now here he was again. And my blood pressure rose just a little bit.

Six

Becoming Americana means no longer packing up with other immigrants, and learning to live in isolation.

LUPE PEREZ

Frozen in place, I stared at Will, the ambush kisser. "Oh, hi."

"Waited for you today to have that cup of coffee."

Oh, man. I forgot. "I'm sorry."

As he shoved his hands into his jean pockets, his pants sagged. "You're just not interested. Is that it?"

Interested it what, exactly? My words to Tracey echoed in my head and I realized how untrue they were. I *was* sort of interested. I just didn't want to be.

"No," I said. But then immediately I realized I made that sound like "no, I'm not interested" when I meant that "no, that wasn't it." So I added, "I really just forgot. But I could use some coffee now." I walked around the counter and lugged my backpack on my shoulder, careful not to graze my achy lower back.

He glanced at my face and noticed the bruise.

"Lovely, huh?" I said.

"Get in a fight?"

"Sort of. I had to move out of my house and leave most of my stuff behind because of this fight. Went shopping with Tracey for some new clothes today. I didn't mean to stand you up, but . . . I had other stuff on my mind."

The tension in his shoulders seemed to ease, then he reached across and took my backpack. He wrapped an arm around my upper back. "Let's go."

We walked to his car. "We'll get your bike later."

"Starbucks?"

"Sure."

But when we got to his black Silverado—which surprised me, because he didn't seem the truck type—he made no move to start the engine. Instead, he made a move on me.

Quite smoothly, he reached across, pulled me closer to him, and his lips began featherlike brushes against my sore, bruised cheek. I stiffened and placed my hands on his shoulders.

"It's okay, Lupe." His winsome voice was like warm honey. "I won't hurt you. I swear to God."

The sweet promise said with such conviction forced me to relax. And this may sound pitiful, but I've had such little tenderness shown to me in my life, that I wanted to close my eyes and absorb as much as he wanted to give.

"I can't believe someone laid a hand on you."

"I'm fine," I whispered.

He touched my face, like I was a fragile piece of pottery. "If you ever need my help . . ."

"I won't."

He sighed and kissed above my eyelids. "Okay. Okay."

His hands roamed my upper back, then got lost in my hair. His mouth finally found its way to my lips, and he kissed me the way I'd seen it done on the old *novelas* my mom watches sometimes. Mouth open. Wet, hungry kisses.

And I began to dip into a sensual spiral I'd never felt before. The sweet, comforting mood of a few moments ago reached its end, and was replaced by something else. Heat. Desire. Physical need unlike anything I'd ever imagined. I wanted his hands to slip under my top, to touch my breasts. And I wanted his lips to follow. A rush of moisture between my legs dampened my panties. And a cry escaped from my throat.

When he pulled back, I was actually dizzy. I wasn't ready to be let go. "Wait," I said and dragged myself over him, dipping my tongue into his mouth and trying to ease this need that suddenly pulled at me like ripping Velcro.

He gazed up at me. "Oh, Lupe, you're so hot."

Hot. Me? I didn't know a thing about being sexy and desirable. In that aspect, I was still very much naive and innocent.

Though I didn't actually want to, I eased out of his arms and wiped my lips, confused. And with distance came slight embarrassment that I'd reacted so strongly to him. "I think I want to skip the coffee." There was no way I could sit across from him at Starbucks and talk. About what? Our college majors? "I need to get home."

"Can I come with you?"

I gazed at him. "No."

"I'm in the dorm and—"

"I'm not sleeping with you."

He swallowed. "No, I know. I thought . . . I mean, if you wanted . . . I'd . . ." He drew a breath and ran a hand across his scalp and drew away from me. "I'd really like to spend some time with you. You know, if you wanted."

As I stared at him, he looked so young and unsure of himself.

Probably a lot like me. He was a boy, unlike Nash, who was all man. I was suddenly ashamed of myself for kissing Will. Nash was who I wanted. I've loved him for so long, and even if he thought of me as his sister, I had to try to make him love me back. With some regret, I reached across and caressed the side of Will's head where his cropped hair poked at my fingertips. "I'm just not into casual sex. Sorry."

He closed his hand around my wrist and brought my hand down, kissing my knuckles. "I'm okay with that. I don't mind going slow. Going out on a few dates." He smiled. "I want you. No doubt about it. But it's not all about getting your clothes off."

This had to stop. I didn't want Will. I had no intention of starting a relationship with him. "Will . . ."

"Well, maybe it's a little about getting your clothes off," he teased.

I smiled.

"Give me a chance."

"I can't right now. I'm sorry. Look at me. I'm a mess." My face had a big blue bruise, I was homeless, penniless, and hung up on a guy who wanted nothing more than to tuck me into bed with a glass of milk and some cookies. How could any guy think I was remotely appealing?

His eyes traveled down my body, but focused on my face. "I don't see a mess. I see strength and beauty and passion and it all turns me on like crazy."

But he didn't know me and all my baggage. Yet, something about Will attracted me too—he wasn't the only one feeling the pull. "Let me think about it," I said finally. Maybe precisely because he didn't see the mess that I was, I found him appealing. He didn't want to fix me. He wanted me—to take me just as I was. And no one else, not Marcela, not Tracey, not even Nash was willing to do that.

• • •

I can't remember where we lived before we moved into the neighborhood from hell. I only remember that for a couple of months we lived with my aunt. She had a two-bedroom home somewhere in the San Fernando Valley. Four girls slept in one bedroom—me and my three cousins. Three boys in the other room. All the adults crashed in the living room.

But the smallness of the house never mattered much to us kids because we spent most of the time playing outside in a huge backyard. They could have fit three houses in that yard and still had room for a swimming pool. We all built forts and had tire swings and chased the pack of dogs that also lived with the family.

My aunt let us run around out there and brought us Kool-Aid and cookies in the afternoon. Then one by one, she called us inside to bathe before dinner. My parents were out looking for jobs or working. I didn't miss them.

I knew that the adults seemed to argue a lot, but as a kid, I didn't know or care why. All I knew was that I felt cared for and loved. When the day came for us to leave, I cried, begging my mother to let us kids stay—which was interesting in and of itself since I didn't ask for her to stay. Of course, that wasn't an option. We were moving to downtown L.A. and that was way too far from my aunt's house for us to even visit.

What always stuck in my mind was that my aunt made us feel so welcome, though I'm sure it was a huge imposition. Immigrants tend to bunch up. They help each other until they each are able to get on their feet. It's cool. And it's the way it should be. And eventually getting your own place is the reward; I guess it's a step toward Americanization.

To me, however, it wasn't a positive step. I liked living with all my cousins, having my aunt around if I fell down and got hurt or just needed a hug. What I got instead was an empty house with my brother in charge until my parents got home from work late in the evening. I walked to school alone, I ate dinner out of a can, and learned my lessons from my brother or other kids on the streets.

Who ever said isolation was a good thing?

I got to Nash's place about ten-thirty. He was in the guest room, removing boxes of CDs and a stereo system. He looked over his shoulder and noticed me leaning against the door frame. "Hey," he said.

Immediately, I was consumed with guilt for unsettling his home. "You can leave that stuff in here. Really. It won't bother me. All I need is a bed and part of the closet."

He lifted the box of CDs onto his shoulder and walked toward me. "You think I'm going to leave this great music in here for you to enjoy?" Lowering his head, he planted a kiss on my forehead. "Get out of my way."

He only said that because the man was into oldies rock like Mötley Crüe and Aerosmith (introduced to him by his older sister) and he knew I teased him about his taste in music. I rolled my tired body away from the door frame and watched him walk away with his stuff.

I was too tired to argue with him tonight about the length of my stay, so I dropped down on the bed and watched him walk in and out of the room. He pulled his computer equipment out next and began to set it up in the crowded living room.

My cell phone went off, but I was too tired to get up.

Nash peeked in. "Your purse is talking."

"I hear it." Kuniva from D12 was urging me to pick up my phone and asking if there was something wrong with my ears—a unique ringer I bought.

"Here." Holding it with thumb and index finger like it might jerk up and bite him, he brought the purse over and walked back out.

I sent him a nonverbal thank-you and pulled out my phone, turning off the annoying rapper. But I wish I hadn't answered. It was my father.

He'd never called me before so I was surprised to hear from him.

"You left. Your mother said you aren't coming back," he said.

"I can't stay there anymore with Carlos in the house."

Nash walked in and picked up a box of cables and wires. I absently watched him. His muscled arms bunched and hardened with the weight of the box.

"Come and get the rest of your things, *mi'ja.* I'll be here."

Carlos wasn't afraid of my father anymore. He knew now that my dad was weak. But Carlos still wouldn't dare do something to me while my father stood watch. "I'm sorry I left without saying good-bye." Though I didn't think anyone would care much.

He sighed. He was probably tired. "I understand why you did. But no matter what, we are your family. You don't turn your back on your family, *mi'ja.* If we were in Mexico you wouldn't have done this."

I've never been to Mexico, but I had this image of women being chained to men—first their fathers, then some abusive, tequila-drinking, unwashed *viejo.* I've seen some of my relatives who moved to this country. The women all look worn and tired after raising a dozen kids and being a slave to their husbands. Women put up with cheating, drunk husbands who beat them, and they accepted it as their fate. Hell, I didn't want that for myself.

Okay, okay, don't throw tomatoes; I know I'm not being totally fair, but when you grow up Latina and watch men act like asses all your life, what the hell are you supposed to think?

"I'm sorry things have been so hard on you, Dad. I'm sure we haven't helped." My father shouldn't be mistaken for a good man, despite my apology. He spent much of his time drunk. He beat my mother more times than I'd like to remember—and Carlos too when he was young. Only I escaped his wrath because I was so little and he chose not to see what I did wrong—maybe because I was a girl.

Yes, he believed that men had to rule their homes like tyrants—with brute force and threats. And yet he had very little control over what Carlos and I did or what went on under his roof. So to me he was a tyrant with no real power. Maybe deep inside he knew this and it's why he drank.

He cared about us like a person might care about their possessions. So I'm sure he didn't like the fact that I'd left.

"You kids don't know what it's like to work. You've had it easy all your lives."

Sure. Easy. "I don't have much to pick up, but if you can be there tomorrow night, I'll stop by and get a few things, and . . . say good-bye."

"Tomorrow. *Sí, sí,* come by."

After we hung up, I lay in bed thinking about things—my father, my mother, my brother. How did things get so bad? I came to the conclusion that my parents never should have had kids. They were totally clueless.

I listened to Nash put the computer together in the other room. At some point, I guess I drifted off to sleep.

When I woke up in the morning, my shoes had been removed and a blanket covered my body. And the room was bare of anything that belonged to Nash.

I met Marcela for lunch on Friday. We sat in the outside garden of the restaurant, because the day was warm and beautiful, and we both needed some fresh air. I told her about my job interview next week. I thought she'd be thrilled, but she had a fit about my dropping out of college. "Are you crazy? This is your future we're talking about. Absolutely not. You're not going to drop out of school, lose your scholarship, and miss out on getting a degree."

"I don't have a choice."

"Yes you do. I told you, I'll pay for you to get a place to live. I'll give you spending money. Shit, you're working at the center for free and have been for years."

"I don't want you to bail me out again."

"I'm not bailing you out of anything. I'm offering to help you for a few years—"

"I want to do this on my own. Why is that so hard for you to understand?"

"Because it's stupid. You don't have to do it alone."

I stood.

She stood as well. "Sit down."

"You sit. I'm not a fucking dog."

"And another thing," she went on, "you should have come to me in the first place. What are you doing going to Ryan?"

We glared at each other across the table. Nothing new. Marcela and I had a love/hate relationship like many real siblings. Except she was a bigger pain in the ass than a real sister, who probably wouldn't care what I did with my life. And I was tired of her telling me what to do. "He's my friend and I knew I could count on him helping me without a lecture."

"I don't lecture you."

"Like hell, you don't."

"Excuse me," the waiter said. "Are you ladies leaving?"

I turned to him ready to tell him to get the hell out of our faces, but Marcela smiled. "Yes, we are. Can you bring the check, please?"

He nodded and glanced uncertainly at me like I might transform into the hulk and begin overturning the tables.

"I know how you feel about Ryan, but give it up, Lupe. He's too old for you."

My attention returned to Marcela. She knew how I felt about Nash? How could she? For a moment, I had lost all the fight inside me and couldn't come up with a response. I picked up my purse.

"You shouldn't be living with him. He's a grown man, and you're . . ."

"I'm what?"

Marcela actually blushed. "You're not a kid anymore." She pointed at my body. "Let's face it, Lupe. You're quite a temptation."

Was I? Would Nash really think so? Her comment had the opposite effect of what she intended. I smiled. "Let's hope so. I've wanted to get him into bed for years, and now he'll be just a few steps away."

Before she could close her big mouth, I left her in her fancy restaurant with her ridiculously high bill. As I roared away on my bike, I felt sort of bad.

Marcela couldn't help butting into my life. She's basically been responsible for me for six years, and old habits die hard. But it was time to cut the apron strings. If I wasn't careful, I could easily depend on her the rest of my life.

I'd call her later and tell her I was sorry. Not that I had to. We could say just about anything to each other, and it didn't matter if we fought a million times, we always made up. Someday, I'd be in a position to make things up to her. But until then, I needed some space from Marcela and her family.

I pulled my motorcycle up to my parents' house, killed the engine, and took off my helmet. Sitting there, I stared at the front door with mixed emotions. Would this be the last time I ever walked through it? I've hated coming home to this dump since I was a kid. It wasn't even ours. We rented. But it was also home, and I wished my family had been . . . I don't know. More normal. There were lots of families who lived in the neighborhood who stayed clean, worked hard, and got out. But not us.

My watch said it was after eight, so I figured my father was home. Carlos wasn't out on the steps, so that was a good sign. I left my bike, squared my shoulders like I was going into battle or something, and headed up the walk.

When I walked inside, it was quiet. No one seemed to be home, but the front door had been unlocked. "Hello?"

The door to my bedroom flew open and Carlos looked out, nervous and jumpy. Great.

He grabbed my arm and dragged me inside the room. Two other guys were inside packing for a what looked like a big drug buy.

Carlos pushed me down to the floor. I moved like a hermit crab, my back to the wall.

"You scared me," he said. "Sit there and be quiet."

"Okay."

The other two guys didn't look happy to see me.

"Just my sister. She's cool."

My heart was beating a little too fast and moisture was starting to collect at my temples and between my breasts. At least he'd said I was cool. That was a first. "Where's Dad?" I asked.

"I said to sit there and shut up," he said, yelling and holding his hand up like he as going to smack me.

I flinched, but didn't back down. "Why don't I just leave you guys alone to finish your business? I'll come by and see Dad another time."

The doorbell rang. He froze, listening for I don't know what. *Paranoid druggie.* Then he grabbed my arm again and pulled me to my feet. This time he took a gun from out of his waistband and placed it flat against the side of my face.

Everything inside me went silent. The Earth stopped spinning. Where the hell had he gotten a gun? I knew that if he'd bought or stolen a gun, he'd use it.

"Good idea," he said. "You leave. But first go and open the door. Collect any weapons, and send them back here unarmed. Got it?"

I got it, but didn't want to get it. Shit. "Yeah." I nodded.

"Don't fuck this up, Lupe, or I swear I'll come after you," he promised, letting me get a look at the gun one more time before he slipped it away. Then he pushed me out of the bedroom.

I carefully opened the front door. "Can I help you?" I asked.

A couple of white guys stood on the porch. They appeared way more alert and with-it than Carlos. They were dressed in shabby jeans and T-shirts that didn't stand out, but something about them didn't strike me as genuine.

They looked at each other like they weren't expecting me, a girl, to open the door. "Carlos here?"

"Come in," I said, opening the door wider.

They walked in and scanned the room. I got the feeling they were visually recording everything they saw.

"Any weapons?" I asked.

Again, they glanced at each other. "Where's Carlos?"

"Come on. Don't make me have to lay my hands on you. Drop your weapons and I'll take you to my brother."

One guy with a tacky earring on his right ear lifted his chin as if understanding my involvement. But the other moved toward the bedroom.

"Hey," I said.

Earring man grabbed my arm and led me toward the room.

Then things happened a little fast and I realized what it was that had bothered me about these two. They drew their guns and announced they were undercover detectives and for everyone to put their arms up.

"You too, sweetcakes, unless you still want to lay your hands on me."

I groaned and lifted my arms up. Perfect. I was going to be part of a drug bust.

Seven

Becoming Americana means learning to live in two worlds and never quite belonging to either.

LUPE PEREZ

The detectives meant business, so I did exactly as I was told, though I glared at Carlos.

But my brother could never do anything easily, so he tossed a box at one of the detectives and jumped out the window.

"Oh my God," I said as glass flew in all directions. Mostly outside, but I still ducked and pasted myself against the wall.

Carlos's accomplices tried to follow, but they were apprehended by the detectives, who, unlike me, weren't startled by a little flying glass. I stood out of the way, pretty sure I was going to get shot by someone in the struggle.

But both guys were eventually cuffed and shoved to the floor. Then one of the detectives called the black and whites and hurried out the window to look for my brother.

I couldn't believe this. Just what I needed. Funny thing was that

I wasn't nervous or scared or worried. I sort of watched all this unfold in front of me and silently rooted for the cops.

Earring man shot me a look. "Don't even try to leave."

I held my hands up again and met his gaze. "Do I look stupid?"

He smirked. "If you're not stupid, what are you doing with these guys?" He stood over the two jerks on the floor.

"You know, some people just manage to find themselves in the wrong place, with the wrong people all the time, no matter what."

He narrowed his eyes and came closer to me. "What you managed to do is get yourself arrested for possession of narcotics for sale. How does that strike you?"

I closed my eyes for a moment as I pictured my future dissolve before my eyes. Then I shook my head and met his gaze. "I had nothing to do with this. I swear."

Maybe he believed me. Maybe he didn't. But he had a job to do. "I need to cuff you," he said.

I held my hands out in front of me. "What the heck. You might as well."

He snapped a cuff around one of my wrists while studying me. "You know the drill, don't you, sweetheart?"

I couldn't speak as I stared at the cold steel I swore I'd never feel again. He twisted me around and placed my hands behind my back. Gently, he finished cuffing my wrists.

Shit. I wiggled my hands, now lightly shackled, and swallowed a lump in my throat. Haven't had this happen to me since I was a kid.

He walked me to the living room. "Sit on the couch and wait. Don't try anything . . . stupid."

I sat on the couch until the uniformed cops came and took the two loser buddies of my brother away. Carlos had managed to escape. He knew the neighborhood well and probably had a hiding spot already staked out, just in case. But eventually the police would find him. Idiot.

Cops got to me last.

Earring man gazed at me like he regretted having to turn me over to the cops. "I think her involvement here was coincidental . . . but she *was* helping her brother."

I was taken to the police station in the damn patrol car. Luckily, Captain Martinez spotted me as soon as I walked into the station.

He rushed over. "What the fuck, Lupe?"

"Carlos. A drug bust. I was there to see my dad and got caught in the mix."

"Shit. Take the cuffs off her," he said to the younger officer.

"But—"

"Take the damn cuffs off."

The second the cuffs came off he pushed me into the interrogation room and forced me to sit in the most uncomfortable wooden chair in all of Los Angeles. Then he scowled at me.

I rubbed my arm. I'd probably have bruises come morning from all the men who'd grabbed me and pushed me around tonight. "Sorry," I said. "But you guys are the ones who let him out of jail early."

"Says here that you were helping with the drug buy."

"Carlos told me to open the door and let the *gueros* in." I sighed. "You know Carlos. You think I could have gotten away from him? He had a gun—"

"A gun? Did he threaten you with it?"

"Of course. What do you think, he was framing it as part of a collection? I did what he asked, hoping I could leave and let him conduct his drug deal alone. But the guys were cops. What can I say?"

Martinez cursed. "So you felt threatened? Feared for your life?"

"Well, I don't know how far Carlos would have—"

"You helped him under duress."

I gazed at my old enemy, the man who was now my pal, the man who wanted me to say the right things. "I don't deal drugs, Martinez. I just wanted out of the house."

"And who were the other two we arrested?"

"Don't know. They were with Carlos."

He threw open the door and ran a hand though his hair. "I'll be back. And you better hope those two are willing to back up your story. Or damn it, Lupe. This isn't going to go good for you."

I sat alone and waited for over an hour. I didn't cry. I should have. I needed to. But I couldn't. Life was unfair. I knew that already. Whatever happened next, I'd deal with it.

When Captain Martinez returned, he sat heavily across from me.

"Well? How screwed am I? Don't keep me in suspense."

"You think this is funny?"

"No."

"Then shut up. This is *not* the time to be a smart-ass."

I knew he was angry, but not really at me. He didn't want to arrest me. A lump grew in my throat. "It's my home, Martinez. I live there—well, I did. I've moved out. But that's the atmosphere I lived in. I can't control what Carlos does—"

"You can control what *you* do, damn it. How could you be so stupid as to get involved?"

"What was I supposed to do? Refuse to help him? Get a few more broken ribs to add to my collection? Maybe a bullet to my head this time." Now tears did spring to my eyes. I held my forehead in my hands. "I was afraid. You want to know the truth? I'm scared to death of the bastard. Okay? Happy?"

"No." He sighed. "No, Lupe, I'm not happy."

"So am I going to be charged with selling drugs?" I angled my head and gazed at him from under my arms.

"Of course not. Those guys were pissed as hell that your brother ran out and left them to take all the heat. So they blamed most of it on him and corroborated your story about him threatening you if you didn't help him."

I released a huge breath of air.

"They also said that Carlos told you he'd come after you if you messed up. That has me worried."

"Don't worry. I doubt he'll do that."

He nodded. "Go give Castillo your report. We've got you down as a witness, not as a participant. Then get the hell out of here."

I stood. "Really. Just like that?"

"False arrest. You're free to go after you tell us what happened."

I wanted to give the chubby, gruff guy a hug, but I restrained myself. "Thanks, Martinez."

"Stay out of the house, and for God's sake, stay away from your brother."

"I will."

Swallowing both my pride and my embarrassment, I had to call Nash to come and get me when I was finished a couple of hours later. He took me back to my parents' house, where I picked up my bike. My father had gone out drinking and had forgotten I'd be coming by, and by the time I returned he was sleeping off the liquor. My mom had worked late. I filled her in on what had happened with Carlos. She gave a distressed sigh and told me to take my things and go. I said good-bye without taking anything. This part of my life was over and I decided I didn't want anything that would ever remind me of it again.

When we got to Nash's apartment, he made me some tea and put his arm around me as we sat on the couch together.

"I'll never go back home."

"This is your home now, Lupe." He looked down at me. "With me."

I met his hooded eyes, and bit my lower lip. Then I nodded. No doubt about it, my home was with Nash. I've never wanted anyone or anything more. We belonged together. Hadn't I always known it?

On Sunday, I dropped by the university library to renew a few books. I was still shaken by the whole experience yesterday and shell-shocked with the too-close-for-comfort near-arrest. I wondered where Carlos had run to, and if he would actually try to contact me. Nash wanted me to place a restraining order on him. But those damn things never worked. A restraining order wouldn't stop Carlos if he wanted to get to me.

After renewing my books, I strolled back through campus and decided to go to Drake Stadium to sit on the track and field bleachers. The day was nice and warm and after facing the fear of being locked up again, I decided that spending a few hours reading outdoors was just what I needed.

Our track team was practicing, so I sat and watched for a while. Down by the field, I thought I recognized Will standing beside the track. He had a clipboard in his hand. I watched him from up above as I studied, finding myself glancing down every once in a while to see if he was still there.

Finally he stretched after about a half hour and glanced up. He placed a hand over his eyes. "Hey." He smiled. "Lupe? That you?"

"Hi," I called back.

Taking two steps at a time, he ran up the bleachers. "Isn't this a nice surprise? Tell me you came to see me."

"And pump up that ego of yours?"

"Admit it, you couldn't stay away. You missed me." He sat beside me and pulled out a pack of cigarettes.

I watched him light one and blow smoke out the side of his mouth. My eyes stayed trained on the red tip of the cigarette.

"What?" he asked

I was staring. "You smoke?"

He seemed to stiffen. "Ah. Sometimes."

"No wonder you had a lighter handy the other night."

He put the cigarette out. "You don't like it."

"No, I . . . it's none of my business."

"Here." He gave me his pack. "Throw it out."

"Will, no, really. I don't care."

"You do care. I can see it on your face. You don't like it."

"No. I guess I don't." We had two programs at The Vibe to help kids get rid of addictions. One was a simple antitobacco program that included smoking cessation, and the other was a more intense cleansing program, which I went through myself.

"Then I don't need to smoke. It's no big deal. I quit. It's bad for me anyway."

I gazed at him, unsure of what to say. He was trying awfully hard to get my approval and it felt sort of nice. "Thank you."

He winked. "Thank *you.* For caring."

I offered him a stick of gum and took one for myself. Then, I looked away. He leaned over my work, his shoulder brushing mine. "What are you studying there?"

"Just reading a little about Latino culture. I'm writing a book about Americanization of immigrants, and decided I need to do some research."

"Cool topic."

"I'm not really sure what I'm going to write about. I've got nothing but thoughts and ideas, and little stories I remember from when I was a kid."

He leaned back, resting his elbows on the bleacher bench behind him. "Sounds like you're off to a good start. Writing starts like that. A few ideas, a few stories, and soon, you've got an entire article or book."

"Really?"

He grinned. "You've got the cutest expressions."

Okay, embarrass me, why don't you?

"I didn't know you liked to write," he said.

"I don't particularly like it."

"Then why do it?"

I shrugged. "Maybe I need to write this. And maybe I *do* like it a little."

"Something else we have in common."

I didn't respond. He sat beside me watching the runners. Then he pushed himself up. "I better get back to work. I'm supposed to be covering this practice and the race next week."

"Okay."

He stood. "See you in class?"

"See you."

He bent down and took the pen out of my hand. Then he wrote down his phone number. "In case you want to see me before class," he said, and with a smile, took off.

When I got out of juvenile detention camp, Marcela and my mother had made an agreement that I would attend a private high school. My mother wasn't really pleased about this, but she saw it as a way to keep me off the streets and out of juvie.

My old friends from East L.A. High School didn't like it either. They made fun of me. Called me a sellout. Said I'd gone weak. I was stunned. "Hey, we can still be tight," I said.

"Naw, you'll be hangin' with white chicks now."

I frowned, trying to understand, but failing. "Man, it's just school. You guys will still be my friends."

"You don't get it," Mari said. "Once you start mixing, you change. You can't help it."

I argued. Told her she was crazy. Downed a six-pack of beer to prove I was still one of them.

But in retrospect, she was right. Private school opened my eyes to the fact that a whole other world existed out there. I realized my barrio speech would have to change if I wanted to be accepted by mainstream society, for example. The change was gradual, but it happened. I became aware that my world was not quite right. That I had to let it go. I had to turn away from the friends I grew up with, and that hurt.

I became unaccepted by Mexicans because I was turning white and unaccepted by Anglos because I was still Mexican. And *that*, I know now, is what becoming Americana is all about—learning to live in both worlds, forever unaccepted. And learning to switch back and forth as easy as flipping a switch in your head.

On my way home from the university, I stopped by Long's Drugs and bought a bunch of magazines. *Glamour*, *Cosmo*, *Vogue*, *Allure*. With my new job looming ahead of me, I decided it might be a good idea to learn a little about fashion, hair, and makeup.

As I was paying for my purchases, the person behind me in line bumped me with her cart. When I turned to look, I saw that I knew this particular female.

"Hey, dawg," she said.

I wish I could say I was happy to see my old friend, but I was never glad to see anyone from my neighborhood anymore. "Hey, *chica*," I said back to my old buddy Mari.

"Slumming?"

I took my change from the cashier. Mari knew I worked at The Vibe, and that I never have abandoned my people, but she always had to rub it in my face that after I met Marcela I moved away from my gang of friends. "Well, you know, I want to remember how the other half lives every once in a while."

As nonchalantly as possible, I picked up my plastic bag with the magazines inside, grateful she didn't see what I'd bought. She'd really have ammunition against me if she knew I was planning to read *Glamour.*

"Wait up," she said as the clerk rang up her Sudafed and candy bars.

I waited, then once she paid, we walked out together. "Saw your brother," she said.

Because she was one of his customers. I tried not to show outwardly how angry that made me. But I'd tried to help my old friends, including Mari, a few years ago and they'd laughed and then shunned me. Although it was never too late for someone to change, there was definitely a fortress that grew higher and higher the longer someone was involved in the drug scene, and hers had become impenetrable to me. "I thought he was on the run," I said.

"He was pretty pissed at you."

"So what else is new?"

"You fucked up this time, Lupe."

"Look, it wasn't my fault he was too stupid to realize he was dealing with cops. He got sloppy and it backfired on him."

"Yeah, well, not how he tells it."

"Whatever." I turned away toward my bike.

"You better watch your back. He said that you led those guys to him. That you and the cops set the whole thing up, and that he's gonna take you out."

Did he actually believe I'd go through all that trouble to trap him? A chill ran up my back, but it vanished as quickly as it came. Carlos was an idiot and lots of times he was out of his mind, but he wouldn't put in the effort to get to me. What for? "He's that afraid of me, huh?"

"He knows you'll testify against him again."

In a heartbeat. "Oh, so he realizes he's going to get caught."

"Hopefully not, but . . ." she shrugged.

"He should turn himself in—they'd probably go easier on him."

She laughed.

"Stay away from him, Mari, he's nothing but trouble."

"Seems to me you're the one that's trouble."

"All I want is to be left alone."

"Maybe if you helped him recover from the deal gone bad, all would be forgiven."

Sure, he'd love it if I incriminated myself. That way I couldn't testify against him without also involving myself. Then he'd feel safe. "Since I want him caught, I'll pass on that offer." I held out my fist in a good-bye wave we used to use as kids.

"Yeah," she said. "Take care."

When I got to Nash's place, I spent a couple of hours reading articles and looking at pictures. Was it me or were these articles just a bunch of superficial crap? I mean, do I really care what Hilary Duff wore to her movie premiere? Or if Hillary Clinton's skin tone has improved since moving out of D.C. and into New York City? Come on.

Though I did find a couple of articles on combining clothes useful. I tore those pages out of the magazines to file away.

Then I noticed an article on makeup. Here's something I was curious about. The title read, "For a Vibrant Outdoorsy Flush." I shrugged, grabbed the bag of cosmetic products I just bought and the magazine, and headed to the bathroom, where I dumped everything in the sink.

The article said to apply a lustrous foundation. I frowned and looked through the mess of stuff I bought and found what I needed. I cleaned my face first with a cleanser, then applied the foundation. Sort of perplexed, I gazed in the mirror—I looked like I'd worked up a sweat or had oily skin. Okay, this was supposed to be good? So far not impressed.

I read on. I had to put on a glistening pink liquid highlighter. Hmm. I wasn't sure about the "glistening" part, but I had a bottle of pink liquid, so I poured some on my fingers and rubbed it all over my face, forehead, cheeks, chin, even my nose. Again, I looked in the mirror and my jaw sagged. I looked like a bubble gum Blow Pop.

The next step called for shimmery apricot eyeshadow. I wasn't sure I had apricot, but I found some orangy stuff and put it on my lids. This time I laughed out loud at the results. "They must be kidding," I said.

The last two things I had to add were blush across my cheeks and berry lipstick.

What was up with all the fruit names? I looked for more red shit and added it to my already glowing face.

Holy shit. This was supposed to look good?

I let my hair flow down across my shoulders and pursed my lips. I shook my head. I was ready for Halloween already.

I picked up all my stuff and put it back in my bag.

As I headed to my bedroom, Nash came home.

He glanced at me and stopped dead. "What the hell did you do to yourself?"

"You like it?" I smiled to show off my bright berry lips.

"Ah, no." He tossed his keys on top of the TV.

"Are you telling me you don't appreciate my artistic skills?"

He sat on the couch and put his feet on the coffee table. He stared at me, then burst out laughing. "Honey, forget your interview with the ad agency. I hear Ringling Brothers is looking for new clowns."

I wanted to laugh, but controlled myself. With only a slight smile, I pulled out my berry lipstick. "Too much red, you think?" I showed him the tube and walked forward.

"Too much is an apt way to describe it. What did you do, empty the makeup bottle on your face?"

You know, I looked bad, no doubt about it, but wasn't he going overboard and being a little mean-spirited? Yes he was. And I planned to fix him. I opened the cap. "Too much lipstick?"

He raised an eyebrow. "Is that what you put on your lips? I thought maybe you were holding one of those Christmas balls in your mouth."

I sat on my knees beside him on the couch, and twisted the stick so he could get a good look at what he'd be wearing in about one second. "Problem is, I need to practice; I don't know how to use this stuff."

He eyed me warily. "What are you doing?"

"If I could apply it to someone else's lips a few times, you know, learn the art by doing, I might do better on myself next time."

"No," he said, pressing his back tighter against the couch.

"Please. No one would know but you and me, that you wore lipstick."

He looked horrified. "You're not putting lipstick on me!"

Oh, yes, I was. Before he could slide farther away from me, I straddled him. "I read that lots of guys have fantasies about wearing makeup. And it's okay with me, Nash. Your secret will be safe with me."

He placed his hands on my forearms. "No."

"I'll never tell anyone. This will never leave this room. I need the practice. Please." I strained my arm to get the lipstick close to his face.

He dipped his head back. "Stop it."

"You'd look so adorable with berry lips."

He laughed. "Cut it out."

Since both his hands were holding my arms, I leaned my face close to his. "I guess I have enough on my lips to do the trick."

I didn't mean this as a come-on, and he didn't take it that way either.

He laughed as my lips hovered over his. "You're evil."

"What's it gonna be, Nash?"

He raised an eyebrow and glanced at my lips as if to say getting lipstick smeared on that way would actually be enjoyable. "You're playing with the big boys here, Lupe. You sure you're going to be able to handle the repercussions of your actions?"

I touched his lips with mine and glided them across, painting his lips a little at a time. I wasn't prepared for the sensations that this action stirred inside me and I suddenly realized the position of our bodies.

He sat there motionless. His hands on my arms had gone slack and his body had tensed.

Then before I realized what was happening, he flipped me onto my back and pinned me by straddling me this time. He also managed to snag the lipstick from my hand. "Here, let me show you how it's done," he said with a wicked smile.

Coming at me like an evil Dr. Jekyll with a syringe, he touched the point of the red tube to my lips. I moved my head to the side and a line of berry slashed across my cheek.

"Tsk, tsk, tsk," he said. "You moved."

I bucked and fought him for the stick.

He laughed. "Wait. You need a matching stripe on the other side."

He managed to mark my other cheek.

With the heel of my hand I hit his stomach.

"Ugh," he said as he lost the air in his gut.

I quickly stole the lipstick back and attacked his lips, making him look like a male Angelina Jolie.

By the time he recovered and was fighting for control, we fell off the couch. I scratched my side on the coffee table and my tattoo ached. But I was laughing so hard that the pain didn't matter.

"Okay, okay," he said. "Time out." He made the hand sign to match his words.

I got one last swipe at his nose.

We sat up with our backs against the couch, catching our breath. He shook his head. "Teaches me to give a woman my opinion."

I gazed at him with a smile. He called me a woman. Okay, so maybe I could forgive the clown comments.

"Let's get washed up, huh?" he said.

I nodded.

"Then I'll take you out for burgers and fries."

"Okay."

"But Lupe."

"What?"

"Stay away from that makeup, man."

"Shut up. I'm going to learn how to do it right, you'll see."

He chuckled as I walked away. I washed up in the bathroom while he did the same in the kitchen. When I came back out to the living room, he was taking a call.

He hung up. "Sorry, Lupe, Ernesto is having girl problems and needs to talk to someone."

It was Sunday, and though The Vibe never closed, it was Nash's night off. But that didn't mean anything. Anytime one of the kids needed him, he dropped everything and went to them. This was one of the reasons I loved him. However, tonight I wished he wasn't so conscientious.

"Here," he said, handing me a twenty-dollar bill. "Go get the burgers. I'll nuke mine when I get home."

"Sure," I took the money, disappointed that I'd be eating dinner alone.

Eight

Becoming Americana means eventually working with those who don't understand your culture or your ways, and pretending your heritage no longer matters to you.

LUPE PEREZ

Wednesday morning, I got up early to dress in my power suit—well, it was a power suit to me. I'd never owned an outfit like this. Tracey said my long hair was perfect and showed me how to pin it up in a bun. I practiced all morning while Nash knocked on the bathroom door every once in a while and asked if I was okay. I also worked on my makeup. Tracey recommended that I use a reddish blush with sparks of copper and gold because it would look good with my olive skin coloring. And to stay on the light side.

So, when I walked out of my bedroom and headed to the bathroom to do my hair and makeup for the final time, I prayed that I'd do it right. Nash nearly spilled coffee down the front of his shirt when he saw me.

"You okay?" I asked.

"Those are some clothes you bought."

"I have to look the part for this interview."

"What part is that?"

"Well, it's an ad agency—I'm not really sure of the position. But I figured I needed to dress as great as possible."

He stared at my body. "Well, you look . . . terrific."

"Thanks. I'm so nervous."

"You'll do fine. Really, you look beautiful."

I walked into the bathroom feeling like a million dollars. He noticed me. And he liked what he saw. For once, he looked at me like a man looks at a woman. I owed Tracey big-time.

I applied some light makeup and fixed my hair. As I looked at myself in the mirror, I couldn't believe the transformation. I felt almost uncomfortable. I didn't look like myself.

Nash waited outside the door. I nearly bumped into him when I walked out of the bathroom. Again, he stared.

"Do you need the bathroom? Sorry I took so long in there."

"No, it's . . . okay."

I smiled.

He didn't return it.

"I'll try to stop by The Vibe later. After my interview."

"Forget it." He shook his head. "You've got classes later."

"Right." But what was the use of continuing with this quarter's classes if I got this job? Of course, I didn't have the job yet.

"Lupe," he said, and cleared his throat almost as if trying to lift himself out of a fog. "How are you getting to this interview? I mean, you're not going to ride your motorcycle with that skirt, are you?"

"Oh, shit, I didn't even think of that."

He pulled out his cell phone and grinned. "Let me have Roberto open the center, and I'll drive you."

"Are you sure? Nash, I—"

"I'm positive." He made the call.

If I got the job, I'd have to invest in a car. Damn, this job thing was becoming an expensive proposition.

We climbed into his old Buick, which had racked up about two hundred thousand miles, but at least it ran and Nash kept it clean, unlike his apartment.

"Where to?" he asked.

I unfolded the paper Tracey gave me with the directions. "It's in Westwood." I passed him the address.

He looked it up in his *Thomas Guide.* "Got it," he said, and took off. Every once in a while he glanced across at me.

"What?" I asked finally.

"You just look so amazing. Like I always knew you would."

What did that mean? "Funny how something like clothes can make even a twig like me look decent."

"You're not a twig anymore and you look more than decent."

A warm blush traveled from my neck to my face and up to my ears. "Yeah?"

He shot me another quick look. "Yeah."

Tell me. Tell me more about what I look like to you.

But his eyes were back on the road. "I hope you get this job. Hell, an ad agency in Westwood where you can dress like that, and work with people with money and class? That's exactly what you need and deserve."

It's what I needed, all right. "I'm a little nervous."

"Just be yourself." Then he thought about it and smiled. "Well, yourself, toned down."

I laughed.

Once we arrived, he jumped out of his seat and ran around the car to open my door. Never had a man done this for me, and at first, I wasn't sure what he was doing. *Why the hell is he hurrying out of the car?* I wondered.

But I accepted the gesture with pleasure.

"I'll wait here. How long do you think the interview will take?"

I shrugged. "Do you want to come with me and wait in the reception area?"

He looked down at his jeans and black T-shirt with The Vibe written in white across his chest. "I'll wait in the car."

To me he looked as handsome as always, but I understood his feeling out of place. "Okay."

He bent down and gave me a soft kiss on the cheek. "Good luck, kid."

"Thanks, old man." If he was going to continue to treat me like a child, I'd give him some of his own medicine.

But he only grinned, then shooed me toward the glass doors.

I entered the building and found the right floor. The receptionist had my name written in her planner, and told me to take a seat while she called Mr. Burton.

As I waited, I tried not to feel intimidated by all the bright, bold colors on the walls. Everything was crisp and in order and shiny, unlike the drab rooms decorated with garage sale items in my parents' home, or even the old classrooms at UCLA. This place was modern and I hoped represented my future.

Mr. Burton called me in and walked around his desk to shake my hand. He didn't look like a lecherous old kook. In fact, his glance down my body was more of a systematic analysis, as if conducting an inspection. His smile was wide and genuine and he had an elegant Robert Redford style.

We sat across from each other, he back on his side of his desk, me on the other.

"Tracey has shared many complimentary things about you, Lupe."

"I appreciate getting this interview."

"You have a resume?"

I'd typed one up at the campus lab, and though it didn't look very professional, it did list all my volunteer work at the center and my restaurant work and my educational background with computers.

He studied it and raised an eyebrow. "So you've got some background in Web design?"

"I do. I've designed The Vibe's website. You can pull it up if you'd like." I pointed to his laptop. "It's the TheVibeKids.com."

Mr. Burton grinned, then reached for his mouse and called up the center's website. I was proud of that site. I kept it tricked out with all the latest features. "I also have my own site, and I did one for Alberto's, a personal chef service."

"This is excellent work." He clicked through the site.

"Thanks."

"Okay." He leaned back. "Let me explain what we need. I'm looking for someone who will be responsible for all aspects of a client's technological development, including design and implementation of a Web presence and other technology solutions. I don't care too much about previous experience or a four-year college degree—I prefer it, but it's not mandatory. What I am looking for is initiative, the look—which you've got—and someone willing to put in forty to fifty hours a week."

"I can do that."

"Good. Do you speak Spanish, by the way?"

"Yes."

"Excellent. Businesses are looking to market to Latinos, so we're going to be putting a lot more emphasis in that area. Maybe you can help out."

I wasn't sure how, but I nodded.

"Are you willing to attend a few development training meetings prior to starting?"

"Sure."

"Because you'll basically be an intern, I can't pay you much. Couple thousand a month. But I'll throw in a complete benefits package, you'll get amazing work experience, and you'll be working with upbeat professionals in a positive work environment. What do you say?"

A couple thousand a month? Was he kidding? That was fantastic! I opened my mouth to tell him what I thought, but all I could think of saying was that he was fuckin' awesome. But I didn't think that would be appropriate.

"Do you want to think about it?" He stood and came around the desk.

Probably my cue to leave. I stood as well. "It's a generous offer," I said, feeling like an idiot. What did I mean? I didn't even know what I meant, I was just trying to sound intelligent and sophisticated.

He chuckled. "Tell you what, after six months, if you're doing okay, I'll give you a 20 percent raise."

Twenty percent?! That was another four hundred dollars a month! "Does this mean I'm hired?"

"If you want the job, it's yours."

The biggest smile I've probably ever had spread across my face. "Thank you so much."

"No problem. Let's have you come in on November first for the first training meeting."

"Great."

"Oh, and Lupe?"

"Yes."

"Get rid of all that glimmery gold eyeshadow. It's not right for you."

"Oh." And I'd worked so hard at it. Back to the drawing board. "Okay."

I left his office floating about a hundred feet off the ground.

When I finally came back to earth, I practically ran out of the building searching for Nash's car.

"How did it go?" he asked as he pulled up and pushed the door open for me.

"I got the job," I shrieked. "I'm so jazzed." I hugged him. "I can't believe it."

Nash laughed and returned my embrace.

I started filling him in on the entire interview and everything they'd offered me. "I'm going to have to get a car," I said.

"I can drive you to work for a while until you get one."

"I'll have to work at the center in the evening from now on, because work starts at nine in the morning."

"Forget the center. When you leave here, you'll have to go to school—take some night classes."

I glanced out the window. "I'm dropping this quarter's classes. It's too late to make any changes to my schedule this far into the year."

He was silent, but I knew he was thinking the same things Marcela had been vocal enough to verbalize about my future and staying in college, and all that good-girl stuff.

"Aren't you going to say something?"

"What should I say? That you're making a mistake? That you shouldn't take this job even if you obviously want it? That you don't have to stress about money? I've already told you all that."

"I know."

"Any way that you can postpone this job until you finish up this quarter? I mean, you're going to lose everything you've done in the past couple of months."

"I'm lucky he's hiring me. I don't want to give him an excuse not to."

Nash drove without comment. Then he reached across and squeezed my shoulder. "Do what you have to do, Lupe."

I was grateful that he was laying off about finishing college. "How about lunch? I'll buy," I said, and it felt great to be able to offer.

"What the hell," he said. "The day's half over anyway."

We drove to the international marketplace and ate Greek food. It wasn't bad. After strolling around for a while, we celebrated my new job with a huge banana split. I didn't want the afternoon to end. Nash had never spent this much time with me outside of the center, and I was loving it.

"How about a walk on the beach?" I suggested.

"I've got to get to work, Lupe."

"Come on. The day's almost over—you said it yourself. And we need to walk off the calories from dessert."

"Oh, yeah, like you really need to worry about that." He poked my ribs.

"So you *are* calling me a twig."

He gave me the look of a cornered man. "I'm saying *you* don't need to worry about getting fat."

"Probably not, but I would still like to take a walk."

As we reached his car, he studied me over the hood.

"Please, Ryan. I don't want to go home or to the center." I rarely used his first name, but when I did it always seemed to have jolting effect on him, as if he realized we were peers now.

He nodded. "Get in."

I called the school cafeteria to let them know I wouldn't be able to work tonight. I felt irresponsible and indulgent and a little guilty, but I didn't want this day with Nash to end. He called The Vibe to check on staff and let them know that for the first time ever, he wouldn't be in.

Nash got on Santa Monica Boulevard and followed it out to the beach. I took my ankle-strap shoes off and walked barefoot on the sand, and he took my hand. We climbed onto a lifeguard shack and watched the waves roll in and out. The sun was starting to set and the pink and purple colors over the horizon looked amazing. Maybe I was just really happy, for the first time in a really long time.

"I remember the first time I saw the ocean," Nash said in a dream-like voice that clashed with his in-control outward appearance.

But then again, everything about him seemed to be a contradiction. When it came to The Vibe and the kids, he cared so deeply, and gave his heart without holding back, and yet I know some of the women he dated called him a complete bastard. And his looks. Wow. He was beautiful. I stared at his profile now and it was as handsome as the rest of him. Long straight nose, perfect eyebrows, strong jaw that was always covered with a light dusting of whiskers. But he advertised none of that—instead he always appeared unkempt, on the edge.

On his long neck, his large Adam's apple bobbed. "I was about your age when I moved out here from Omaha, and I'd never seen the ocean."

Actually, he hadn't been my age. He'd been seventeen. Full of testosterone and ego, he'd run away from home before his eighteenth birthday. He shared with me once how he'd thought he was so smart and independent that he didn't want his parents controlling him. Arrogantly, he thought he could survive on his own, but when he came to Los Angeles he realized he'd made a big mistake. His parents refused to allow him to return home. The way they saw it, he'd left and now had to make it on his own.

Faced with that fact, he'd lived in a shelter while he got his GED, then got a certificate as a physical trainer online and got a job at the health center where Marcela eventually discovered him. She'd always said she'd picked him out because at twenty-one he'd vibrated with energy and enthusiasm and he had leadership potential written all over him.

"I felt so small and weak staring out at the waves," he said, "at this mass of living, breathing water that had, to me, tremendous, life-altering power. Continents were formed and mountains were destroyed by the power of the ocean, you know?"

"You aren't small or weak, Nash," I said. "You help to mold people. That's way better than forming continents, in my book."

He leaned back against the gray wooden post and stretched out his legs, crossing them at the ankles. "You think we really make much of a difference? Sometimes I wonder."

"I know we do. It's just that those kids have a lot to overcome. They have to hear about the possibilities lots of times before they believe it." I looked out at the water. The sun had almost disappeared. "When all you've had is shit in your life, it's hard to believe there can be anything else."

When he didn't respond, I turned to him and noticed that he'd been gazing at me pensively. Studying me. "You believe though, right?" he asked.

"Took me a long time to realize I could have and be more. Part of me didn't think I deserved better."

He flinched as if my words hurt him. Then he reached across and took one of my hands. "Lupe. You deserve so much more than what you've gotten, kiddo. You're a brilliant, beautiful young lady and . . ." He looked away. "I'm proud of you for turning your life around."

"Thanks." I wanted to scoot closer to him, for him to hold more than just my fingers, but I was too inexperienced to make the first move. This wasn't sex; it was love, romance, and I didn't know how to act like an interested woman and not appear like a slut. I couldn't throw myself at him.

He looked deep into my eyes. "You know, I never told you, because you were so young, but my older sister had a drug problem."

"The one you told me died of diabetes?"

He nodded. "Yep. She was four years older than me. She started doing drugs real young. Think she was about twelve. By the time my parents caught on, she was so hooked there was nothing they could do to help her."

"Mmm." I didn't know what to say, so I just listened.

"And with her diabetes . . . it really took a toll on her body."

I noticed he spoke in an unusually emotionless voice. "What did your parents do?"

"Gave up. Kicked her out of the house so she wouldn't 'infect' me. I was their golden boy. I was going to be everything Trish wasn't."

"Was that why they were so pissed when you came to California?"

"Pretty much. They gave up on me too. It's either all or nothing with them."

And he'd chosen nothing. Rebelled. Showed them. "Maybe they've changed their minds," I said.

Nash shook his head and looked back out at the ocean. "Trish overdosed when she was seventeen, six months after they tossed her out. I blamed them for a while, but now I realize it wasn't their fault. She was lost. And they aren't people who can deal with life when it gets messy. That's just a fact. I have no interest in seeing them again."

I placed a hand on his knee, feeling a warm current move from his body to mine. "Man, I know how that is."

Probably in the spirit of solidarity, he covered my hand with his. "Yes, you do. We're on our own, the two of us."

I can't tell you what those words did to my insides. "I feel that way too." Me and Nash against the world.

"I'm sorry your family sucked, but you can count on me from now on. I promise you that, Lupe. I'll never let you down."

My heart flip-flopped at all that intensity directed at me. He'd done this before, mostly when I was younger and he was promising me that I'd get through whatever drama was making me crazy. I'd get through it, he'd say. He'd help me. I was more than I could even imagine. And when he said it, I believed it.

"So, we agree. Fuck our families," I said, taking an emotional step back before I did something stupid and declared my love for him again.

He grinned. "Fuck 'em."

"Enough about the past then. What are your dreams for the future?"

He chuckled. "I'm the one that is supposed to ask you that."

"You have. Many times. Now, I'm asking you."

"I don't know. I might want to teach one day."

"Gag."

He grinned. "I just want to make a difference. I guess I'm living my dream at The Vibe. You're looking at a guy with no ambition, kid."

No, I was looking at a guy who wanted to save the world, and the truth was that I had the same impossible dream. But I said, "I want a dog."

"A *dog*?" he asked as if I'd said a bad word. "That's *your* life ambition? To own a dog?"

I moved my hand off his leg. "A real cute, little dog."

"That's even worse."

"Really, I'm serious," I said and smiled. "I've never had a real dog. We've had these ugly guard dog types and they've lasted a year or two and either gotten run over or died in a fight with another dog or run away. And they weren't my dogs because they were mean. They were my brother's dogs. I want a little poodle or a little terrier who is sort of tough, but is small and likes to cuddle."

Nash stared at me with an amused look. "That's an okay goal."

"And I want peace. To live in a quiet neighborhood that has a backyard for my dog."

"Peace," he said and nodded. He gazed at me as if he really saw me for the first time ever; like he understood me—but then I've always felt that Nash understood me—and like he loved me. Again, I was overcome by an urge to lean against him and kiss his bright red lips.

"Come on. Let's go." He stood abruptly.

We walked back to his car and the moment was gone. I'd blown it.

Back at his apartment, we worked together in his little kitchen to prepare some food. I worked on a salad, and he was defrosting some hamburger.

"I'm going to change so I don't get my clothes dirty," I said.

I slipped into the bathroom first, to undo the tight bun. "Not bad," I said to myself.

Nash walked past, paused and smiled. "Talking to yourself?"

"This came out pretty good." I loosened the clips, and strands of hair started to fall.

He walked closer, braced a hand on the door frame, and peeked inside, looking at my image in the mirror. "Pretty good? Your hair looks fabulous. Classy and . . . shows off your neck. Very sensual."

I smiled, then shook my hair loose. It felt good to let it down. "Maybe I should cut some of it. It's so long."

Nash came in the rest of the way and grabbed a handful of my hair. "No way." He took a brush and began to brush out the waves created by the bun.

"Just a little, so it's not so heavy."

"It's gorgeous the way it is."

If he liked it, it stayed. I turned to face him and took the brush out of his hands. Our eyes locked. "Thank you," I whispered.

He bent forward and I could tell he was going to kiss my forehead, but at the last second I decided to be bold and I tipped my head back until our lips . . . touched.

Nine

If all else fails, become an Americana by marrying a white guy.

LUPE PEREZ

Immediately, at the first meeting of our lips, he jerked back. But I hooked a hand on the back of his head and held him in place and kissed him provocatively. I'd dreamed of this moment for so long that I wasn't going to let him escape so easily.

He hesitated for a second or two, then began to kiss me back. With a trace of curiosity maybe, but he allowed our breaths to mingle and indulged in the taste of my lips.

His exploration ignited a million illusions in my mind. Illusions of happily ever after and of forever. The pressure of his lips against mine exposed a longing to be loved buried so deep within my soul that I actually heard the strumming of a harp in my head.

Our moist lips slid against each other, back and forth, up and down, until we both seemed to sigh with pleasure. His hands held onto my shoulders, but mine were buried in his hair and pulled him closer. He deepened the kiss and backed me against the sink, inflaming the passion I'd saved up especially for him—for this exact moment.

I was floating in outer space. Oh my God. Was this really happening after all these years? I moaned as his arms wrapped around my back and his lips parted mine. His tongue was hot and insistent as it plunged into my mouth.

I wanted to give him anything he wanted. Everything.

He arched me back against the sink and his hips rested against mine, his arousal stiff and ready. A feeling of power swelled inside my body knowing I could induce that kind of reaction from him. The pounding of his heart when his hard chest pressed against my breasts delighted me even more because he wasn't just responding to me sexually. His whole body was into this, into me.

My hips moved to accommodate him, to arouse him. And I was rewarded with a groan and more pressure from his own hips as he demonstrated the pleasure that could be gained by losing our clothes and taking this to a more comfortable place. But his sensual thrusts only lasted a second before he twisted free and held me at arm's length—again, his hands were on my shoulders.

"Oh, shit, I'm sorry," he said between heavy panting.

"Sorry?" I asked, dazed. I could still smell the spicy scent of his cologne on my skin. I wanted his scent everywhere on my body.

"What the fuck am I doing?" he turned and bolted out of the bathroom.

Barely able to take steady steps, I followed after him. "What's wrong? You—"

"I shouldn't have done that and we both know it. Damn it!"

"I hope you're kidding," I said.

But he wasn't listening. "I can't believe I allowed that to happen." He looked disgusted with himself and angry.

But? "What's the big deal?" I frowned. Sure seemed like he was getting into it.

"You're . . ."

"What?"

"A kid from the center. Jesus."

That hurt. Was that all I was to him? "I'm not a kid. And I thought I was more to you than a member of The Vibe."

"But you're nineteen. Nineteen!"

"And you're twenty-seven. That's not such a huge age difference."

"Are you fucking kidding?" He ran a hand though his long strands of hair, digging into his scalp. "Marcela was right. I had no business allowing you to stay here."

Momentarily, I was devastated. I'd just gotten settled in, I didn't want to have to leave again so soon. And Marcela had said *what* to him exactly? "You want me to leave?"

"No. Damn it. Just . . . that can never happen again. Ever. Got it?" He was shouting at me like *I'd* done something terrible to *him.* Nash had never shouted at me before.

"Fine." I was angry now. "If that's how you feel about it."

I whirled, went into my room, and slammed the door. Afterward, I wondered if I'd reacted too much like a teenager, and maybe I should have gone back to the kitchen and forced myself to finish dinner. But I couldn't sit across from him, and I definitely couldn't eat anything.

I'd made my move, and I'd failed. How could I ever face Nash again?

Want to really blend into American society? Marry into it. A nice descendant of the good ole Pilgrims maybe. A New Englander or a Kansas farm boy. A white boy. A black boy will do too, but then you've still got the minority issue to deal with. Don't think it didn't cross my mind that part of the attraction with Nash is that he is one heck of a handsome white boy. I've asked myself if I'm trying to erase my Mexicanness by being with him. If, by marrying Nash and having kids with him, I could one day pretend that my rotten childhood was just a bad nightmare and that it didn't really happen.

Was that just one more phase of my Americanization?

If I didn't love him so much and it didn't hurt so deeply to be rejected by him, I'd say maybe. But, no, I'd love Nash no matter what his nationality. I love him for the tenderness he'd always shown me, and for the wonderful person he is inside. Skin color has so little to do with who a person really is.

Since I couldn't take out my hurt on Nash, I decided to take it out on Marcela instead.

I didn't exactly barge into her home the next morning, but she knew when she opened the door that I was pissed.

"Great, just what I need this morning. To see you," she said and stepped back to allow me to enter.

She didn't look very good. Maybe she hadn't had a good night's sleep.

"Hi," George said as he walked to the front door.

"Hey," I said, checking him out for the first time ever. Here you had a Mexican boy who, after several generations, was completely Americanized. Other than his dark skin and wide nose, there was nothing left of the Aztec empire in this guy. In fact, for this reason, Marcela almost didn't marry him. At first, she was dead set against marrying a Latino, until she decided the best way to please her family was to marry into *La Raza.* But poor George, who couldn't even say *gracias* without sounding like Lucy Ricardo, didn't match. Personally, I think she got the best of both worlds.

Anyhow, race plays a big part in the marriage decision. And whether you're trying to become more American or more Latina, if the guy doesn't fit the category you're looking for, he's doomed.

"Remember what I said," George called out to Marcela and slipped past me.

"Go to work, George."

"If you don't listen to me, I'm going to send you off to live with your mom."

Marcela cringed. "You really know how to threaten a girl. Go on. I'll be fine."

George left with one last warning look.

"What's wrong?" I asked.

"Just morning sickness, but he thinks I'm dying. Wants me to lay in bed, not work, not breathe. You know how he is. So, what are you doing here? Did you come to apologize?"

I came to lay into her for telling Nash he shouldn't let me stay at his place, but now that I saw what she looked like and remembered she was pregnant, that didn't seem like such a good idea. "Yeah, sort of."

"Good. I'm listening."

I took a seat even though she didn't offer one.

She stretched out on the couch and put a hand to her forehead.

"Want me to get you something?"

"No."

"Well, I know you're not going to congratulate me, but I got the job."

Marcela eyed me from the corner of her eye. "Aaand? What kind of job?"

"At an ad agency, handling the tech part of clients' marketing programs."

She forced herself to sit up, but I could see it was an effort. She held her stomach.

"Lie back down. I'm going to go and let you rest."

"Shut up, Lupe, and listen to me."

I smiled because she'd gotten a lot tougher when dealing with me than she had been when we'd first met and I'd been a little hellion.

"If you wanted a job, I could have given you a job at Panoply. The point wasn't for you to work. It was for you to get a degree and build a career."

I know what she wanted. I wanted it too, but it would take a little longer. "You can't create my future like you do your movies, Marcela. I have to do this my way and make my own choices."

"You're making the wrong choice," she said simply, as if anyone with half a brain could see that.

"In your opinion."

"My opinion is the only one I've got." She raised her voice.

"Look, I appreciate everything you've done for me. Really. But this is my life."

She glared at me and shook her head. "How much are they paying you?"

She'd just tell me it wasn't enough, so I shrugged. "Enough."

"Enough? Meaning, not much."

"It's a lot for me," I snapped. "And I'll tell you something else. I don't want you butting into my personal life—"

"What personal life?"

"You told Nash not to let me move into his place."

"Lupe, honey, I know how you feel about him. *He* knows how you feel about him. It was damned stupid for him to offer you a room."

"I needed him. My brother had just attacked me."

"That first night, yes, of course he should have helped you. Then he should have sent you to me."

Like a stray dog. Feed it for the night then send it on its way. "Why wouldn't you want me to hook up with Nash? He's a great guy."

"He's too old for you."

"That's ridiculous."

She pushed herself up and walked across the room to pick up her remote. "I'm going to follow my husband's orders and watch mindless TV. As for Ryan, I've warned him to keep his hands off you. If he doesn't, I'll fire his ass."

"Are you serious?" I couldn't believe she'd do something so shitty.

"Very."

I stood. "You have no right, Marcela."

"I do. He's my employee."

"But what he does with me is none of your business," I shouted.

"He's not going to do anything with you." She held her stomach. "First of all, he's smart enough not to ruin your life by allowing you to get attached to him. He wants more for you than he could ever give you. But he's a guy, so just in case he lets his hormones get carried away, I put out the gentle warning."

I was so angry I wanted to slap her. Or at the very least pick up one of her precious foreign trinkets she bought when she traveled and toss it against a wall. "You bitch."

"Don't you swear at me. You ungrateful—"

"And to think I thought you were my friend."

"What would you know about friendship? Why do I waste my time and energy with you?" She gripped the back of a chair and swayed.

Before I could respond, she pushed me out of the way and ran past me.

"What the hell? Where are you going?"

I followed her to the bathroom, where she dropped down on her knees and vomited into the toilet.

"Shit," I said as she gagged.

Gripping the side of the bowl, she drew in deep breaths once her stomach stopped heaving.

I hurried and got her a wet towel. "Here." I wiped her mouth and helped her get up. She looked weak and pale. "Come on." I helped her to her feet and told her to lean on me until we got back to the living room. "Sorry, Marcela. Damn it, *I'm* the bitch."

"Shit, I knew I didn't want to have kids. Look what I have to go through."

"It won't last long." I helped her sit on the couch. "Will it?" I couldn't help being worried. Maybe I should call Marta.

"A few months. But lately it's really bad."

I brushed her hair out of her face and wiped her mouth and chin again. Then I went into the bathroom and grabbed a scrunchie. With her brush, I gathered her sweaty strands of hair and put them up to get them away from her face. "I'll make you some tea."

When I brought back the tea, Marcela had fallen asleep. I sat beside her and looked down at her pretty face. She wasn't a cruel ogre. On the contrary, she was actually a very cool and fun person. And all she'd ever tried to do was help me. How was I going to make her understand that I didn't need her to be a parent figure anymore? I just needed a friend.

Her eyelids floated open and she reached for my hand. "Sorry," she said as if she'd read my mind. "I'll back off."

I clasped her hand with both of mine. "Don't worry about me. You need to take care of yourself now. Okay?"

"I've made a second career out of worrying about you, Lupe. I love you, girl."

"I love you too."

We stared at each other for a few moments, then I released her hand. "But I really want to take this job and not rely on you. I'll go back to night school next quarter. I promise." I needed her approval, even if I wished I didn't. Marcela meant too much to me to be able to brush aside her opinions.

"Okay. Guess we'll see." She blinked her eyes and drew a breath.

"And as for Nash, I'll put my feelings for him aside. He doesn't want me anyway."

She frowned.

"I made a pass at him and he turned me down."

"I'm sorry," she said again. "But it's for the best."

Right. For whom? "Okay. Get some sleep. I'm going to hang around for a while and make you some soup. Think you can keep that down?"

"I don't know, Lupe." She groaned. "Man, I don't want to be pregnant."

"Don't say that." I stood. "Sleep."

I checked in with her a while later and she was sleeping. I made some soup, called Marta, who said she'd come over, and sat to watch TV.

Later, when I left her house, I went to The Vibe to work. Nash was polite, but distant. Only I noticed. To everyone else, I was sure he appeared as involved and passionate as always. He drove Angel home when she came in drunk or stoned, clearly under the influence of something. Then he got back and eased an arrest when the police walked in looking for Michael. Nash became the intermediary, indicating to the officers how well Michael had done recently and how much he had progressed, and convincing Michael to go quietly and not fight the arrest. He tackled everything with his usual energy. The only thing missing was his usual playfulness when he passed by me or the winks and smiles across the room when we both realized a kid had made progress. He barely looked at me.

Which was just as well. As much as I wanted him and cared about him, I had to stay away from him. Not only because he'd made it clear he didn't want me, but because I didn't want to upset Marcela. I doubted she would actually fire him, so it wasn't that.

But I didn't want to add to her stress right now. Besides, she was probably right, Nash would never see me as girlfriend material.

As we closed up a few hours later and I was reorganizing the CDs in the computer area, he walked up behind me. "Mad at me?"

"No." I stacked the cases that held about twenty-five CDs each against the shelf on the back of the room. Then I took the keyboard vacuum and ran it across the keyboard of the first computer.

"I lost my head," he said, raising his voice over the hum of the vacuum.

I moved on to the next computer, sucking up anything the kids may have dropped on the keys.

"You looked so pretty in that outfit. I mean, Lupe, you're a knock-out."

Resisting the urge to roll my eyes, I continued down the row. We had ten computers.

"I was seeing you, but I wasn't seeing you, you understand? I was seeing this gorgeous young woman with this amazing body and soft skin. But I wasn't connecting it with you. I mean . . . this is complicated."

I considered letting him stumble all over his words a while longer, but it was too painful to listen. So I turned the vacuum off and placed it back on the shelf. I gave him a cool, passing glance. "It was just a kiss," I said as matter-of-fact as I could.

"Yeah, but I know what that meant to you."

I laughed to hide the pitiful ache somewhere in the center of my heart. "It meant we were attracted to each other and we kissed. Shit, I kissed Will a few nights before that. Big deal. Get over it."

He raised an eyebrow. "Will?"

"A guy from school. In fact, we have a date tomorrow night," I said, and wanted to kick myself for making up such a stupid lie. But I had to salvage some of my pride. If I could manage to make him think that I hadn't been as crushed as I was, then maybe some of my humiliation would fade.

"Oh. Well, good." He leaned his butt against a computer table and crossed his arms. "So, we're okay?"

"Sure." Great. Now I had to call Will and hope he still wanted to go out with me. Was I an idiot or what?

"I'm glad to hear that, Lupe. Because, to me, you're more than one of the kids that passes through this center. You know that. I never should have said differently. You're my friend. You're family. Hell, you're the only one I'd give my life to save."

To my horror, I felt the threat of tears behind my eyes. I didn't want to be his family or friend or a kid in his eyes. I blinked and shook my head. "That's sweet, and I appreciate it," I said, trying to pass my emotions off as being touched by his words rather than disappointed and hurt.

An awkward silence stretched between us. This was something new. "Let's go. I'm hungry. Are you?"

He nodded.

"I'll make you dinner."

I went to UCLA the next day and tracked Will down. I sat beside him in class.

He seemed genuinely happy to see me. "Been thinking about you," he said.

I smiled.

"Don't you want to know what about?"

"Sure."

"Since you were reading about the Latin culture, I decided to join you and bought a book on Latino traditions."

I was so surprised and touched that I stared at him dumbfounded.

He pulled out a laughing skeleton. "I found out that in Mexico they celebrate the Day of the Dead on November second. Not at all like our Halloween. The skeleton is symbolic of the circle of life. Cool huh?"

I thought Will was pretty cool. I took the skeleton he handed me.

He chuckled. "First time I've given a girl a skeleton."

"My family never kept up with any of the traditions. But once we went to a *Dia de los Muertos* party at a relative's house and there was this *pan de muerto*, which is a sweet bread molded into the shape of a skull. All the kids wanted to eat through it because baked inside was a plastic skeleton."

Will grinned. "I read that people actually have picnics at grave sites."

"Pretty creepy, huh?" I felt self-conscious being from a country with such bizarre cultural traditions.

"No, that's the thing the book was saying about that holiday. It's not creepy at all. Not like our scary Halloween. It's a celebration to show that life goes on."

We stared at each other and I tried to remember what I wanted to talk to him about.

"Yeah. Listen, I came to let you know I got the job with Tracey's uncle. I'm going to be dropping out of here for a while," I said.

"I see." Like everyone I've mentioned this to, he looked disappointed.

"I thought I'd come by and give you my cell number, in case you . . . so we can stay in touch."

He took the piece of paper I passed to him. "Thanks."

As the instructor walked in and began his lecture, we stared at each other.

"So. Do you believe life goes on?" Will asked.

Will was a nice guy and my age, which according to Nash was the most important thing in a relationship. I should give him a chance. I had to do something to get Nash off my mind. And Will seemed to be someone I could trust.

As a child, I was raped, many times. I don't dwell on it. It was something that happened to me, like my broken leg—it hurt me, but I survived. But as a result of that, as an early teen, I slept with many guys to prove to myself that the early experiences hadn't affected me. One of the last times was when I was fifteen. It was in the guy's garage, up against the wall. He was a slimy neighborhood creep, and the experience had been dirty and humiliating as he ejaculated inside me and zipped up his pants without once treating me like I mattered. After that I gave up guys and sex.

I met Will's deep brown eyes. "Life definitely goes on," I said.

His gaze probed gently and seemed to seek everything I wasn't giving away.

Maybe I was ready to try it all again.

"Call me," I whispered to Will. "Tonight?"

"You got it," he said, gazing at me like I'd just given him an all-expense-paid trip to paradise.

Ten

You know you're truly becoming Americana when you start to notice how many others are less fortunate than you, and that it's your turn to be charitable.

LUPE PEREZ

Today I volunteered for something even more uncomfortable than dating. I agreed to go with Carmen to a family planning clinic for birth control pills.

Carmen is fifteen, and I know better than most that she should not be having sex. Especially with a guy like Diego who has issues of his own to deal with.

But a promise is a promise and so on the back of my bike, I lugged her and my guilty conscience to a place where they would not counsel her against having sex. They would only load her up with stuff that would protect against a pregnancy.

I remember going to these places myself. When I left the clinic I had the feeling I had been treated very similar to how pet stores treat pets. The nurses repeated over and over that I should make sure I took my birth control pills and that my boyfriend should use a condom. Spay and neuter them so they will not reproduce.

I could have as much sex as I wanted—no one told me that was wrong. But for God's sake, don't have any babies.

When we got to the clinic, Carmen and I waited. I decided to be the sole voice of reason. "You've been having sex already?" I asked casually.

"Yeah. You think it's too late for this?"

"No," I said immediately. "It's never too late for birth control. Well . . . actually, that's not true. I suppose, there can be a time when it's too late but . . ." I was rambling. "If you're having sex, this is a good thing to do."

She nodded, looking sort of nervous.

"They'll give you an exam, then prescribe the pill. No big deal."

"Good. Good." She nodded and looked around. "Thanks for coming with me, Lupe."

"Sure." I drew a deep breath. "Diego your first?"

"No."

Hell, she was lucky she hadn't gotten pregnant already. "Go ahead and get the pill, but Carmen, you should think about maybe abstaining."

"Ab what?"

"Not having sex."

"Why?"

"Ah." What would Marcela have said to me? "Okay, here it is. The truth. At your age, and Diego's age, sex is basically only going to get you into trouble."

"That's why I'm here. Because I don't want trouble."

"Do you think he'd be around to help you if you *did* get pregnant?"

She shook her head. "That's why I'm here."

"Right, but think about this. If he isn't man enough to stand by you if you *did* need him, why would you sleep with him?"

"Because." She frowned. "He's my man. I love him."

Oh crap. "He's not a man. That's the point. He's a boy. You're a girl. And neither one of you is ready to handle the complications of a committed relationship. Getting birth control is good, but . . . why let yourself be used?"

"I'm not getting used. I like it."

"But in a few months after you've given him your love, he'll be gone. Then you'll give your love to another guy and sleep with him. And this will go on and on. How many guys will you go through and how will you feel about yourself when you get older and realize none of those guys cared about you at all? They just wanted sex."

I know how I felt. My self-esteem had been in the toilet. Luckily, I stopped playing musical sex partners when I was her age.

She stared at me. "You think Diego is going to dump me?"

"Someday. Or you'll dump him. You don't think it will last forever or want it to, do you?"

"I don't know."

"Well, I only wanted to let you know that you don't have to sleep with every guy you date. We girls think sex is a given. That we have to. We don't."

She nodded. "Okay."

"Okay."

She took out a mirror and checked her lipstick and face.

"Where did you learn to do your makeup?"

"My mom."

"Oh."

"What about you?"

I laughed. "Magazines."

"Cool."

"Yeah."

They called her name and she looked at me.

"Go on. I'll wait right here."

"What if Diego dumps me because I won't have sex with him?"

"Then you'll concentrate on your school work and eventually find a guy that likes you even if you don't have sex."

"Have you?"

I smiled thinking of Nash and how he wouldn't touch me even though I'd thrown myself at him. He liked me and refused to have sex with me. "I stopped having sex until I figured out what I wanted. Since I still don't know, I don't have sex."

Her eyes widened. "Don't you miss it?"

I sure as hell didn't. But she didn't need to know why. "I want it to be what it should be next time I have sex. With a guy who really loves me. Since I've never had that, I don't miss it."

They called her name again. She turned and took off.

I sat to wait for her, paging through a magazine. Had I given her good advice? The fact was that as an adult sex didn't have to be about love, and many times it wasn't. But as a kid, she shouldn't be doing it at all.

Kids need to enjoy being kids without all the drama and problems of an adult. Just the fact that Carmen had to be here today, with people probing at her private parts, was sad. She shouldn't even have to worry about getting pregnant at her age. I crossed my fingers that she'd listen to me. She needed to be a kid, go to concerts, learn a sport, play a musical instrument, learn to speak French, German, Korean. Why not? Come to think of it, I needed to do all those things too.

With college courses and a full-time job, I wouldn't have much time for all the things I should have done as a teen, but I would put them on a list, and one by one, I would begin to live and have fun. All of a sudden, I couldn't get the crazy smile off my face.

At least until Carmen and I got back to The Vibe and Carlos walked through the door a few minutes later.

With a purpose, he waltzed straight toward me, showing enough macho strut to draw every guy's attention in the place. I vacillated between a fear that urged me to hide behind something and a rage that told me to prepare to defend myself.

Before he reached me, Diego jumped in between us. Carlos stopped and looked at him like he was nothing but a tin can in the street that he could kick to the curb.

I picked up the phone. "Get out, Carlos, or I call the cops. You should be long gone if you know what's good for you."

"The cops find me, Lupe, and this time, believe me, you won't testify against me."

"Look, *Vato*, why don't you leave?" Diego asked, though his tone was more of a warning than a suggestion.

"Get out of my face before I rub yours on the ground."

Diego was about to respond physically, so I eased beside him and motioned Carmen to coax him away. "I can fight my own battles," I told him.

He frowned. "Hey, I know."

"Really. This is my brother and we're having a little sibling disagreement," I lied. "It's cool."

Diego stepped aside, though he kept a bad-eyed look on Carlos.

"That's all I came to say," Carlos warned. "Don't open your mouth. And stay out of my business."

"I want nothing to do with your *business. You* involved *me.*"

He sniffed. Then with cold calculation, his gaze examined the center. "Saving the world, huh Lupe?"

For some reason, I felt threatened, and I wanted to lash out at him. A guy who was capable of doing the things he'd done to me was evil to the core, and would do just about anything. I didn't care that we were related; if I ever got the chance to repay him for the pain he'd caused me, I was sure I'd take it and enjoy every moment. "Someone has to. Especially with people like you out there."

This was the first time I'd deliberately provoked him. I had learned to stand up to him, even if inside I was trembling with fear, but I'd never tossed out the first dig.

When he turned back to me, I could almost smell the brimstone. He lifted an eyebrow. "You think because you're standing in here that you're safe? That any of these kids are safe?"

No, I didn't think that.

Behind me, the door to Nash's office opened.

Carlos stiffened as he and Nash locked gazes. With less fire he said to me, "You're not. Remember that," and he turned around and left.

Nash walked up beside me. "Was that Carlos?"

"Yeah." My voice sounded weak.

"What the hell was he doing here? Why didn't you come get me?"

"He was warning me." I shook my head, but Carlos was permanently imprinted in my mind. "Stay out of it."

"Out of what? If he steps foot in here again, I want the police called. He's violent and dangerous and if he's threatened you—"

"Stop it." I faced him. "Carlos is a threat I live with daily. Big deal. Nothing new here. I'm going home. I have better things to do than spend one more second thinking about my dear brother."

"Lupe," he called after me. "Lupe, come back here."

But I kept going.

Will called, as he promised he would.

"So you want to get together tonight or what?" he asked.

Of course I did. I told Nash I had a date this evening, so I needed to be gone when he got home. "Sure. I'll meet you."

"I know a great club, but you're underage, right?"

"Yeah, I'm pretty much still in the Chuck E. Cheese's crowd."

He laughed. "How about we meet in Westwood Village—Barnes and Noble? Or I can pick you up."

I agreed to meet him at the Village. We picked up a cup of coffee from the Starbucks in Barnes and Noble and strolled around the Village, window shopping.

I found out Will was twenty-two. He came from an upper-middle-class family in Carlsbad. One brother, one sister. Would go into pediatric medicine next year. Wanted to drive a Humvee. He was a Republican.

"None of that shit really matters though, right?"

"What do you mean?" The chilly air tonight gave me a tiny shiver, so I held my coffee cup with both hands.

"Facts." He took a sip of coffee too. "They don't tell you anything about who I really am."

"It helps."

"Naw. I mean, I think you and I are a lot alike even though up until now, our facts have been completely different."

"We're nothing alike." We walked past a candle store and were treated to the scent of cinnamon and spice, reminding me that Thanksgiving would be here soon. My favorite holiday because there was so much good stuff to eat.

"Sure we are. We're both jumping to get on with our lives. I see you in class. It's like you can't sit still. You want to get through all that bullshit so you can start living your life. Am I right?"

Completely, but I just looked at him, encouraging him to continue. I let pumpkin pies drift from my mind.

"I don't know." He shrugged. "I'm not the college student type. I know I have to have the knowledge before I can be a doctor, but I want to get out in the real world and do stuff. Maybe I've been at it too long already."

"No, you're right. I just started and I feel the same."

He grinned and stopped strolling. "I feel like screaming. 'This isn't who I am. I'm not *going to* be a doctor. I already am.'" He held both arms up in the air looking like a preacher giving a sermon, except for the coffee cup in his hand. His jeans rode low on his hips and I got a peek at his firm belly and decided he didn't look like any preacher I'd ever seen before.

"But I'm in limbo," he finished.

"Did you always know you were going to be a doctor?"

"No, I was also going to be a race car driver, a champion surfer, give Tiger Woods a run for his money, and become a monk."

"A monk?" I raised an eyebrow in surprise. Was he messing with me?

"They seem really smart, like they know all the secrets of life and aren't telling the rest of us. But I couldn't handle the no sex part."

He made me smile a lot and I decided I *really* liked Will. He wasn't just someone to help me forget Nash. He was a guy I'd be interested in even if Nash never existed. In fact, he had none of Nash's intensity, but was laid back and easygoing and I liked the difference.

We strolled and he stared at me. "I like what you did with your eyes."

Oh, no. Was he going to make fun of me too? "I used the lavender color eyeshadow because it didn't seem so bright."

"Makes the brown of your eyes stand out. It's pretty."

"You don't think I overdid it and put on too much?"

"Nope. I think it looks sexy. Like the lipstick too." He eyed my lips with definite interest.

I didn't add any blush or foundation or any of that crap tonight. Maybe I'm getting the hang of this after all. "Thanks."

We paused at Bath and Body Works.

"Want to go in?"

"Okay," I said.

As we circled the counters, I picked up various lotions and

smelled them. Will seemed to humor me and smelled them too. We decided the creamy cucumber scent was the best, so he poured a huge glob of the sample on his hands, then rubbed them onto my hands, entwining our slippery fingers together. "Seeing your hands all greased up like that makes me wish you were rubbing them on another part of my anatomy."

I laughed.

"Sorry. That was crass."

"May I help you?" a sales clerk asked when she saw us having too much fun.

"Ah, yes," Will said. "We'll take a dozen of this kind."

The girl raised an eyebrow. "A dozen?"

"Too many? Okay, half a dozen." He looked at me. "Can you use a half dozen in the next few months?"

"Me? I don't want—"

"Half dozen," he repeated to the girl.

She shrugged and went off to ring up his purchase.

"What are you doing?" I asked.

He squeezed his fingers against mine. "Buying you some lotion. I like the way you were smiling just now."

I slipped my hands out of his. He went off to buy the lotion. Then he handed me the bag.

I didn't know what to say. "Thanks, but that was a little crazy."

He smiled. "I'm walking around smelling like a sweet cucumber. That's crazy."

We walked side by side in silence.

"Can I ask for something in return?"

"What?" I wasn't rubbing any other part of him, so he could forget that idea.

"A ride on your bike."

I checked out his expectant smile and the way he held out his arms like he was holding on to the handle bars.

"You want to drive my bike, don't you?"

"How did you guess? Will you teach me?"

I looked up at the sky. "Not in the dark. Some other day."

"You've got yourself a deal. So tonight, just give me a ride. I even bought myself my own helmet.

He did? "Presumptuous."

"Hopeful. Besides, I like sitting up close to you and wrapping my legs around your hips."

"And I thought you were only after a thrill ride," I said, attempting to tease him and lead the conversation away from him holding me.

But his gaze turned darker. "No, I'm after way more than a thrill ride." He took my hand. "Let's go."

We left the shops and went off to ride my bike. I drove out toward the beach, took him on a nice long ride. And this time, it didn't feel bad at all to have his arms around me and his body pressed up against my back. In fact, when we got back to Westwood Village and I leaned back and looked over my shoulder and he kissed me good night, I didn't mind at all.

I confided in Tracey that I didn't know the first thing about makeup. My idea of makeup had always been black eyeliner—what can I say?

Unfortunately, along with makeup advice, she insisted on giving me Will advice. We strolled the Clinique, Chanel, and Estée Lauder counters, but instead of explaining the difference between Sparkle Dust and Champagne eye shadow, she decided to sell me on Will's various qualities, namely that his family was loaded.

"I don't care about that," I told her repeatedly. "What's with the ten million kinds of brushes?" I picked up a lip brush.

"Painting your lips gives them a sexier definition. Buy one. And, I'm not suggesting you date him because of the money. But it *is* great that he's well-off." She picked up another brush for contouring eyes. "Here, this one you absolutely need. You can apply eyeliner with one end and shadow with the other."

"But shadow already comes with those little applicators. Why should I spend money on a brush? Jeesh, this one costs thirty-six dollars."

"Because those applicators are useless. The angle of the brush will allow you to fit in the crease between your lids. Trust me. Buy it."

I shook my head, rolled my eyes, and took the brush.

"Will wouldn't be wasting this much time on you if he didn't like you."

"I *know* he likes me."

"Then call him. Tell him how awesome you thought your date was. I still can't believe all you did was walk around a strip mall and make him ride that nasty bike of yours. He could have done that with his buddies."

"He *wanted* to ride my bike."

"Probably to get you the hell out of the mall."

"Can we change the subject please?"

She handed me a big ole fat brush. "For your face," she said.

I looked at the flat-top, stubby thing. "Forty-five dollars!"

"It'll give you a shine-free face."

"I can buy a brush like this at Home Depot for $4.99. Are you crazy?"

She shrugged. "Suit yourself. And all I'm trying to say about Will is that he's nice, he's cute, he's got money—which you desperately need, honey, so stop making it so hard for him. Show some interest. Instead of going to a strip mall, you should have stripped."

I turned to her. "I should have taken my clothes off? That's your idea of what a girl should do to interest a guy?"

She flashed a bad-girl grin. "Works every time." Then she added. "He needs a reward for all his persistence."

"Tracey, look, I may be poor, but I'm not a slut." Not anymore anyway.

"I'm not telling you to be a slut."

"You're telling me I should jump into bed with this guy." I slapped all the brushes on the counter. "And you're telling me I should cough up almost two hundred dollars on brushes. You're fucking crazy. See you around school." I left, frustrated by my makeover—one that everyone I knew was participating in, except me.

"Hey!" Tracey called after me.

I sent her one last glare.

"Lose the gum. I've been meaning to tell you, it makes you look like a Jerry Springer guest."

I narrowed my eyes, about to really let her have it. But she was being so tough, I decided to let her have the last word instead. I took the gum out of my mouth and set it in a wastebasket beside one of the cosmetic counters.

We had decided that our walls needed to be overhauled at the center. Actually, last time Marcela had been in, she decided that she was going to have a bunch of animators come by and decorate the walls. This was before she found out she was pregnant and was throwing up all over the place.

She did this kind of shit all the time—showed up every couple of months and said, "change this, do that" and left.

So in anticipation of the artists coming in, we were going to paint the walls with nice, fresh, clean white paint. The kids were excited, and so on Halloween afternoon we got a couple dozen of them to agree to come in and have a party and help move furniture away from the walls.

I was washing the paint off some brushes, daydreaming about

my date with Will and contemplating going out with him again, when I heard some boys getting loud.

"What you lookin' at, bitch?" Diego shoved Samuel.

Samuel puffed out his chest. "Not your sorry ass, that's for sure."

"Hey," I called out over my shoulder. But they ignored me.

"He was trying to look down my shirt," Carmen said in this pouty, cutsie, little-girl voice that made me want to ring her neck.

Diego put a protective arm in front of Carmen. "Is that right, *hermano*? Lookin' to get your eyes cut out of your head, *pendejo*?"

"You callin' me *pendejo*, cocksucker?"

I dropped the brushes and stood in a hurry. Here I was with my hair sticky and sweaty and pinned up all over my head, paint stains all over my clothes, dead tired, and now this? No way. They weren't going to fight at this center tonight.

"Cut it out," I said, getting between the two boys, who outweighed me by more than fifty pounds.

Diego reached over my shoulder and pushed Samuel. Samuel started to retaliate, but I shoved him hard. "No, Samuel. Stop it."

"Get out of the way, Lupe," he said.

"Just let it go." Sam was always nice to me, always listened, so my best bet was to work on him.

"He thinks I care about that stupid ho of his. Shit."

Diego lunged at Samuel, knocking me out of the way.

I crawled away as the two started throwing punches. Diego threw serious blows and connected twice before Samuel was able to push him off and hit him back. Yelling for them to stop was pointless. So I did the only thing I could thing of. I picked up a three-gallon bucket of paint and doused them both with it.

They stopped immediately, heavy white paint dripping from their heads and faces, and down their bodies.

"Ah, shit," Diego shouted. "What did you do that for? You stupid . . . ahg," he growled, keeping the rest of the insult to himself.

Carmen laughed. "Oh my God. Look at you."

Nash walked in. He'd gone to his car to get more drop cloths. "What in the world?"

"We had a small disagreement, but it's over. Right boys?"

"Man," Samuel said. "Lupe, you're crazy, man."

"Go home. Get washed up before it dries."

Both boys and Carmen filed out, cussing and complaining and promising each other their fight wasn't over.

"Lupe, you can't go around pouring paint on kids," Nash said.

"They were fighting."

"And that's how you stopped them?" Nash gave me an astonished, slightly amused look.

"What else was I going to do?"

He burst out laughing. "You've got a point. You okay?" He reached across and brushed his thumb on my nose. "Aside from needing a hot shower."

I'm sure I looked a mess. "We'd better replace the drop cloths on the carpet before this paint seeps through."

He nodded and laughed some more.

We got it all cleaned up in an hour. I dragged out two bags of trash and tossed them in the Dumpster. My arms ached and I wondered if my muscles were growing.

Next to our Dumpster was a guy about in his midforties so wasted on drugs he barely knew I was beside him. He blinked and tried to focus. Damn, what a waste. I pulled one of the drop cloths that didn't look too bad back out of the trash and covered him with it. "Here you go, dude," I said. He mumbled something incomprehensible and I went back inside.

Eleven

Becoming Americana means finding the strength to be yourself and not letting your background, your race, or your gender stop you from achieving your goals.

LUPE PEREZ

When Nash and I got home from The Vibe, we took turns in the shower. Nash was nice enough to let me go first. Afterward, we sat in the living room to eat the Chinese food he'd ordered.

"How did your date go the other day?" he asked right before I was about to bite into my second egg roll.

I glanced at him, wondering why he'd ask. "Fine."

Our living arrangements had gotten a bit strained. We were too aware of each other now. I know he noticed what I wore around the apartment these days, when in the past his gaze had never rested on my body. So I made sure my shirts weren't too tight or my shorts too short. You'd think I'd do the opposite, but no. I didn't want to make him uncomfortable. And if I was ever going to get over wanting Nash, I had to avoid situations where we could be tempted to repeat that sexy bathroom kiss.

But there were certain intimacies that a man and woman shared when living together that were unavoidable. Tonight was one of those. Both of us freshly bathed and dressed for bed, sharing dinner on the couch like a newly married couple.

"Why didn't he pick you up here?" Nash persisted.

"I met him in Westwood Village."

"Why?"

I exhaled, unable to hide my irritation. "What do you mean 'why?'"

"I guess I'm trying to say that it's okay for him to pick you up here. I don't mind."

I tossed my egg roll back onto my plate. "Why would you mind? It's not like you'd be jealous or anything." I stood.

"Hey." He frowned. "Where are you going? Can't we talk?"

"Not about Will. Not about you and me. Not about . . ." I placed a hand on my hip and sighed as I looked down at the floor and shook my head.

"Lupe, I'm trying to make things easier for you. I don't want you to be shy about having dates is all."

I raised my gaze to meet his. "Do you know how humiliated I feel that I'm so pathetically in love with you, and you . . . I can't believe this, you're sending me off to another guy like you're grateful to get rid of me."

Now he stood. "Whoa, that's not what I'm saying at all. I don't *want* you to date anyone else." He stopped and shook his head. "I mean, I want to encourage you to . . . oh hell." He kicked his couch then tried again. "Since I feel protective of you, I don't like the idea of you dating some guy I haven't even met. But as you've told me repeatedly, you're old enough to do what you want and that includes dating. So it's okay with me if he comes here. I prefer it, so I can meet him. There. Clear?"

Clear? Didn't he notice the smoke coming out of my ears? Did he think he was going to take on the role of my guardian? Big mistake. I stepped up close to him and pointed at his chest. "You can stop feeling protective of me. You're not family, and you're quickly becoming less of a friend. So what I do and with whom is my own damn business."

"I know. I agree. You can do whatever you want. It's all okay with me," he shouted right back in my face.

Suddenly, I paused. Was it okay with him? Maybe he was angry because it wasn't so okay? Maybe he wanted to see Will because he *was* jealous? No. I had to stop fooling myself. Nash didn't want me. "Fine. Thank you for being so accommodating," I said, my voice tight and brittle from trying to control my anger.

"You're welcome," he grumbled and sat back down.

I sat down again too, more hesitantly, and picked up my discarded egg roll. I was going to finish my dinner even if I had to choke it down with soda.

"You don't really love me," he said after some silence. "You just think you do."

Great, now tell me I don't know my own feelings. "I love you," I repeated, though the tone I used probably did little to convince him it was true.

"Not the way you think."

"Exactly the way *you* think."

More silence. He was uncomfortable and so was I.

I reached across and placed my hand on his knee. "I'll admit that at first, it was a little-girl crush," I said, my voice sort of quiet and raspy. "You were the first one to ever hold me when I cried. You were the first guy to pay attention to me. To listen to my dreams. Your beautiful blue eyes looked at me like I was someone that mattered. As a child, I didn't see that you did that with all the kids. I just knew you did it with me, and I fell in love with you."

"And one day you'll grow up and you'll get over that crush, and you'll be grateful that I didn't take it seriously."

"No." I stared at him. "I *am* grown up and it's not a crush anymore. It's deeper and it's real. It's the only thing I'm sure of in my life. How could I not love you? We have the same interests, we're best friends. And physically, I think you're . . ." I ignored the blush that warmed my body. "Spectacular."

He reddened too. "Thank you. I—"

"Ryan, I'm sorry that I love you, but I do." I pulled my hand off his knee and finished my egg roll. We were both silent. I chewed and swallowed, determined to clean my plate. He simply watched me. I picked up the half-full can of Coke and took a drink, then met his gaze. "You don't have to love me back. It's okay."

The tortured look he gave me was almost too much for me to take. When he reached across to touch me, I stood, backing away from him. I couldn't take it if he showed me any tenderness.

"Are you okay?" He sighed.

"Of course. But I'm tired. I'm going to bed."

"Okay." He nodded. His body language said he was exhausted with this whole topic. "I'll clean this up. Go on."

"Thanks." I placed my can of Coke on the coffee table.

"I'm sorry, Lupe. I wish things were different."

I folded my arms around my body and stared at the sexy, scraggly-haired man who'd stolen my heart. "They don't have to be different," I whispered. "All you have to do is change your mind and decide you want me . . . and I'm yours." I shrugged. "In every way."

"That's a hell of a thing to say to a man."

"It's the truth."

He reached for me and hooked an arm around my waist. "It would be very easy for me to take advantage of what you're offering. Very easy. Don't think I'm not tempted—it's a big turn-on to have a girl hand herself over to you the way you just did." His eyes smoldered a deep passionate blue. "And you know I love you back."

I nodded.

"But first of all, you're not just 'a girl' to me—you're you. You're special. And secondly, I want you to have better than . . . me."

In my heart there wasn't better than Nash. He was perfect. "You mean someone with what? More money? A better job? None of that matters to me."

"It should. It did once."

"I *never* cared about any of that when it came to you. Those were things I wanted for myself, because I thought they would make me . . . I don't know, more valuable, more important, like I mattered in this world."

"Exactly. You wanted out of this neighborhood. You wanted more out of life. I can't give you any of your dreams—"

"But—"

"No buts, Lupe. I'm not going to let you toss it all away for me. I'm the wrong guy for you."

I didn't know what to say to any of that. I let my hand fan over his shoulders, and I looked into his eyes. Why didn't he get it that I didn't need him to support me? I could go out and make my own money. I could get the college degree and the great job just like he wanted. "You're wrong about not being able to give me my dream." Because he *was* my dream. The rest I could get on my own.

"Let's face it, kid. I'm not the kind of guy that wants to be tied down to a woman and a family. I love my job. I get off on being . . ."

"The big savior." He was mine for sure.

"Maybe. And when you take your place in society, I'd be a weight around your ankles. I'm not cut out to be the one who gets taken care of."

In other words, he didn't want to be with a woman who would one day make more money and be more successful than he. I nodded and stepped out of his arms. "Okay. I got it."

One of his heavy hands fell on my shoulder. "So after tonight, I'm going to forget we had this conversation."

My heart dipped then picked up speed when he leaned in close. After tonight? What was going to happen tonight? I glanced at his lips. "Don't worry. I *will* get over you if we can both go back to pretending we don't know how I feel about you."

He smiled and touched his forehead to mine with a growl. "You're everything to me, Lupe. Don't ever doubt that. Okay?" Then he eased me away from him.

I went to my room, but I didn't sleep until very late. It became clear to me tonight that I had to choose. My life with Nash and the barrio and The Vibe. Or the world outside—the world flashed at me on every commercial and in every magazine, the world that included a college degree and a heavy bank account. I had to choose, because I couldn't have both. I guess I've known that for a long time. And I've also known which one I was expected to choose. But did I want to?

Racism. You know, I never really experienced racism. When you grow up in Boyle Heights and 98.999 percent of the population is Mexican, well, there isn't much racial diversity. The only exception to this was at my exclusive, full-of-tight-ass-teachers high school.

I had this guidance counselor, Ms. Lewis, who couldn't stand me. She was looking for ways to prove to herself and to me that I just didn't belong in that school. And back then, I managed to give her the reason to believe she was right. My grades were in the toilet, so she summoned me to her office, and, along with the assistant headmaster, told me that if I didn't ace my final exams I'd be failing most of my classes. I already knew all this. It wasn't because I couldn't do the work. I simply had too many other issues to deal with and schoolwork didn't matter to me.

Once the assistant headmaster left, Ms. Lewis lost her fake smile and stuck her face right up to mine.

"Face it, you don't have a hope of graduating from this school. You'll never be able to pass all those exams."

I stared her down. I wanted to say, "wanna bet?" because I could if I wanted to. But I just blinked and shrugged.

She smirked. "You people are all lazy. You don't want to make anything of yourselves. You'll always be dishwashers and maids."

You people? From deep inside, I felt this slow boiling rage begin to swell. But it wasn't my usual explosive rage. This was different. I stood. "I'll pass all those exams," I said.

"Sit down. No one told you you could stand, young lady." Ms. Lewis was very old. Probably in her seventies. She was wrinkled and her eyebrows slanted down toward her nose, and I wondered if it was because she was so mean that she looked like an evil witch.

I glared at her. "I'm going back to class."

"Why don't you admit that this program is too difficult for you, and go back to the public schools where the education will be more suited for your . . . level?"

I had to wear this stupid uniform with a plaid skirt. I hated it, hated all skirts and dresses. Made me feel awkward and not myself. But I stood there in this lame uniform and decided I was going to learn to love it, because I'd be graduating from this school with the best grade point average they ever saw.

"May I leave now?"

"You certainly may."

I turned around, and though I felt like running away, I walked out and back to my class and spent the next two weeks cramming information into my head. I did well enough on my finals to pass those classes and the following semester my grades skyrocketed and I joined every extracurricular activity I could. I graduated with a 4.6.

Ms. Lewis and I never again had another conversation.

• • •

When November first rolled around, I was a nervous wreck. Nash kept telling me I'd do fine. I knew I would, but still, the first day of work was a big deal.

He drove me to work. "I'll pick you up this afternoon."

"Thanks."

He took hold of my arm. "Lupe."

"What?" Distracted, I looked across the car at him, with my hand on the door handle.

"I know I'm the one who keeps reminding you that you're a kid, but . . . you're not. You're a competent, talented young *woman.* You'll do great. You're ready for this, okay?"

Oh, Nash. I leaned across and kissed him on the cheek. "You have to stop being so wonderful," I scolded. "Or I'm never going to be able to fall out of love with you."

He chuckled and I was glad we could start to joke about this.

"All right," he said. "As of tonight, I become a bastard."

"There you go. Start kicking the cat or something."

"We don't have a cat."

I offered an exasperated sigh. "Can't you do anything right? Go get us one."

"I'll pick you up after work. Now go."

I nodded, got out of the car, and closed the door. "Wish me luck," I called as I walked around to his side.

"I *wish* you'd just get in there and stop stalling."

I hurried across the sidewalk and walked into the building. Once inside, I turned around one more time and saw Nash start to pull away. He'd watched me walk all the way in.

I shook off all thoughts of Nash, of school, of the center, of everything except impressing the hell out of everyone here today.

But as it turned out, I had nothing to be worried about. After a brief tour of the offices and introductions I was sure to forget, I began training on their equipment. I learned about their software programs and practiced for half a day. Then Tracey's uncle spent the afternoon discussing some of his top clients and showing me the first I'd be working on. I'd be designing their website, then a multimedia presentation that they would be able to use to market their business. Piece of cake.

After work I was so excited that all I talked about that evening with Nash was my new job. I dished up a big bowl of ice cream and sat on the arm of the couch and chatted while he sorted his laundry. "So how did it go at The Vibe today?" I finally remembered to ask.

"Okay. Paramedics and cops were there when I got to work in the morning though." He paused, picked up a T-shirt off the ground, smelled it, then shrugged and tossed it in the clean pile. "Some guy died right outside in the alley overnight. Drug overdose."

I stared at Nash, a lump forming in my throat, cold cookie dough ice cream almost burning as it got lodged and I couldn't swallow. I forced myself to let it slide down. "That's the guy who was propped up against our Dumpster."

"Yeah, I think that's where they found him."

"I covered him with a dirty drop cloth," I mumbled.

"What?"

As best I could, I ignored the wave of nausea and sadness that suddenly overtook me with a cruel power. How easily that could have been me or one of the kids at the center if someone hadn't intervened in our lives. But I'd been helped so it wouldn't be me. I was on my way out of the ghetto. It was some other poor washout that no one cared about. "Nothing," I said to Nash, who was still waiting for clarification. "One less druggie on the street."

Nash cringed, and so did I. I didn't mean that. Honest. It hurt to say it, because I could still see the guy's face. I placed my bowl of ice cream on the coffee table, and buried my face in my hands and tried to rub away the image. "Sorry," I said.

"It's okay. You've had a long day," he said. "Go to sleep."

He slid the dish aside and sat on the coffee table across from me, then wrapped a hand around my wrists to ease my hands away from my face. "Hey, your hands are shaking. What the hell's the matter?"

"I . . . I don't know. He was alive yesterday, and today he's dead. It's crazy. It's . . ." I felt myself shaking and I couldn't stop. "Not surprising. Expected. But . . ."

"Lupe?" His worried frown made me feel like an idiot.

"I'm just so tired of it. The pain, the crimes, the drugs. I'm . . . tired."

"You don't have to work at The Vibe anymore, Lupe. Take some time off. It's hard to see that stuff day in and day out. It gets to you after a while."

"I'm okay."

"No, take some time away. I insist. Concentrate on this new job, which sounds awesome."

I did need a break, and this job really would require most of my time for a while. But I didn't want to leave The Vibe. I loved it there. Some things were too important to brush aside. "I can't."

He placed a finger under my chin. "You've put in your time. Now you need to move on."

I shook my head.

"Lupe," he said, with that strong authority he'd used on me since I was a kid. "I *want* you to move on. It's what we've worked for all these years. To get you to this point. You're not the lost street kid anymore. You're a new person and you need to start living that life."

A new person? Was I becoming something new? Then why did I feel so lost? So out of touch with who I am and what I want to be? But I saw that look in Nash's eyes. The look that said, "do this for

me, please," and I knew my success was as much his as it was mine.
"Okay," I said. "If you don't mind, I'll take a break from The Vibe."

The tension in his shoulders visibly eased. Then he smiled. "Nope, don't mind." His thumb stroked my cheek, but immediately he seemed to realize what he was doing and let his hand slip down. He got up and began sorting through clothes again.

The thought of leaving The Vibe left me with a hole in my heart. I took my ice cream dish to the kitchen, washed it, and put it away. "I'm going to bed," I said as I walked back into the living room.

"Sleep well."

I nodded. In my room, I said a silent prayer for the soul of the dead man by the Dumpster. Then I got to work on my book, because I knew I'd just taken another major step toward becoming Americana today.

Twelve

Becoming Americana means no longer needing the security of belonging to minority group clubs or organizations.

LUPE PEREZ

The ladies in the admissions building, who had read the article about me a few weeks ago, were horrified. "You can't drop out."

"I have to," I explained.

They pulled me inside and called counselors, the dean of my department, hell, I was expecting the UCLA chancellor to make an appearance.

They all said the same things I'd already heard a million times. Without an education I didn't have a hope in hell to make something of my life.

"But I need to make money," I explained.

"Money will come later. You've been through too much to give up now."

"I'm not giving up. And I need money now, not later."

"You have financial aid."

"That helps with tuition and books and a little food, but I can't pay rent and gas and buy clothes, and live."

We all decided I would think about this for a few more days and they wouldn't drop me from my classes. By the time I left I was totally frustrated.

So when Mr. Reyes sat me down in his office and stared me down, I lost it. "Stop looking at me like that. I'm not like most of these college kids. I don't come from a perfect family. I don't have money. I need to work."

"No one comes from a perfect family. You have to charge ahead regardless."

"That's what I've been doing."

"Then keep doing it, Lupe. If I can arrange for you to take your final exams this quarter and keep you enrolled without attending classes, would you be willing to study on your own?"

"Yes, but . . . I don't think I can pass without attending lectures."

"If you can, will you try?"

I sighed.

"If you drop out, you'll never come back. I can almost promise you that. And you have a thesis to complete."

I wanted to finish, I really did. But I was so tired. Life was so hard and—oh hell, just what I needed, a pity party for myself. "I'll try. I'll try to do it all."

"Good girl."

Later that night, I met Will. He ushered me into the back seat of his truck.

Then right there in the university parking lot, we had a romantic meal, complete with soft classical music. He'd bought takeout at the Olive Garden. It was sweet and thoughtful and fun, and I decided I wanted to make this work with him.

"I'm going to try to pass finals without attending lectures this quarter," I said.

"Great. That means you'll still be around campus."

"Sort of."

"No 'sort of' about it, girl. I think we need to start seeing a lot more of each other."

I wiped tomato sauce off my lips. "You do?"

"Like exclusively. What do you think?"

What did I think? "I'm not 'seeing' anyone else if that's what you're asking."

He chewed on garlic bread and eased closer to me. "I'm asking"—he pretended to share a great secret with me—"if you'll be my girlfriend."

I smiled. Girlfriend? Did people really use that term? "I've never been anyone's girlfriend. What does that mean?"

He gave me a curious look, then reached across and traced my lips with his thumb. "I guess it means we date only each other."

"Oh."

He raised an eyebrow. "And have lots of sex."

I matched his look. "Is that what this is about?" Was Tracey right about what he expected?

"Absolutely not."

"Good."

"Well, maybe just a little."

I hid my amusement at his enthusiastic, yet shy and hopeful expression. "I think I understand now."

"Mostly it means I'm really starting to like you and I want to know you'll be around. So what do you say?"

Not sure what I was agreeing to, I said, "Okay."

He finished his bread and wiped his lips. "You realize I'm going to have garlic breath."

"Yeah, so?"

"Will you still kiss me?"

"*Still* kiss you? Did I say I planned on kissing you tonight?"

He eased the plate off my lap. "I really think you should."

"Why?"

"Because, you just promised to be mine. We should seal this moment with a kiss."

"I promised to be yours?"

"Mmm hmm. And to have lots of sex with me."

I rolled my eyes. "You're really silly. You know that?"

He shrugged. "And you're much too serious and mature. You need to make out in the backseat of a vehicle like most girls your age."

He made me laugh. "*Most* girls my age? So that's what they're all doing when they ditch class."

"Yep. All of them. You're totally missing out. And you're working on that Americanization paper, right? So—"

"It's a book."

"Book. Right. Well, making out in the backseat of cars is definitely American."

I smiled. He was so cute.

"Come on," he said. "Time to play catch-up. Let's get to it. I'll help you by showing you how it's done."

"How kind of you."

He slid right up against me. "Yes, I am. Very kind. And very determined. Tell me all this corny manipulation is working on you."

I rested my arms on his shoulders and angled my lips so that they almost touched his. "It's absolutely working."

So we abandoned our meal and feasted on each other—nothing too risqué—mostly kissing, some touching, but it all felt amazing.

Though I agreed to stop volunteering at The Vibe, I still had an obligation to train a couple of volunteers to take over my job. So after work, I went into my old neighborhood and spent a few hours at the center.

I also intended to show up for and participate in the rape prevention workshop. The topic was too important to me to walk away from it. In all honesty, everything at The Vibe was important to me, and I wasn't happy to be leaving.

As I sat behind the reception desk, I watched Diego and doodled on a notepad. Diego sniffed every few seconds and spoke super fast. He seemed unable to focus on anything for long.

I knew the signs. I'd been around people who took drugs way too many times. Leaning back in my chair and putting my feet up on the counter, I considered whether to confront him about it.

"Why the frown? And if you squeeze that pencil any harder it's going to snap." Nash rested his elbow on the counter.

I tossed the pencil on the counter. "Just thinking." I stood. Promising myself to pay closer attention to Diego in the next few days, I pushed all thoughts of him out of my mind. I had studying to do and I wanted to see Will.

The last two weeks, Nash had been driving me to work and Will had been picking me up in the evenings. In a way, this was nice. I spent every evening with Will, and I was actually starting to feel like maybe I could fall in love with this guy. I would always love Nash, but I was hoping that in time that love would fade. He'd become an old friend and my heart wouldn't ache for what might have been. I hoped.

But, I disliked not having my bike and being free to come and go as I pleased. "I was thinking maybe you and I can make a deal."

"What kind of deal?" Nash focused on me.

"What if you drove my bike to work and I used your car?"

He wrinkled his nose. "That doesn't sound like a good deal."

"Please. I need my independence. It's driving me crazy having you and Will cart me around everywhere."

"I kind of like knowing where you are and not worrying about you on that bike."

"You need children, Nash. Seriously. You've got parenting down to a science."

The warm, sexy grin he touched me with was so unfair.

"So what do you say?" I asked.

"Well . . . okay."

I fisted my hand over his. "Thank you, thank you, thank you. I'll drive super safe. I promise."

And I did.

The next morning though, I was thinking maybe I hadn't made such a good trade. I didn't realize how boxed in I would feel inside the old clunker. I hated to wait behind other cars. A motorcycle can go between other vehicles and inch to the front. Cars can't do that.

As I was hurrying to work, the yellow light turned red just when I was crossing an intersection, and a jerk in a white bug zoomed in front of me, cutting me off and leaving me smack in the center of the intersection.

Damn. Cars blew their horns and swerved around me, avoiding the rear end of the car and calling me names. Then a siren sounded and a cop on a motorcycle pulled up beside me. Oh, damn, not again.

I rolled down my window. "Hi," I said.

He lifted his helmet visor. "You need to pull off to the side as soon as we get a green light."

"That bug in front of me cut me off. I would have been okay if he hadn't done that."

By the look on the officer's face, he wasn't buying the excuse. "Miss, a yellow light doesn't mean to speed up and cross an intersection."

"I know, but—"

"The light has changed. Pull over, please."

Great.

I pulled over to the side, then handed him my driver's license and Nash's registration. "You really should have ticketed the white bug instead," I complained.

He wrote out the ticket and handed it to me. "You both created a dangerous situation. Next time, if the light is yellow, stop. Don't try to rush across the street."

"Right."

Jerk. After he was gone, I stepped on the gas and sped all the way to work.

During my lunch hour, I went back to the university in search of Tracey, deciding I'd forgiven her for suggesting I seduce Will. Especially since lately I'd had the same idea way too often.

The physical attraction between us was exploding. Although I've always thought Nash was sexy and I've loved him, I've never drooled over him the way I do with Will. Maybe because Will's always touching and kissing me and telling me the things he'd like to do to me. Come to think of it, I didn't have to seduce Will. He was doing it to me. Anyhow, I hadn't touched base with Tracey and I wanted to. She had tried to help after all, and I shouldn't have dissed her. But I got stopped by these Mexican chicks who belonged to a Chicana organization on campus.

They congratulated me on that stupid article and I simply

thanked them, tired of explaining to everyone that I had nothing to do with it.

They went on to tell me all about their organization. "Why didn't you join? We have to stick together, you know?" one girl said with a smile.

"We?" Who the fuck was she?

"Yes, we. Chicanas."

"I'm American, dude. I've never been to Mexico, okay?" Perhaps I said this a bit too defensively—when you grow up in East L.A. and you look totally dark, and, well . . . Mexican, you get tired of people asking you where you're from or assuming you can't comprehend the English language or that you're an illegal alien and thus barely human.

She looked at me like I was stupid. "Well, sure you're American, but you're also Chicana."

I continued to walk across Wilson Plaza toward Ackerman, where Tracey and Madison met to gossip between their morning and afternoon classes.

The Chicanas followed me. "We've got a great support group here."

UCLA was sponsoring a career fair today, so I had to weave around groups of students and display tables. "Listen, I'll be sort of dropping out of university life. If I come back next quarter, I'll check you out." Yeah right. Hope they don't hold their breath.

"We're a strong advocate group for change here on campus and in the community, and what you're doing at The Vibe is perfect. We'd love to have you."

Didn't she listen? I just told her I was leaving. The noise and commotion on campus was disorienting, and I was starting to get the feeling that everything was spinning around me. "Yeah, cool. Maybe next quarter," I said. I stopped in front of one of the tables to try to figure out the best way to get around this fair.

"We recently had the first Chicana rights conference. Maybe you'd like to speak at the next conference?"

"Speak?" I looked at her. Shit, I didn't want to be involved in some Chicana group. I wanted to get away from *La Raza* thank you very much. "I don't think so," I said.

A couple of the girls exchanged looks. "You're not one of these *Chicana falsas* are you?"

No, I wasn't a fake. And as far as being Chicana, that was a big deal when I was a borderline gang member, because the tag gave us a political-sounding reason to gather into groups and be socially negative about everything. Today, I don't give it much thought. If people wanted to think of me as Chicana—cool. Mexican-American was fine too. Just American was probably the best. I think we'd all do much better if we stopped sorting ourselves into little groups.

For a second I thought I spotted Tracey at one of the booths. Great, I wouldn't have to try to work myself out of this maze.

The guy sitting at the table where we stopped was from the L.A.P.D. "Interested in joining the force?" he asked.

"What?" I took the pamphlet he shoved into my hand. "Oh, no, I don't want to be a cop."

"She doesn't want to be a Chicana either," the chick said to the Mexican-looking cop.

I glanced at her again. Shit, I'd offended her. Couldn't people just leave me alone? "Dude, I grew up in the barrios, okay? I've had it up to here with Chicana bitches fucking jumping me, stealing from me, trying to twist my arm to join their *clicas*. I know this is different and what you're doing is awesome, but I can't be a part of it now. You understand?"

They took a step back. "Yeah. Sure."

I felt kinda guilty for rejecting them. But I was tired of being different. I didn't want to group myself into a subgroup and continue to be a minority. That was one of the main reasons I hated that the article about me was published. "For the few hours I'm here at the university I want to be just a student. Not a Chicana. Not the girl that was lucky to make it out of the barrio. No tags, just me."

"Hey, okay. We just wanted to offer a friendly invitation."

And that was nice, I guess. But I didn't want friends that only liked me because I happen to share the same heritage as them. "Thanks."

They left, and I tried to spot Tracey again, who seemed to have left the booth where I thought I saw her standing.

"So you grew up in the barrios, huh?" The cop said, a warm smile on his lips.

I sighed. "Yeah."

"We need good cops in L.A. Kids like you who have personal experience on the streets."

His poster above my head said, "Join the Blue, Change a Life," but it was my life I was attempting to change. I gazed at him. "But I'm trying to get off the streets," I said quietly. In a way, I was pleading for him to understand.

The noise of students talking and music blaring out somewhere on the lawns and the bright sun on my back started to make me dizzy. And the scent of grilling hot dogs in the air turned my stomach.

"What's your name?" he asked, and held out his hand.

"Lupe Perez. My juvenile records are sealed, but you all had a huge file on me once."

We shook hands and he chuckled.

"Now I'm collecting a bunch of traffic tickets. I don't suppose you can do anything about those, can you?"

Again, he laughed. "'Fraid not."

Out of the corner of my eye, I saw Tracey again talking to some lady from a fashion school, and this time I was sure it was her.

"I better go."

"Good luck, Lupe," he said. "And when you graduate, keep us in mind."

Keep the police force in mind? No way. But I was distracted and wanted to leave. So I nodded. "I will."

Then I hurried over to the fashion school table and patted Tracey on her shoulder. "Stay at UCLA," I said. "Your parents would probably kill you if you went to something like this."

"We've got a very good school," the woman at the booth defended.

"Well, well, well," Tracey said. "It's the college dropout." She checked my clothes out and I could tell she approved today. "My uncle says you're awesome."

"And you told him you'd made a huge mistake and that he should fire me immediately. Right?"

She placed her thumb on the strap of her new purse. Obviously getting jumped didn't teach her anything about carrying an expensive purse around campus. "I told him he was lucky to have you and to treat you well."

Time dragged as we both stared at each other.

"Sorry I lost my temper at the store the other day," I said.

"Yeah, well, my advice stinks sometimes." She jerked her head for me to follow her and we walked off to the next table. "Going to a beach party this weekend. Wanna come?"

"Maybe."

"It's a three-day weekend, we all deserve a break. Say yes. It'll be fun."

Tracey knew how to have fun, that's for sure. I agreed to go to her party if Will went too.

"Perfect. Then you're going."

"Hey, Trace, will you come somewhere with me?"

With a questioning gaze, she said, "Sure. Where?"

"The Vibe. I'm giving a workshop on rape the Saturday of Thanksgiving weekend. We're going to have a few guest speakers, and, well—"

"Yes. I'll go. Of course."

I felt our friendship and bond grow. I was trying to fit into her world, and she was doing the same for me. This was cool and exactly what I needed.

Getting ready for the rape prevention workshop, I walked the neighborhood in my comfortable jeans and black Vibe T-shirt and boots that I had missed wearing. Tracey and my new job had me looking like a damned wannabe magazine cover model.

I posted flyers and talked to girls on the street. From them I got lukewarm interest. I even jumped on my bike and went to my old high school, knowing that girls that age were the most susceptible. As I was heading back to the center, I decided that though I may be crazy, I should invite my old friends. I headed to Mari's house, which was about two blocks from my parents' house. Yes, I was nervous, and twice I changed my mind and turned back to The Vibe, but I couldn't let fear stop me from doing the right thing. I parked my bike in front of Mari's house.

I knocked on her door but got no answer. As I was about to leave, a guy walked out. He scanned me. I returned the frown and a don't-you-dare-touch-me look. Then without a word he walked away. "Mari?" I called and cautiously walked into the house. I heard movement in a bedroom, and when I looked inside I froze.

"What the hell?"

Mari lay naked on the bed, pretty much passed out. A couple of tens lay beside her on the bed.

I shook her. "What are you doing? Prostituting yourself for drugs now?"

She moaned, barely awake.

Having no idea what she took, I checked out the room but saw nothing. I looked into her eyes. Shit. Some kind of barbiturate; she was going to pass out.

"Hey, Mari. It's Lupe. Can you sit up, girl?"

She mumbled something I couldn't make out. I tried to help her up by placing one of her arms around my shoulders and gripping her around her waist, but there was no use.

"You switching from uppers to downers? What's up with that?"

She still didn't respond.

I pulled out my cell and called 911. "Not good, Mari. But I'll get you some help. Okay?"

I talked to the 911 operator and told her to send an ambulance, then hung on with her until I could hear the sirens. "You'll be fine," I said to Mari, pushing away temporarily the pain of seeing someone I grew up with in this condition. "You buying from Carlos? Hmm?"

She seemed to be trying to focus on me.

"Or is he giving you the stuff for free? You hiding him out?"

"Dawg," she said.

"Yep, it's me." I smiled.

But she didn't seem to be getting better. Instead she was going out.

The paramedics knocked on the door I had left open and called out to me.

"In here."

They rushed in and got to work. I stood out of the way, trying to control my shaky nerves. After administering blood pressure tests and a few other things I didn't recognize, they hurried her into the ambulance.

• • •

Once everyone had cleared out and Mari was on her way to the hospital, I ran out to my bike, climbed on, and rode away. Absently, I passed endless streets that all seemed to have the same stupid strip malls: gas stations, grocery stores, coffee houses, liquor stores.

I drove around, looking for something. Not sure what. Answers. A pain reliever. But not the kind Mari had resorted to. No. I wanted revenge.

In a wave of sudden rage, I hung a U-turn and headed back to the neighborhood. To my parents' house. It was payback time. I needed to let loose and release some of the garbage I'd held inside for too long. I wanted to find Carlos, and if anyone would know where he'd run off to, it would be my mother.

She sat at the kitchen table and glanced at me, then back at her dinner.

I pulled a couple hundred dollars out of my wallet and tossed them on the table.

This time she gazed at me a little longer. "This is supposed to make everything all better?"

"Sure. It's what you want, right? For your kids to bring you money. Doesn't matter how they do it. Legally, illegally."

"I don't want your money. You are no longer my daughter."

"When was I ever?" I shouted.

My mother frowned. "What do you want from me? I work, day and night. All you had to do was go to school and be good, and help out your family."

"You wanted me to be good? Help my family? By doing what? Sleeping with my brother? Running his drug deals?"

"Get out of my house." She stood, almost knocking over the kitchen table.

"Are you that blind that you didn't see the living hell I had to endure while you were at work?"

My brother burst through the bedroom door, surprising the hell out of me. My heart almost jumped out of my chest as I turned to look into his eyes. I was actually afraid. These two people who were related to me were strangers. Worse than that—they were monsters.

"What the fuck is going on, and what are you doing here upsetting Mom?"

"You're *here*? You're stupider than I thought. The cops are looking for you and probably watching the house."

His complexion darkened and his eyes turned cold. "And what are *you* doing, scoping things out for them? Reporting back?"

"I just got back from Mari's house, where she was practically in a coma, you fucking dirtbag. What did you sell her?"

His glare held no life, no sympathy. "She was having trouble sleeping so I gave her some yellow jackets. What's the big deal?"

"The big deal is she could die, and it would be your fault."

He laughed. "I didn't shove the pills down her throat."

I hated him. "I hope when they catch you, they lock you away forever."

The smirk on his face said it all. Even if he was caught, he'd do a few years and when he got out he'd be even stronger.

"Little sister, if I go down, I'll make sure I take you with me. If you don't want to end up servicing my contacts like your friend Mari, you'd better smarten up."

Without even a last glance at my mother, I said, "I'm leaving."

Carlos focused in on the cash on the table, then turned to me and grabbed my elbow. "Not so fast."

But my mother gave me the second shock of the night. Putting her whole body into it, she slapped his face so hard that he let me go and stumbled back against a wall.

"Sucio," she accused.

Cursing, he held his face and glared at our mother as he slid down the wall and sat on the floor.

"Go," she said to me.

I felt great pleasure in watching him down there on the floor. The burning rage inside me that has never really gone away urged me to do something really terrible. Break a bottle over his head, light a match to his sorry ass, take a baseball bat and beat him with it until there was nothing left but a pulp of bloody flesh and splintered bone.

I walked over to the kitchen cabinet and took out a bottle of tequila. Grabbing it from the mouth I spun it in the air the way bartenders do in movies. Then without stopping to think what I was doing, I caught it and hurled it at Carlos's head. He moved to the side and avoided getting hit. The bottle exploded against the wall, sending glass and clear alcohol all over the kitchen.

"*Estas loca?*" My mother screamed.

"You fucking bitch," Carlos roared and scrambled to his feet.

I grabbed another bottle, knowing I was dead if he got ahold of me. But my mother yelled for him to stay back and she took me by the shoulders and shook me. "Lupe."

"You were a terrible mother," I hissed.

Tears clouded her dark brown eyes. "So go. Leave us and make a good life for yourself. Don't come back."

I knew that years later I would wonder about those last words of hers. Was she finally thinking about my welfare as she booted me out of the house and out of her life? I looked down at the bottle of tequila in my hands and took it with me as I pushed her out of the way and stormed out of the house.

Thirteen

Becoming Americana calls for decisiveness and courage.

LUPE PEREZ

Nash found it hard to calm me down when I burst through the front door of our apartment and told him what happened.

I was charged. My old destructive tendencies were resurfacing and I could feel them coming back full force, but there was nothing I could do to stop them. I didn't want to stop them. It felt too good to take out my anger and frustrations on people like my brother. Or anyone else who crossed my path tonight.

"Want some tequila?" I sat on the couch and pulled the bottle out of my purse. "Two hundred dollar bottle of booze. We should enjoy it," I said, thinking of the money I'd dropped on my mother's table.

He sighed and stood. "Where'd you get that?" Standing in front of me, he towered above.

"I took it from my brother's stash. Would have had two, but I threw one at his head. I missed though. Bad shot."

He frowned. "Give me that."

"Go get some glasses."

"Don't be stupid."

I shot to my feet and got as close to nose-to-nose to him as I could. "That's right, I'm just a stupid kid, right? Why don't you try fucking me once and give me a chance to change your mind."

"Why are you doing this? Why did you go back to your parents' house?"

I laughed. "I had this urge to kill my brother."

Nash shook his head and reached for the bottle. "Maybe you've already been drinking."

I shoved him. "I haven't been drinking. I've been rescuing my friend Mari who overdosed on drugs Carlos sold her."

He yanked the bottle out of my hands and walked away with it. He stored it up on a high shelf. When he returned, he looked angry. Screw him. Part of me wished he would throw my ass out. Then I wouldn't have to face him every day knowing he'd never want me, never love me the way I loved him.

"Your brother's an ass. No doubt about it. But your friend did this to herself. We see this all the time at the center. You know that."

Yes, I knew that, but I hurt so badly inside, I needed to take it out on someone. Someone who was responsible for selling drugs to kids like me and Mari and those that came to the center. I stalked back and forth in front of the coffee table, feeling like I was going to explode.

"Do you know Diego is using?"

"Yes," he said in a subdued tone.

I cursed.

"I've talked to him about it. He's considering going through the cleansing program."

"Perfect. He's considering it. That's just wonderful." And where the hell was he getting the drugs? Not from Carlos. Not when he tried to defend me against him.

"You can't let these kinds of things get to you, Lupe."

"What the hell do you suggest? That I rip my heart out and stop feeling?"

"That you stay the hell away from The Vibe. You're too close to this stuff. You're not able to deal with any of it properly. You're too young."

"Fuck you, Nash."

His jaw tightened. "You're immature, and it shows."

I hated him. I hated everyone and everything. I wanted to bury myself in the sand somewhere and disappear.

He placed a hand on my shoulder, gingerly. "Your brother can *not* hurt you anymore. It's over. You've got to let the anger go if you want to help others."

"Is that what you've done? You're not angry with your parents? You're not angry that your sister died of an overdose?"

When his eyes flashed, I knew he was angry all right, with me. "Yes, I am. But that's over. I'm putting my energy into giving other kids a chance now—if they want to be helped."

"And what if they don't? We let them kill themselves?"

"Yes."

"Is that what you would have done with me? You'd let me get back into the gang and drug life if I chose?"

"I wouldn't *let* you. I'd tell you every day to get out of that environment. But if you didn't listen, there would be nothing I could do."

As always, he was right. And I had so much to learn. I sat down and dropped my head back. Nash sat beside me.

"I can't believe you said I was immature," I muttered. "That was mean."

He sighed and smiled. "I can't believe you told me to try fucking you."

I smiled back feeling a small flush of embarrassment. "I am *so* screwed up, it isn't even funny."

"You're getting better." He caressed the top of my head. "And you're making a difference. You did what you could for Mari. Maybe this episode will scare her into cleaning up. You can make the offer again."

I nodded.

"But don't be hurt or angry if she turns you down. She probably will."

What would I do without Nash? I leaned across and kissed him softly on the lips. "I'm sorry."

He patted my back. "Don't be. You're a strong, amazing, wonderful young lady, Lupe. I take back the immature comment. That *was* mean."

But I wouldn't take back the fucking me comment—though I wish I could rephrase it, because I wanted him. Like always.

Going to a beach party was well and fine, but Marta wasn't having any more of me missing Sunday lunches. So before going to the party, I had to agree to attended the family barbecue. As I was walking out the door, I felt sort of strange leaving Nash behind. After all, he knew Marcela as well as I did. "Want to come?" I asked.

Reclined on the couch in shorts and no shirt, his hair in disarray, the man looked like the ideal calendar model, I swear.

He hesitated. "I don't know. I'm not really family. You are."

But he had no family, except me. I pulled on his arm. "Come on. Please. You're family to me."

"I was going to work on the leak. You notice we've got water dripping into the bathroom from the apartment above us?"

"Put a bucket in there and call the landlord. That's not your job."

"Neither is wasting the day at a barbecue."

"That's where you're wrong. I'm your protégée, and it's your job to keep me happy."

Sitting up and draping an arm along the back of the couch, he narrowed his eyes. "That's the way you see it, huh?"

"Sure." I flipped my hair in stuck-up Tracey fashion. "You can be my arm candy."

He laughed, reached for a piece of paper and a marker from the coffee table, and wrote a big ten, holding the number over his head like an Olympic judge.

"So come on. We'll be late if you don't hurry."

He nodded and disappeared into the bathroom, where I heard the shower start.

Together we drove to the valley and spent the afternoon with the Alvarezes. I left him with the other husbands and boyfriends and joined the women.

Marcela had to give me the third degree, of course, about bringing Nash.

"Butt out," Marta advised.

"No, I won't," Marcela said. "Besides, I'm just asking."

"You didn't like it when I dated Gilbert either because he was older. She has something against older men," Katie said, motioning me to ignore Marcela.

Marcela sighed as if the whole thing were hopeless and she was never going to win against us all. "This is different. He watched her grow up. The entire time she was a child, he was a man. It's wrong."

"There's nothing going on."

"You don't get it, Lupe. He's never going to hurt your feelings. He cares too much about you. That's why he's allowed you to fantasize about him all these years. He'll do anything you want, anything for you. He's told me so."

"So?" I wondered what Nash had said. And what he would do?

"So, don't make him do something wrong."

I took that in and let it sift through my mind. I couldn't make Nash do anything. I knew how he felt. He *had* told me after all. And this was why I'd moved on. "I brought the man to lunch because he's our friend. That's it. Shit, Marcela. Can we drop it already?"

She held her hands out to her sides. "Dropped."

"Thank you."

"*Pobrecito,*" Marta said, ready to adopt another child. "He's welcome every Sunday, *mi'ja*. Even if you foolishly listen to Marcela and don't date him."

Marcela gave her mother an evil look.

"Okay, okay," she said. "Bring your dishes outside and let's eat."

Women and men all met again during lunch at the outside picnic bench, and I sat beside Nash.

"Having a good time?"

"Great. I can see why you like coming here."

"She doesn't like it, but we make her come anyway," Katie said.

Marcela nodded and pushed away the meat as if it were grossing her out. "They do that to all of us. Be careful or they'll be hunting you down too, Ryan."

George replaced Marcela's plate with just rice. "That's right, pal. This family sucks you in and before you know it, you're trapped."

Marcela arched an eyebrow. "Do you feel trapped?"

Oh man, she was totally hypersensitive lately. I passed Nash some rolls, because I knew what was coming. A ten-minute argument between those two about how much George loves her and how much she takes him for granted.

But Nash seemed oblivious to all the little annoying quirks of my substitute family. He just grinned and ate.

Later as we cleaned up and washed dishes, Anna shared her experiences in meditation class.

"That's a bunch of hogwash," Marta said.

"No, *Mami.* It's not," she said reasonably. "You guys have to try it."

"I'd fall asleep," Marcela said, carrying a stack of dry dishes to the hutch.

"Let me do that," Marta scolded. "Go sit down."

"I've been sitting. I'm starting to get sores on my ass," Marcela complained.

Katie turned off the water and frowned. "Don't share."

Anna dried the last of the plates, then turned to us. "Let's try some meditation."

"Give me a few months and we'll do belly dancing instead," Marcela said.

Abandoning the plates on the kitchen table, Anna took a seat across from Marcela and grabbed her hand. "It would be really good for you."

I put the leftover meat in a Tupperware container. "What would be good for her?" I set the container in the fridge.

"Meditation."

Katie rolled her eyes. "Don't tell me you're stuck on that again. The other night she called me to tell me she'd connected with IT." She directed that comment to Marta with a warning look that said she'd better take care of this before it got out of hand.

"You didn't understand what I was trying to explain to you," Anna defended. "And it was the most magical feeling." She turned to me. "Lupe, you'll try it with me, won't you?"

She had to be kidding. "Me?"

"Come on," she said, Marcela forgotten, as she left the table and took my hand.

"Hold on a minute," I said, digging my heels into the linoleum.

But we were headed to the living room whether I wanted to or not. Probably out of pure curiosity, Marcela and Katie followed.

"Let's sit in a circle," Anna said, urging her sisters to participate.

"You need serious help, *hermana*," Katie said, but sat on the floor just the same.

Marcela sighed. "I've done this before, you know. Didn't do a thing for me, except put me to sleep."

"You probably did it wrong," Anna said.

"How can you meditate wrong?" Marcela sat beside me and let out another long-suffering sigh. "If I fall asleep, pinch me."

"Don't tempt me."

"Shh," Anna said. "Now, sit comfortably and—"

"On the ground? That's impossible," Katie complained.

"Shh. Sit comfortably, close your eyes, and breathe."

We sat in silence for about ten seconds, then Marta walked in. "*Ahi, Dios,* you're not humoring her, are you?"

"Don't let any outside *distractions* bother you," Anna said. "Just breathe."

My nose itched. I wiggled it, but it only got worse. Could an ant be crawling on it? Maybe I brought one inside from the picnic. "Anna?"

"Just breathe, Lupe, and think of nothing."

"She's good at that," Marcela said.

Was she referring to me or Anna? I never thought of nothing. And right now, I was really thinking of that ant. Now it was crawling along my cheek. "What if my face itches?" I asked.

"You're resisting," Anna said in a chanting-like voice. "Breathe. Clear your mind."

"Psst, psst," Marta tried to get our attention. "I'm going to serve the flan," she whispered. "Who wants some?"

"Me," Marcela said.

"We're going to begin our chant now," Anna said. "Begin to say or think the word, 'calm'."

"Anyone else want flan?"

"I do," Katie said enthusiastically.

"Chant," Anna said.

"I dooooo," Katie repeated.

Marcela chuckled.

I was afraid to talk, but I finally swiped at my face. Couldn't stand it anymore.

"How about you, Lupe?"

"Okay," I whispered, opening one eye and peeking at Marta. Everyone else had their eyes closed so I closed mine again.

"I'll get you some too, *mi'ja*," Marta said to Anna, and walked out.

Then it was finally quiet as we all breathed. I tried the "calm" chant and started to feel sleepy. What happened if I fell asleep and tipped right over?

"Let thoughts filter past you. Don't attach to them," Anna instructed. "Let them pass and get to nothingness."

Why? I wondered. What was so good about nothing? I heard footsteps.

"What the hell are you girls doing?" George asked.

"I think they're sleeping," Nash said.

"Meditating," Marcela said.

"Reject outside distractions," Anna reminded.

George laughed. "You mean she can't talk? This could be good."

"How long does this last?" Nash asked.

"Not much longer. My legs are going numb," Katie whined.

"And I have to pee," Marcela said.

"Shh."

I really think I'm going to fall asleep.

"Hey, Lupe, you're swaying," Nash said.

"She's reaching her private sanctuary," Anna said. "Shh."

I yawned. "I need a pillow," I murmured.

"That's it," Katie said, and stood. Then all of a sudden a pillow hit me on the head and I opened my eyes.

"Take a nap," Katie said.

Marcela tried to get up. "Bathroom. Fast. George, help."

He hurried to her side and helped her up. She wasn't even showing yet so it wasn't a huge belly that was keeping her down, just a full bladder.

Anna had finally shut up.

Marta walked in. "Okay. Flan. Should we eat it in here or outside?"

"Outside," Katie said, and headed out the sliding glass door. Marta followed.

I looked at Nash, who shrugged.

"Do we leave her here?" I whispered.

George and Marcela walked back in. "Where is everyone?"

"Eating flan on the patio," Nash said.

"Well, let's go. What are we waiting for?"

"She going to be okay?" I asked Marcela.

Marcela kissed her sister on the top of the head. "We're going out now."

No answer from Anna.

"Love you," Marcela said, then winked and waved for us to follow her.

And we all did, leaving Anna alone with IT.

Fourteen

Becoming Americana means taking the plunge into the unknown—even when it's frightening.

LUPE PEREZ

On the drive home, Nash told me over and over again how much fun he'd had.

"They're great," I agreed.

"They argue about the stupidest things, but they all love each other—that's pretty evident."

"Yep."

"And Marcela's middle sister is a little wacked, isn't she?"

I laughed. "Naw. She's okay. This meditation thing has helped her become more in tune with her inner self."

Nash shook his head. "She's wacked."

"Aren't we all?"

"I guess," he agreed. "I had a great time. Thanks for inviting me."

"You can come with me every Sunday, if you want. Marta said you should."

"No, I can't do that."

"Of course you can. Why not?"

We both knew why not. He wasn't my guy. But he was my friend and I was sure he got lonely having nothing but The Vibe in his life.

"Did you see the look Marcela gave us, when we walked in together?" he said.

"If she wasn't pregnant, I'd say, who cares. But I don't like to upset her these days. Besides, she got over it pretty quick."

"She worries about you and she doesn't want me to take advantage of you."

"Like you would."

Something akin to an electric zap crisscrossed between us.

"I wouldn't. But she still worries."

"I know. Still, our relationship is none of her business."

"No. You're right."

We parked the car and strolled to our building. "Wanna catch a movie?"

"I'm going to a party with Will tonight," I said, feeling my face warm.

"Oh." He seemed speechless. "Okay. Cool."

"Some other time?"

"Sure."

Will picked me up, looking like the typical California boy. Khaki pants, a soft pastel Hawaiian shirt, and extra-short brown hair. He was gorgeous, actually.

And the second he arrived, I had the urge to run right out the door, to get us out of the apartment and the neighborhood. He didn't belong in this part of my world.

But Nash invited him inside. I knew I should've introduced them, but they were doing pretty well on their own.

Nash held out his hand. "Nash," he said.

"Hi, nice to meet you. I'm Will."

I stepped back and watched the two men. One that I loved with all my heart, and the other who made me laugh and feel beautiful and special and who was occupying more and more of my thoughts every day. I realized at that moment how much I wanted them both. But I shook away the crazy thought and picked up a sweater.

Will pointed to the TV. "How are they doing?"

Football. I had no idea who the teams were.

"Raiders are kicking ass," Nash said.

Will grunted.

"Don't tell me you're a Chargers fan."

"Oh yeah, I'm a San Diego boy all the way."

"Yeah, well, at least the Padres got a new stadium. That's something to be proud of. But the Chargers? Come on." Nash shook his head in sympathy. "They've got nothing going for them."

Will sort of smiled, then glanced at me, and his smile grew. "For the last couple of years the Chargers have done better than the Raiders, so we're plenty proud."

Why they were arguing about two sports teams was beyond me. Some girls get into sports, but not me. Every time Nash and George get together, they do the same thing, and Marcela and I walk away knowing we've lost them for at least thirty minutes.

"Ready?" I asked Will.

He placed an arm around my waist. "You look amazing," he said.

I had on a plain yellow sundress. Nothing special. Though I have to admit, me wearing a dress at all *is* special. Makeup was minimal. I'd learned that a little makeup goes a long way. And I even had a couple of citrine earrings.

"She does look pretty fantastic," Nash agreed and winked at me.

"All right, cut it out, both of you. I can't handle compliments."

Will nuzzled my neck. "Well, you better get used to them, because you're going to be getting lots more from me."

With Nash watching us, I wanted to crawl under the couch and hide. "Let's go," I said, and slipped out of Will's arms. "See you later, Nash."

Will offered his hand again, and Nash shook it. Then he reached across and kissed me. "Have fun," he said.

I gazed into his eyes and my face warmed. "'Kay. Bye."

As we walked down the stairs, Will took my hand. "So, that's Nash?"

"Yep."

"I thought you worked with him."

"I do. He's sort of like my brother." I lied. Nash could never be anything like a brother in my eyes. Our steps echoed as we made our way down the steps.

"He's not the one who hit you, is he?" Will opened the door and motioned for me to step outside ahead of him.

"No, no. He's the one who took me in when my real brother . . . can we talk about something else?"

We climbed into his truck. "No, actually, I'd like you to tell me more about Nash."

"Why?"

"You're living with him."

"So?"

"I didn't know your roommate was a guy."

"He's my best friend, like family. And he's doing me a big favor by letting me stay with him."

"Mmm." Will pulled into traffic, and got on the freeway before he spoke again. "How long are you planning on living there?"

"I don't know." I was starting to get annoyed. "Does it matter?"

"Sort of." He shrugged.

"Well, it shouldn't."

He glanced at me. "Did you notice how he looked at you?"

I didn't notice anything unusual. "I don't know what you're talking about."

"Lupe," he said. "He acted like he owned you. Like . . . he was an ex-boyfriend or husband or something."

"The something is brotherly."

Will raised an eyebrow as if he didn't believe me. "If you say so."

"He's a little overprotective. That's what you're sensing. And that's only because he's known me since I was a young kid and, well, he's still trying to save me from my past."

"Well, you're right, that certainly sounds brotherly." After a few moments of silence, he asked, "Mind if I put the radio on?"

"Go ahead." I knew it was a mistake to invite Will to the apartment. I just figured it was time he saw where I lived. I didn't realize he'd focus on whom I lived with.

When we got to our destination, he draped an arm behind the seat and reached for my chin with his other hand. "Sorry. I didn't mean to interrogate you."

"It's okay." He hadn't acted jealous or angry. He just had questions and he deserved answers. I should have told him ahead of time about Nash.

"I was just a little surprised that you were living with a guy, and it seemed like he was interested in you, and—"

"He's not. Of that you can be sure."

He smiled. "Good, because I certainly am."

"I know." I leaned forward and kissed him.

His mouth covered mine and he returned the kiss. When he pulled back, he groaned. "Let's continue this later."

• • •

The party was at a beach house in Newport, and it was extravagantly wild. Not like you see in movies, where hundreds of teenagers are milling about, filling up every corner of the house or passed out in the backyard. There were maybe thirty people and almost everyone was in the backyard. The weather was beautiful, which for November was a little odd. And though everyone was probably in their early twenties, I was definitely the youngest.

Will and I found Tracey talking to three guys and passing a joint around. Great. Just what I needed to see.

"Hey!" she said, hugging me first, then Will. "Come here." She dragged us to the side into a new circle. "This is Brittany and this is her place." Meaning she'd inherited it from her parents, my cynical brain deduced.

"Nice," I said.

"Here. Do you still smoke weed?" Tracey asked.

"No, I'm clean." No drinking. No smoking. No drugs. Even if every other stupid person in America seemed to do all three.

"You sure?" she asked, passing me the joint.

"Dude, I work to get addicted people off this shit. Get real."

She nodded, as if my comments sobered her up. "Sorry."

I glanced at Will, who also refused.

"Well, there's beer in the ice chest," Brittany said. "The hard stuff is inside in the wet bar. Food on the table by the fire pit. Get in the hot tub, enjoy yourselves." She winked at Will. "Lots of bedrooms, guys."

Will chuckled. "Come on," he said and took my hand. He opened the ice chest. "What do you want?"

I glanced inside. "A Sprite is fine."

He pulled out one beer and a soda. I took it and held it in my hand so no one would hand me anything else. The food was obviously catered—lots of seafood, sushi, fancy salads. I took a carrot stick.

We strolled for a while and Will found a few of his buddies to chat with. I headed back to Tracey and her group of friends. They were all wasted.

"How's it going with Will?" Tracey asked.

I glanced over at Will, who was laughing with his friends and had his hands all over the ass of a girl in a string bikini.

"Okay until now," I said, a sharp feeling of jealousy tightening my stomach. Now I knew what he must have felt about Nash.

All three girls watched him act like a pig. "Go give him a blow job in the bathroom and he'll forget all about her," Brittany said.

Yeah, like that was going to happen. I took a sip of my Sprite, trying not to show how horrified I was by her suggestion. I always thought rich white girls were different—didn't fool around, didn't do drugs. Guess I was wrong.

"You can change, get out of all those clothes."

"I didn't bring a swimsuit." I didn't even have one. The only old suit I had, I'd left at my parents'. Didn't seem like something I needed to throw into my small duffel bag as I was fleeing my home.

"Oh, too bad."

"I'm going to go for a walk," I said.

"You sure?" Tracey asked. "Want me to go with you?"

"No, no, stay here. I'm fine." Alone, I headed down the wooden steps, out to the beach, and onto the sand. I didn't stop until the waves came close to my feet. The moonlight shimmered off the water and it smelled fresh and salty out there. The music from the house filtered down, but it was still peaceful.

"Hey," Will came up behind me before I got too far.

I didn't bother turning to look at him. "Finished feeling up other chicks?"

"What?"

"Nothing." What did I care anyway?

He put an arm around me. "This party's not your style, is it?"

"It's okay. But I don't know anyone." And probably would rather not know most of those people. How different this was from the quiet Sundays at Marcela's family house, drinking lemonade and eating good food with people who were kind and funny and sane. Who needed all this outrageous partying? Where was it written that drugs, alcohol, and indiscriminate sex were fun?

"You know me." He smiled. Then he ran a fingertip along my exposed collar bone.

"Do I?"

"Mmm hmm."

"What are you doing?"

"Touching you."

"Why?"

He grinned and raised an eyebrow as if to tell me I should know why.

"Who was the girl?" I pushed his hand away.

"What girl?"

"The one whose ass was filling up your hands."

He laughed. "Oh her. She had implants and all the guys were feeling them."

"Implants?" Who would want to make their butt bigger? Jennifer Lopez syndrome—was that it?

"Yeah, crazy, huh? I told you all these girls are fake. Why do you think I like you so much?" He placed his hands on my shoulders and massaged lightly.

"I really don't know."

He scooted closer and kissed right below my ear. "Sure you do. With you, what you see is what you get. And hell, you're perfect."

"I'm not perfect."

"To me you are."

"You don't know me. I've got a bad temper and—"

"I don't care."

"I've got a rap sheet that's about a ream of paper thick."

"I don't care."

"I'm not sweet and innocent like other girls you've probably dated."

"Lupe, you're the only one I want these days," he said. "Don't you get it?"

I stared at him.

"You've got zero reason to be jealous, trust me. I have a million. You're sexy and beautiful and smart, and I worry every day that you'll decide you don't want to bother with an average guy like me. There's nothing special about me at all. Nothing."

"That's not true," I said, wondering if he seriously didn't recognize that girls saw him as amazingly handsome. When he walked by, he turned heads. But even putting aside the physical, he was kind and sweet and polite. And yes, he had money, but he didn't flaunt it. Then there was what drew me the most—the way he could be adorably insecure sometimes, yet confident enough to be himself. I stared at him and realized he was the one who was perfect. Too perfect for a flawed person like me. I pulled him into an embrace and held him.

"I can think of little else but you, Lupe," he said into my ear. "And I'd like to make love to you."

He'd like to do *what*? I pulled back. "Will—"

"In a Jacuzzi in my parents' weekend condo in San Diego."

"Why there?" I asked, surprised, to say the least, that he could be so specific about what he wanted.

"Because it would be romantic and memorable, and I want to remember every moment of our first time together."

My face was on fire. But my tongue had frozen. I couldn't speak.

"Then we could lay out on the balcony and stare up at the stars and the city lights until the sun comes up over the ocean."

"Boy, you've got it all planned out."

He caressed my back. "I've been thinking of it since the day I met you."

"Ah." I nodded.

"What do you say? Will you make the drive out to San Diego with me?"

I didn't know what to say. This was the first time a guy had presented a sexual experience to me in this way. Also the first time one called it "making love." But I couldn't sleep with Will. "Now?"

"Now."

"I can't—"

"Don't say no. I want to make love to you and hold you naked in my arms, Lupe."

Even though he was being sweet, and not at all acting like he just wanted to get lucky, I laughed bitterly. "I'm sure you do."

He tipped my chin gently and firmly. "I'm a guy in the prime of my sexual maturity," he teased. "So yes, I'm a dog who wants you bad, but—"

"Stop it." I wasn't in the mood for his stupid teasing tonight, and I didn't like when he made light of his wants or needs. "You're not a dog."

"I am, believe me. I've thought of little else but getting you naked for weeks. But even so, I want more than sex with you, Lupe. I want to bring you pleasure and to watch you smile and be happy. I know you haven't had a lot of that, and I want you to have it. Please, let me hold you and make love to you."

I needed someone to hold me and make love to me. I needed to erase all the terrifying, humiliating experiences of the past and replace them with something better, something sweet and new. But I didn't think I was ready. "It's not so easy for me."

"If you'll trust me, I'll make it easy. I'll make it magical. I'll make it anything you need me to make it. Just let me get close enough to you to try."

In a moment of bravery, and maybe insanity, I agreed and we left the party together.

Fifteen

When becoming Americana it sometimes helps to think in terms of sports. At times you may be winning, at times you may be losing, but if you keep your eye on the goal you have a better chance at a good score.

LUPE PEREZ

Three hours later Will and I arrived in San Diego, at his parents' condo. He took me into the lavish bathroom with a huge Jacuzzi tub in the center and looked expectantly at me. "What do you think?"

What did I think? Incredible. Elegant. Opulent. "I've never seen anything like it," I admitted.

Keeping his eyes on me the whole time, he ran the water and began to fill the tub. Then he took his clothes off. As if in a trance, I took off mine. We got into the tub and he took me into his arms.

His hands traveled over my body, swishing water over my skin. I got goose bumps.

"You're even more gorgeous than I imagined. You've got the softest, most beautiful skin I've ever seen. You're like a golden goddess."

I touched him back thinking *this girl is far from a goddess*. But *his* body was majestic. Strong and lean and powerful. My breath became uneven just by looking at him and feeling him under my fingertips.

He kissed my shoulder, and his fingers traveled down my spine. "Angel wings?" He gently traced my tattoo. "How appropriate."

"No," I whispered. "I'm no angel."

He pulled me closer. "You're the most angelic girl I've ever seen, sweet Lupe."

He started to kiss me and my body melded to his. Until this moment, I didn't realize how hungry I was for this kind of contact. I gasped for air. "Will." My body was shaking because of the intensity of my feelings, my desire, and my fear.

He turned on the jets, and held me. "It's okay. I'm sorry. I'm going too fast."

"N–no." I couldn't stop shivering.

He settled me into the hot water and kept his arms around me. With a smile, he smoothed out my wet hair. "I've never had a girl tremble with passion before."

I tried to smile back, but I felt like a fool.

"Though I think I'll have to let my ego take a hit here. You're just plain afraid, aren't you, Lupe?"

"No." But I was.

"You sure?"

I let my hand travel down his chest and belly, feeling and learning about each ripple and plane of his body, until I reached his penis. I held it and caressed its length.

He moaned.

As I watched the pleasure on his face, I got more bold and kissed him as I stroked.

After a short time, he gently eased my hand away. His lips left mine, but only to work their way down to my breasts.

The first touch of his tongue to my nipple inflamed every nerve ending in my body. So wonderful. So sensual. No one had ever kissed my breasts before. I caressed the back of his head.

This encouraged him to extend his kisses to other parts of my body.

For the next hour I felt things with Will I'd never felt before. He was tender and kind and my body came alive everywhere he touched. We made love in the tub, then again on the balcony, and again in bed.

In the morning he woke me up gently with tiny caresses and butterfly kisses on my breasts. I was momentarily caught off guard and stiffened, ready to push him off.

"It's okay. It's just me."

I smiled. "Good morning."

"I'm sorry. You looked so delicious sleeping next to me, I had to touch."

I still wasn't very comfortable with cuddling or too much closeness, but this was nice.

He made little circles on my stomach above my belly button. "Someone really hurt you, huh?"

For a second, I wanted to shove him away and tell him it was none of his damned business. But I resisted the urge to flee and nodded. "Yes, but I don't want to talk about it."

He stretched over me. "That's fine. I really don't want to talk anyway. I've got a way better idea."

"Let me guess what that might be."

He smiled wickedly. "Kissing."

As his lips parted my mouth, his hand continued to travel down my stomach and between my legs.

"Stroking," he said.

His fingers worked at arousing me as they dipped inside me and pulled back out. I loved the way he touched my body. When he replaced his fingers with his penis I thought I'd climax right then and there.

"Ah, that feels fucking great," he said as he sank into me.

Yes it did. I kissed him.

His hands cupped my face. "Oh, Lupe. You're so beautiful."

"Ah," I said as intense feelings made me shiver in the cool morning air coming from the balcony's sliding glass door we'd left open last night. "So are you."

"I could make love to you all day and night."

No he couldn't. He was very close already. So was I. "Try it."

He laughed.

When he came, he said my name over and over and made promises about how he would always be by my side to take care of me. "You're never going to suffer again, baby."

"Oh Will." I couldn't get enough of him. He was cute and sweet and generous.

"I'm going to make your life better than you've ever imagined. I promise."

I held him tight as my body convulsed and gave in to his. And though I knew his words were spoken in a moment of passion and he didn't mean them, they still touched my heart. He held me for a long time and we stayed intimately joined, then fell asleep and didn't awaken until late in the afternoon.

I entered the apartment in a state of bliss, only to find Nash fuming with anger when I walked through the door.

"Where the hell have you been?" he roared.

"I was with Will. You saw me leave yesterday," I said, startled by his temper.

"Yesterday! You stayed out all fucking night. You've been gone for twenty-four fucking hours."

"Two fucks in one breath. You must be pissed." I put my purse down and took a seat on the arm of the couch.

"I called the damn cops, Marcela, your parents. Everyone. I don't know this Will guy. I thought . . . I don't know what I thought. Shit, Lupe. How could you be so irresponsible?"

"Irresponsible?"

He reached into my purse and pulled out my cell. "Did you forget how to use this?" He looked at it. "Perfect, the damn thing is turned off."

I counted to ten and practiced controlling my temper. I tried to see it from his point of view, like he'd taught me. I tried to feel compassion for his feelings rather than the burning desire to tell him to fuck himself. "I'm sorry. I didn't realize you wanted me to check in with you." I tried not to make that sound sarcastic.

He ran a hand through his hair and cursed.

"Next time, I'll call you. Will that make you happy?"

"I don't need this crap from you, Lupe."

"I'm serious. I'll call. I didn't mean to worry you. But right now, you're acting like an ass."

"Yeah. Maybe." But in his eyes I read genuine concern.

Suddenly it was very easy to stand in his shoes and see that because he cared about me, he'd been worried.

"I'm glad you're okay," he said, turning his back on me.

"I'm fine," I said quietly. "Will and I drove out to San Diego and spent the night. It was too late to come back. That's it."

"Yeah. Okay." He grabbed his gym bag. "See you later."

"Where are you going?"

"Self-defense class."

"Didn't know you were taking a class."

"Just started."

I didn't like to see Nash angry. He was too good a friend. And his friendship was one thing I never wanted to lose. "Hey," I said and touched his arm. "I should have called. This roommate thing is new for me. Back home, no one ever cared where I was or with whom. I'm sorry if I worried you."

He glanced at me, then shook his head like he didn't know whether to hug me or strangle me. "I'm not used to our living arrangement either. And I'm sure as hell not used to you dating. I'll be honest, it bugs me."

I smiled. "Ryan? That's the nicest thing you've ever said to me."

He chuckled. "Come here." He hugged me. "I could *never* stay angry with you. It's not fair."

And it wasn't fair that I loved being held by him so much. Not fair, especially not right after making love to another man all night. I stepped back. "Go on to your class."

I was in my PJs, studying, when I heard a crack and a crash. My attention snapped away from the books and I hurried out of my room. The noise came from the bathroom. When I opened the half-closed door and felt the wet puddle at my feet, I realized what had happened.

Water no longer dripped, it poured from the apartment above.

"Shit."

A piece of the ceiling was missing, the chunk now lying on our bathroom floor. I hurried inside and dropped towels on the floor, then grabbed a bucket and tried to catch the downpour. Water splashed all around me, spraying my hair and clothes with cold water. There was no way I was going to be able to keep our apartment from flooding.

I heard the door open and close. "Nash?"

He peeked inside and dropped his duffel. "Holy shit."

"The whole ceiling caved."

"Damn it. The landlord was supposed to have that fixed." Staring at the hole in the ceiling, he cursed. "Keep catching what you can and dumping the water in the tub. I'm going to go shut the water main off."

"Okay."

About fifteen minutes later he returned and the water above had stopped falling. I was mopping up the soaked bathroom floor with towels when he walked in. "Let me help." He took off his shoes and threw them into the living room. Then he got down on his knees with more towels. "I can't believe this mess."

"I know, neither could I. I was in my bedroom when I heard the crash."

"The bastard should have fixed it. What if you had been standing at the sink?"

I rung out my towel in the bathtub. "I've been hit with worse than a little paint and plaster," I said jokingly.

But he gazed up at me, not amused. "Don't remind me."

I bent down to soak up more water and lost my footing and started to slip.

He reached for my legs and steadied me. "Slippery. Be careful."

I laughed and held on to the sink.

He picked up pieces of chalky and moldy plaster. "Look at this, and look at you."

I glanced down at myself. My white sleep shirt was so wet you could see right through it. My dark nipples stuck out like pebbles. I looked like a contestant in a wet T-shirt contest. I'm sure I turned fifty shades of red.

Finally, I lifted an eyebrow. "Well, don't look," I said.

With a chuckle, he said, "Sure, spoil all my fun."

But he took his gaze off me.

"I'm going to go change." I stood, took one step, and again started to hydroplane on the cheap linoleum floor. This time he had to catch me, because I was definitely going down.

He opened his arms and I landed on his lap. Again his eyes

traveled up my legs and to my breasts. "Lupe, honey, I thought we had a deal. You were going to stop throwing yourself at me like this."

I pushed on his shoulders. "Very funny."

He helped me ease off him. "Now, be careful before you break something of yours; or worse, something of mine."

I tried not to show my embarrassment at being so exposed. Though I was grateful that he was joking about it at least.

I climbed over him and went into my bedroom, where I dried off with my bed sheets, since all our towels were soaked. I changed into some real clothes this time.

"I'm going to take these to the laundry room," he called.

I opened my bedroom door. He held all the wet towels in his arms.

"Let me help," I said.

"I got it." He gazed at my chest. "You've changed—as unfortunate as that is for me—so I don't want you to get wet again."

"Cut it out. You act like you've never seen a naked woman before."

"I've never seen *you* naked before."

"I wasn't naked."

"Pretty damn close."

I felt my evil streak rise, and shrugged. "So, what did you think?"

"Honestly?"

"Sure."

"You gave me a hard-on."

"Oh yeah?" I shouldn't be happy about that.

"Don't look so smug. It's purely physical. I've been celibate for way too long."

Though my cheeks burned, I smiled. "Been a while, huh?"

"A long while," he admitted.

A couple of weeks ago, I would have suggested I help him out with that problem, but things had changed. After making love to Will, and finding it so wonderfully romantic and special, for the first time ever I didn't want Nash. And for once, I felt like we were sharing intimate roommate things like I would with a girlfriend—talking about dates and sex. He wasn't acting like an authority figure and I wasn't fantasizing about him. "I hope I'm not cramping your style."

"Only a little."

"You don't have to stop dating because of me, Nash."

"You sure?"

Was he asking my permission? Damn, I loved him. And he knew it and he wanted to spare my feelings. "I . . . will deal with it."

"Lupe, Lupe, Lupe," he said with a sad smile. But he didn't have to say more, I knew the rest. If only I were older. If only he hadn't attached brotherly feelings to me. If only.

"Better take those away. You're dripping on the carpet."

He winked. "I'll be back. But not until I find out who's going to fix this. Keep your clothes on and dry in case I need to bring a repair guy in here."

"You got it." I winked back.

Tuesday morning before going to work, I stopped by The Vibe. Still had things to prepare for the workshop, but mostly, I wanted to talk to Diego.

I dragged him outside to the alley.

"Wassup?" he asked.

"I know you're using."

He rolled his eyes and looked away. "What are you talking about? I—"

I shoved him hard and he straightened his back, no doubt wanting to shove me back.

"Where are you getting it?"

"What the fuck do you care?"

"If I didn't care, I wouldn't ask."

With a disgusted look, he tried to move past me, but I grabbed his arm.

Instantly he grabbed me by the shoulders and pushed me against the wall. My head bounced off the brick and I saw stars.

"You've been busting my balls since the beginning. I let you play that knife game, and let you pour paint all over me, but don't touch me. Got it?"

I shook my head to get my vision clear. "Don't stop, Diego." I rubbed the back of my head. "Hit me some more."

"What?" He looked at me like I was crazy.

"This is only the beginning. You keep doing drugs and you'll start beating up Carmen. You'll stab people. Shoot them."

He took a step away from me. "You don't know shit."

I recovered enough to stand up straight, and I reached for his T-shirt, grabbing a bunch of it in my hand. "I *know*."

His eyes met mine and I saw just a tiny bit of fear with all the hostility.

"Would you like to see some of the scars I have thanks to my drugged out brother?"

"He's an asshole, I'm not."

"Everyone is an asshole when they're on drugs. You'll lie, you'll steal, you'll hurt people. Eventually you'll do whatever you have to to get what you need."

"It's no big deal. Just a little partying, I'm having a good time."

"A friend of mine almost overdosed. She started out just having a good time too. We used to have good times together." I sighed. "If you're not learning anything at The Vibe, why do you keep coming back?"

"Carmen," he said.

"She's a good girl. Don't do this to her and to yourself."

He batted my hand away from him and turned his back on me, but he didn't walk away. "Nash said you have a cleansing program."

"Yeah. And it's a good one, but you have to be strong. When you walk out of The Vibe, there will be no one to hold your hand."

With a look over his shoulder and a smirk, he said, "I'm plenty strong."

"Your buddies won't like this."

"I'm not sure I'm going to like this either."

"Are a few good times worth ruining the rest of your life?"

"What kind of life am I going to have, Lupe? I'm a straight F student. I know nothing. I've got a dad who works construction sites and is gone most of the time. I'm probably going to end up doing the same."

"So get clean, work on your grades, and think about what you'd rather do." He hadn't been doing drugs long. He wasn't an addict, yet. He still had a chance to make a U-turn and head down a different road.

"I'd rather *do* Carmen," he said and headed back into the center. "But you told her to stop having sex." He threw me another glance. "Anything else you'd like to do to fuck up my life?"

I know he was trying to act cocky and tough, but he looked like a frightened little boy and I wanted to wrap my arms around him, even if my head was now pounding like crazy thanks to him. I touched the back of my head and it felt wet and sticky. Great. "I should kick your ass. I'm bleeding."

"Sorry."

I shrugged as we walked back into The Vibe. "I'll heal."

I got cleaned up, changed into appropriate work clothes, and took a handful of Tylenol for the headache. Today I was more than ready to sit behind a computer all day and not be bothered.

Will usually met me at the ad agency after work and we either went out to eat or found a place where we could have sex. Sometimes we studied together afterward, or he studied and I worked on my book. Tonight, I wasn't in the mood to do either. My head was no longer throbbing, but I was physically and mentally exhausted. "I want to go home," I told him.

"I thought I'd go shoot some hoops. Want to come with me?"

"Oh." That, I could do. "Sure, but let me drop Nash's car off at the apartment."

So I sat on the edge of the court while he ran around and tossed the ball again and again, hoping each time that it would land in the net.

The day had been warm, but now the afternoon had cooled and a chilly breeze blew out of the Pacific. The air smelled of fresh-cut grass, and I could hear the sprinklers watering the lawn around the residential buildings in the distance.

I watched Will dance around the court, but my mind was on my thesis. Writing this book was harder than I thought. Boiling things down to the basics wasn't easy. What was American anyway? I wasn't sure. The more I thought I knew what I was talking about, the more I realized I didn't.

So instead of writing, I stared absently at Will. He was trying hard to impress me with his athletic skills. I didn't know if he had any or not. I didn't know anything about basketball except that the ball was supposed to go through the hoop. But he counted down seconds on an imaginary timer and dribbled to the left and to the right, dodging pretend opponents. Then he'd ring a buzzer and shoot. "Yes, he scores!" he cheered for himself.

I clapped and he loved it. Then I tried to write another sentence or two while he played more calmly for a while.

"How about we do it on your bike?" he asked as he threw the ball for a long shot.

"Do what?"

"It." He winked and chased after the ball.

"Oh." He thought about sex an awful lot. Didn't bother me—much.

Sweaty and slightly out of breath, he crouched down and wiped his face on the towel beside me. Then he leaned across and kissed the side of my neck. I'd pulled my hair back with a butterfly clasp, so he had easy access. And by the way, I'd sort of given up on the makeup thing. I'd found one eyeshadow and one lipstick color that worked and stuck with those every day.

"What do you think? Would it be hard to do?"

I gazed at him, no idea what he had just said. My mind had returned to my work.

An overwhelming percentage of second-generation Latinos ended up losing their language, though not their heritage. I read that in the library the other day. I wondered if that was due to the stigma of speaking Spanish. Was that something Latinos purposely chose to do—lose their language?

"Am I interrupting your train of thought?" Will asked. "You're staring right through me."

"Sorry." I shook off my thoughts and closed my notebook. "Were you saying something important?"

He smiled. "I guess not."

I took his towel away from him and wiped his face and neck again. "You want to do it where?"

"On your bike."

"On my bike," I repeated using a teasing tone. I got up on my knees and gripped his wet shirt. "What about right here?"

"Here?" he asked with a nervous laugh.

"Here." I pushed him back and climbed on top of him. "Don't tell me you're losing your sense of adventure?"

He laughed again, a little surer of himself. Then he let go of his ball and wrapped one arm around my waist and the other behind my head. Hungrily, he kissed me.

I pushed him until his back was flat on the court. We continued to lock lips for a good five minutes. When I pulled back to look at him, he didn't make a move to get up. He just stared back.

"Man, Lupe. You are so beautiful."

"You're just saying that because I would sleep with you on a basketball court."

He placed both hands behind his head and simply stared. No smile. No response.

I slid off him. "It's starting to get dark."

"Hey, Lupe," he said.

I stood. He sat with his legs open and his ball by his side. He looked adorable. "Yeah?"

"Thanks for watching me play ball."

"You're welcome," I said and reached for his hand. Will Preston was an easy guy to please. I couldn't believe he was thanking me for such a small thing as spending time with him.

He took my hand and walked beside me toward the parking lot. "No girl's ever just hung out with me. They all want to go out to fancy dinners or to some other bullshit event. I like just hanging out."

I thought about that for a second. "That's funny."

"What?"

"No guy has ever taken me to a fancy dinner. They all just want to hang out."

We walked hand in hand, swinging our arms a little. "You've never had the pleasure of dining at some stuffy restaurant and had to endure a boring seven-course meal?"

"The guys from *el barrio* somehow managed to miss those places. But I did get to share a shake at Jack-in-the-Box."

When we got to his truck, he opened the door for me. "You know what I want to do?"

"Yes, you want to have sex."

"No. I want to take you out to a fancy dinner."

I smiled. "You don't have to do that."

"Sure I do. Because you think I'm exaggerating or making up stories about those seven-course meals. But don't say I didn't warn you."

I knew what he was trying to do. But he didn't have to. "I'm not the fancy restaurant kind of girl, Will."

"I know. Probably why I like you so much. But I'm going to take you anyway. Because you should get a chance to do everything in life. Okay? Tell me you'll go with me. Not today. But soon."

"Get inside and take me home. I'm tired." Besides, I wanted to call the hospital and check on Mari. She had probably been released already, but maybe I could get some information. I didn't dare go back to her house.

He nodded. "And by the way? Do you need help with that thesis? I'm a pretty good writer."

Sixteen

Sometimes becoming Americana has nothing to do with what you're working to become, but what you're learning to give up.

LUPE PEREZ

Burton, his team of advertising executives, and I met with one of his clients, a software support company called Fish Net. I sat in on all the preplanning meetings and listened to the ideas everyone tossed back and forth. The over-arching theme we wanted to get across to Fish Net's customers was that this company would "catch" all of the software issues that normally fell through the cracks. Their target market was other software companies that didn't want to offer support for their products.

After a month of rehashing idea after idea, the team of advertising executives came up with their campaign pitch, and I developed a website that would hopefully blow them away. Since this was my first big chance to show them what I could do, I went for it.

Though I was nervous, I tried not to show it as I walked a roomful of people through my PowerPoint presentation. As a navigational sidebar, I had a fish that dove into the water and pulled up whatever was clicked. I incorporated all the images and ideas that the ad experts used in their brochures as part of the campaign.

When I was done, I felt pretty good about the reception I got, both from the client and the ad execs.

I went back to work at my cubicle after receiving lots of pats on my shoulder and thumbs up. So, I was pretty happy.

Burton called me into his office a few hours later and asked me to sit down.

"First of all, your skirts are too long. You're young. Dress young."

Unable to help myself, I lifted an eyebrow and stared at him. This was not what I expected. Everyone else had congratulated me on a job well done. I thought he'd do the same.

"Don't look at me like that. I get to control your wardrobe during the hours you work for me."

"Maybe you'd also like to buy my wardrobe?"

Slowly, he took a seat, keeping his eyes glued to me.

Shit. Why couldn't I keep my big mouth shut?

"Deal," he said as he leaned back in his seat. "I'll give you a thousand-dollar credit card for you to use for your expenses. Things like clothes, lunches, you know, work-related stuff."

What? I stared at him in disbelief.

"So shorter skirts, a little more cleavage—not too much. We want provocative, edgy, not obvious."

I wasn't sure I should accept this "deal." I hadn't meant it quite the way I'd made it sound. I thought I was being a smart-ass.

"That'll do it for now. You can go back to work," he said.

I still hadn't moved or said a word.

"Anything else, Lupe?"

"What about the presentation today? Did you notice any of that or just my skirt?"

"Your presentation was flawless. You captured exactly what the ad executives wanted."

And? So?

He grinned. "If that hadn't been the case, I wouldn't care about your skirt, because you'd be fired. But I want to keep you. Hence, the skirt suggestion and the credit card. Congratulations."

"Thanks." I think.

"I'll have a few revisions for you to do. Things the client wanted touched up. Other than that, we're ready to start our next project. Take the blue file on your way out and start looking it over."

"Mr. Burton?"

"Yes."

"What if I don't want to wear shorter skirts?"

He lifted an eyebrow. "Did you hear me say it was a suggestion?"

"Yes."

"Good. The rest is up to you. Just realize that I don't make suggestions for the heck of it. I know what looks good. I know what sells. And we're not only selling our services, we're selling ourselves. I also know what image I want for the company. You can be in sync with that image and be part of the company or . . . not. You decide."

Clear enough. I guess I'd look at it as a uniform. I nodded.

"Oh, and Lupe?"

"What?" I was a little pissed.

"My secretary has your first paycheck. I've included a little bonus, because I'm happy to have you on our team."

My first paycheck. Cool. "All right. All right," I said. "I'll wear the damned short skirts, but just know that it's not me."

"It is now, my dear."

As I left his office, I sighed and headed to the secretary's desk. *It is now*. I wondered how much of myself would be left if I continued to give an inch here and an inch there.

• • •

The first time I met Nash, I was thirteen and he was twenty-one. I was recently out of juvenile detention camp and determined never to go back. I was also set on helping Marcela start up The Vibe. The three of us worked day and night trying to get kids to trust us. But no one worked harder than Nash. While I was at school and Marcela was at her real job, Nash ran The Vibe alone.

But after school, I was right there beside him until we closed at midnight. He and Marcela let me stay so late, not because they were into child labor, but because they knew I was better off there than at home. And Nash always drove me home.

One night, he took me out for a burger, and after talking to me about my dreams for the future, he outlined exactly how *we* would go about reaching them.

I told him I wanted out of the ghetto. I wanted lots of money. And I wanted an important job where people would look up to me.

"Those are great dreams," he'd said.

"I'm going to do it," I said. My brother was in jail, I was at a new school, and I had Marcela on my side. Nothing could stop me.

"It won't be easy. And there will be times when you'll want to give up."

I knew he was right. I reached across and touched his hands. "Don't let me, Mr. Nash. If I want to give up, kick my ass and make me keep going."

He squeezed my hand. "I will, but on two conditions."

"What?"

"First, you stop calling me Mister. I'm too young for that. And second, when you make it out, we go celebrate."

I nodded, probably already in love with him. And through the years, Nash kept his promise. Only, now that I was an adult, I wasn't sure I still wanted what that scared, desperate little girl had seen as salvation.

• • •

I called Nash at work and told him about my first real paycheck after two weeks as a working adult. I was so thrilled.

He laughed at the way I tried to keep my excitement in check so the rest of the office wouldn't hear me act like a fool. "Well, that calls for some celebrating, young lady."

"That's why I was calling. I'm taking you out to dinner tonight."

"Don't waste any of your money on me." He sounded distracted, and I wondered if someone had walked into his office or if he was walking around the center.

"Don't be ridiculous. I've been living and eating for free at your place for almost two months."

"Yes, and I've been taking note of the extra you've cost me. Let's see. You owe me a Starbucks coffee. Not one of the those small ones either. Make it a venti."

"Look, I get to be the smart-ass in this relationship."

He laughed.

"So, dinner? Will you leave work at a reasonable hour tonight?"

"Actually, it's movie night. Roberto is walking the kids to the theater and Tito is going to hang out just in case someone drops by. I planned on leaving early tonight."

"Perfect. Then it's a date."

"Whatever you say, Lupe."

So I went shopping and bought a couple of new dresses. And yes, a few slut skirts for work too. Stupid man gave me a five-hundred-dollar bonus. Since he wasn't an actual pervert and barely paid attention to me physically, I decided not to let his clothing demands bother me.

This time as I breezed through the racks, I didn't have Tracey's input, but I'd been reading my fashion magazines regularly, so I figured out what to buy. Then Nash and I went out to a nice steak house in Hollywood.

He dressed up too, and looked fabulous. We'd managed to stay away from each other for the most part lately. I know he took me up on my suggestion that he date, though he didn't bring dates home. And Will and I were getting so close that I'd been able to put aside my feelings for Nash anyway. Though nights like tonight, my heart still ached for what I wished could be.

Every time I looked at Nash and remembered everything he'd done for me, and was still doing, I wanted to wrap my arms around him and never let go.

"The Learning Channel is doing a piece on youth empowerment centers and they want to feature The Vibe," Nash shared during dinner.

"That's great." This was the first time I'd heard of it. "Did they call you?"

"Marcela called. I have a feeling she's known about this for a while. The new paint job, a delivery of new furniture last week, now this?"

"Well, could be good. Maybe it'll generate an influx of donations."

"Yeah," he said, not sounding convinced and absently rubbing his chin.

"The kids will be excited to be on TV."

"What about you?"

"Me? I won't be there."

"I might want you to be."

I thought about it for a second. "You're the one with the personality. Not me."

He leaned forward and took my hand. "But you've been through the program. You can give a different perspective."

He wanted me there as a success story. As a kid, not as a volunteer, not as an equal. Even though I've spent most of the last six years helping to run the center.

I looked down at my dessert, hurt and disappointed even if maybe I didn't have any right to be. "You're right," I said.

"Thanks, Lupe. I know you don't want to come back."

"Now you're wrong. I'd love to come back."

He shook his head. "You're serious, aren't you? You don't want to let The Vibe go?"

"I'm trying, but I miss it. I felt like I was doing something important there. Now . . . I'm building websites."

"But you're so close to—" He broke off whatever he was going to say and smiled. "Let's not talk about this tonight."

After we were finished, he slipped his arm around my waist. "As gorgeous as you look, and as much as I enjoy looking at you in that dress, are you willing to take it off?"

I took a step away from him. "What?"

He chuckled. "I thought you might be willing to slip back into your jeans and go with me to see one of my old favorite bands. Styx is playing at an Indian casino about an hour and a half away and I've got tickets."

"Tonight? Why didn't you tell me?"

"Because you wanted to go out to dinner and celebrating your first check was more important. But we've got time to make it if we hurry. We should get there just after the warm-up band wraps up."

"Let's go," I said, then paused. "You bought two tickets?"

"Yep."

"Shit, you had a date tonight, didn't you?"

He took my arm. "Nothing that couldn't be rescheduled. Besides, I'd rather take you. You need exposure to good music."

For the first time ever, Nash drove over the speed limit. "Better be careful. You're going to wind up with a ticket to add to my collection."

"I noticed those on the entertainment center. I meant to talk to you about that."

The car was dark as we headed east down the 10 Freeway. "Let me guess, you want to pay them for me."

"Not on your life. If you're not a careful enough driver to avoid getting tickets, I'm not bailing you out."

"Marcela would," I teased him.

"She's a sucker. I'm not."

I leaned back in the seat, completely relaxed and happy. "I'll drive more carefully. It's not like those tickets were my fault."

"So says every traffic violator."

"Are you acting like my dad again?"

"I'm giving you a serious warning. Drive safely with my car, or I won't let you use it anymore."

As my pride took another bruising from the love of my life, my back stiffened. "Someday, you're going to be really sorry that you couldn't stop treating me like a child."

He glanced at me, then frowned at the road. "Someday you won't be a child, and then I'll stop."

That only made me angrier. Damn him. "And by then it'll be too late."

This time he looked like I'd hit him. "Oh, hell," he said.

We drove in silence.

He ran a hand through his hair. "What am I supposed to treat you like, my buddy?"

"Sure, we're roommates, aren't we?" I snapped.

"Yeah, sort of. But it's different."

"It's not different. If I were Roberto or one of the guys you wouldn't play this protective crap with me."

Intermittent light moved across his face and I could see the frustration building on the hard muscles beneath his cheeks. "You're *not* one of the guys."

"Try me."

He laughed, though without humor. "Fine. You want to be my pal? My roommate?"

"Yes."

"Start taking out the trash once in a while."

"Fine."

"And don't give me money after I've put gas in the car. Put the gas in yourself."

"You think I can't? You're just always rushing out and doing it before I get the chance. All I can do is repay you."

"And stop cleaning everything up and cooking for me. Roberto sure wouldn't do that."

I sort of liked cooking for him. I'd been cooking for my father and brother since I was five. I was used to it. But cooking for Nash was different. I wanted to take care of him, make him happy. "Okay."

He glanced at me. "I went out on a date the other night."

"I know."

"The sex was terrible."

I was a little surprised that he was sharing, but I figured since the other stuff wasn't getting to me, he was going to up the stakes. "I'm sorry."

More silence.

"You and Will . . . you know?"

I turned on the air conditioner because though the air outside was cool, inside I was burning up. "Mmm hmm."

He grinned. "Not a child, huh? You want to have an adult discussion or not?"

"Does it have to be about sex?"

"Sure. Just so you know, I think about it a lot. But since you have been a *child* most of the time I've known you, I've never brought it up before." His voice was hard.

Okay, so this was actually a battle. A test. Okay. Unlike the lipstick fight, I'd win. "Actually, you have talked to me about it. Remember when I was sleeping around with all the guys in my neighborhood?"

His jaw tightened. "You were a frightened, hurt little girl."

"I wasn't that little and the guys I slept with were sometimes way older than me."

His fingers gripped the steering wheel tighter.

"I'd do it just about anywhere, and any way they wa—"

"I never date women more than twice," he interrupted, looking like he wanted to tape my mouth shut. "If they sleep with me the first time, once. All I'm after is sex."

"Good for you. Do they put out?"

"Usually."

"Men are scum."

"Yes," he agreed.

More silence.

"I believe that was the extent of what I told you when we 'talked' about sex when you were a teen. Men are scum, they can't be trusted, and all they're after is sex."

"Actually, you told me that none of those guys loved me and that someday one would."

He glanced at me, his expression softening. "And I was right. Wasn't I?"

"Are you referring to Will again?"

"Yes."

"I don't want to talk about him."

"Why?"

"He's off limits."

"Why?"

"Damn you, Ryan."

He grinned. "Come on. Roommates share things like this."

I glared at him as I realized I couldn't do it. I couldn't be his buddy. Besides, that wasn't what I was really after. I wanted him to see me as a woman. "You win. Okay? You want to be big brother or daddy, then fine. I give up." My voice cracked and I realized I was ridiculously close to tears.

"I know I hurt you every time I push you away."

"No, you don't—"

"Sure I do. But I have to. For your own good."

Was he right? Would I thank him one day for continually rejecting me? "Are we going to a concert tonight, or what?"

"We're almost there."

"Step on the gas. Do something wrong for once in your life."

He chuckled. "You're going to love this band." Then he reached across and caressed the back of my head in a tender way that told me he was sorry.

We made it to the concert as Styx was taking the stage. The band was awesome, though I wouldn't admit it to Nash. They sang a song called "Miss America" about the decline of the United States and others about not being fooled by the TV, radio, and magazines because they all present illusions of what life should be, and none of that is real. How *deep inside we're all the same.*

I was inspired by their music and wanted to hurry home to work on my thesis. Deep inside we *were* all the same. Yet, unless we conformed to American society, we Latinos seemed to feel inferior.

When Nash and I got home, I changed into sweats and an old T-shirt and grabbed my notepad. He changed as well and sat in front of the TV.

"Not tired?" I asked.

"Too wired. Gonna watch a movie. What are you doing? You're not planning on studying, are you?"

"Going to work on my thesis."

"Put that down. Relax for once."

I turned off all the lights for Nash. "I need to get my thoughts down. You enjoy the movie."

My cell phone rang and I got it, noticing I'd had three calls from Will. It was him again.

"Hi," I said, walking into my bedroom.

"I've been calling all night."

"I see."

"Why didn't you call back?"

"I went out with Nash to celebrate my first paycheck. We just got back."

"It's after one in the morning."

"I know." And his point was?

Will was silent for few seconds then finally spoke, and I wish he hadn't. He said, "I don't like you hanging out with him so much."

"Excuse me?"

"Damn it, you live with him, work with him, are you fucking him too?"

"What kind of question is that?" After how close we were getting, why would he ask something like that?

"Are you?"

"What do you think?"

"How should I know?"

"I've already explained that it's not like that between us. Besides, I'm with you." I slept with Will almost every day. If that wasn't enough to show him I was with him, what was? Never mind that I was still in love with Nash—that would never go away—but I would never cheat on Will.

"Then why is it you chose to celebrate with him tonight instead of me?"

I sat on my bed. "Because he . . . he's like family, Will. He's supporting me. He's been by my side since I was very young. He knows what I've been through."

"I know what you've been through too. Why don't you lean on me more?"

I couldn't answer "why" questions. "Okay, I will. But Nash and I have a history and that's not going to change." And any guy I was ever with would have to accept that or leave.

"Just as long as it stays history. I want to be your future."

I didn't respond. My future had been spoken for for years and it didn't include guys. Education and work, yes.

"Lupe, I really like you. I want to introduce you to my parents. I want there to be more between us than what goes on in the back seat of my truck."

"Okay."

"I love you," he said.

He what? "Oh, ah . . . you love me?"

"I know it's soon, but I do."

"I think real love takes longer to develop than a few weeks."

"I know what I feel."

And since I'd said the same thing to Nash and he brushed it aside, I wouldn't do the same to Will.

We made arrangements to meet the next day and then I sat on my bed alone for a while feeling overwhelmed and confused. I was falling for Will, but I didn't love him. Damn it, I still loved Nash, even if I didn't want to. Was I stupid to believe Will would make me "get over" that love? Was I making a huge mistake dating Will while living with Nash?

"Lupe?" Nash called. "Want some ice cream?"

"Ah. No." I slid off the bed and went to sit beside him on the couch.

"Changed your mind about the movie?"

"I guess so."

He frowned. "You okay?"

"Yeah. Sure." I turned to him. "I had an awesome time tonight."

"Even though it was an 'oldies' band?"

"Even though."

"Good." He stood. "I'll be right back."

He returned with a huge bowl of ice cream.

"Ryan?"

"Hmm?" He dug into the ice cream and pushed a button on the remote.

"Are you really a jerk with women?"

Surprise made him freeze with the spoon in the air. "Yes."

"Why?"

"I don't want a relationship." He shrugged. "And I don't want anyone to expect that, because they're not getting it."

He turned the volume up and stared at the TV as if he didn't have a care in the world.

Was he waiting for me to grow up? I wanted to think so. And he wouldn't be a jerk to me. Would he?

As always, I was a confused mess. I thought of Will's declaration of love and of his accusation before that. Was he wrong or was something actually going on between me and Nash? Nothing sexual, but something? Of course there was; who were we kidding?

I gazed at Nash. "You know Marcela said you told her you'd do anything for me."

"I would."

But so would Will—in a more equal sort of way.

"Why, is there something you want?" Nash asked.

I wasn't sure what I wanted anymore. It had always been him, but now, I didn't know. "Maybe. I'll let you know."

What the hell was I doing? If Will really was falling in love with me, then I didn't want to risk hurting him. He deserved better. He didn't deserve me. If things got any more serious and I couldn't return his love, I'd have to break things off with him.

Seventeen

When becoming Americana, it's important to trust in yourself. And to give those around you everything you've got.

LUPE PEREZ

For the next two weeks I avoided Will and buried myself in work. We spoke on the phone and I reassured him that things were cool, even if I wasn't so sure they were.

Thursday, Nash and I drove to the Alvarez's house together for Thanksgiving dinner. As much as he argued that he didn't belong like I did, everyone knew he did. Besides, I enjoyed going together.

Marcela and George arrived late. Her morning sickness was getting better, but she was always tired. She still wasn't showing. Still looked thin and athletic and beautiful.

I decided to confide in her about Will. I left my confusion over Nash out of it.

She seemed glad that I had a boyfriend.

"He wants me to meet his parents."

"So, meet them."

"Look at me. You think they're going to like me for their son?"

"I *am* looking you," she said, acting like I'd cursed. "You're quite a catch."

I laughed. "Sure."

"You're cute, intelligent, kind, and Will likes you. What else matters?"

"That's another thing. He told me he loved me."

She raised an eyebrow. "And what did you say?"

"That you can't really love someone after a few weeks."

A smile crept to her lips. "I'm with you there, girl. Well, he's young, impulsive. He probably just likes you rather intensely."

"Do you think it's bad that I don't tell him I love him back?"

"I didn't tell George I loved him back for months. In fact, I didn't tell him until after he left me. Doesn't matter when you say it, as long as you really mean it when you do."

"I don't know if I love Will. I like him a whole lot."

"That's enough. Honey, you're nineteen and you've been through hell. I know how hard it is for you to trust people, especially men."

My heart leaped to my throat. She was right. I tried to be honest and open, but trusting someone enough to let them get too close—that didn't happen.

She leaned in closer. "Don't rush into anything. Take it slow. You'll know if he really loves you in a few years."

"If we're still together."

"If you're still together."

I nodded.

Since it was a holiday, things were different in the Alvarez household. First of all, Marcela's aunts and uncles, grandmother, and cousins were all packed into the house and our usual intimate gathering was swallowed up in chaos.

I pretty much stayed out of the way. The older women ran the show in the kitchen today, so Katie and I hid out in her bedroom.

"Are you ever going to move out of your parents' house?" I asked her. She was twenty-seven, after all.

"Would you? I've got it made."

"You've got a point. Still seeing Gilbert?"

"Uhh," she said and shrugged, changing the channel. "He's too serious. Always talking marriage and shit."

"So? You've been dating him for six years. What did you expect?"

"I don't know. Maybe that's the problem. I've been dating only him for six years. I want new blood. Nash is pretty cute."

Should I scratch her eyes out now? "Don't even think about it."

"Not for me, *estupida*, for you."

"Shut up. And I have a boyfriend."

"Why don't you bring him then?" she challenged as if she didn't believe me.

"He wouldn't . . . you know, fit in."

"Are you ashamed of us?"

"God, no." I was horrified that she'd even think that. "I'm just not ready for it to get that, I don't know, serious."

Nash peeked in after a little knock. "Hey can I come in?"

"No. Go away," I said. "We're talking about guys and Katie will just embarrass me."

"Come in," she said, smiling at him.

Where Nash was, George was close behind. He walked in without asking his sister-in-law if it was okay and took the remote.

"Hey!"

He scooted her out of the way and changed the channel to a football game.

"We don't want to watch football."

He kissed her and told her to shut up. "Marcela is taking a nap next door."

"You're smothering her again."

"That's my job. Where's Gilbert?"

Nash decided to take a seat and watch the game too.

"None of your business," Katie snapped.

George shrugged.

Anna pushed open the door. "So this is where you guys are hiding out."

Katie groaned. "Can't a girl get a few moments of peace and quiet?"

Anna sat on the bed and it sagged. "Not in this house."

"This is a double bed. You're squishing me," Katie complained.

Marcela padded in. "How am I supposed to sleep when you all are having such a good time in here?"

"Come here, baby," George said.

She crawled onto his lap and curled close, wrapping her arms around him and kissing him like she hadn't seen him in months.

This was ridiculous. I decided to get up. But Nash pulled me back by grabbing the waistband of my pants. Big mistake. As I fell back, the bed collapsed.

Marcela looked up at George and smiled. "Mmm, honey, when you kiss me like that, the whole world rocks under me."

"Shit, I can't believe this," Katie shrieked. "You stupid fat-asses broke my bed!"

Marcela got up and pulled George with her. "Let's go to mine, babe. I'm suddenly tired, but I don't want to be alone."

George immediately tossed the remote back to Katie and followed his wife out.

Katie got off and tried to see where the bed had buckled. "You guys are going to buy me a new bed."

"Shh," Nash said, reaching for the remote and turning up the volume.

"I don't believe this. This is my room. I can talk if I want to."

"Give it up," Anna said. "Let's go back downstairs. Between

football in this room and the moaning that's going to start next door any second, we're better off sitting outside listening to *Abuela*'s stories for the umpteenth time."

I followed Anna out.

"Wait for me," Katie called, leaving the entire bed to Nash, where he was probably as content as . . . well, as a guy on a bed watching football.

The rape prevention workshop had five attendees. To say I was disappointed would be an understatement. Didn't young girls want to learn how to be safe? Didn't they realize the dangers of the streets, of dating, of being uneducated?

Tracey walked into the bathroom where I stood brooding, and placed a hand on my shoulder. "Thanks for inviting me."

"Yeah, sure. Thanks for coming. Right now I'm willing to go out in the street and pay girls to sit through this."

With a gentle squeeze, she released my shoulder. "Did I ever tell you that my uncle—the one you're working for—once invited me and my cousins on an African safari?"

"*What*?"

"Back when I was in high school. You know how he is. Loves to have fun and is into adventures, and he wanted to share this with us."

I wasn't sure what the hell Tracey was talking about, but I didn't want to get to know my boss better today. "Trace, look, I need to get out there."

"Let me finish."

I drew in an irritated breath. "Can you speed this up?"

"I didn't go to Africa. Only one of my cousins went. The rest of us had better things to do."

"Great for him."

"It was. He loved it. And since then has gone back countless times. He's involved in some kind of conservation thing. He totally got into it."

Impatiently, I nodded. "So, you blew it. He didn't. Though somehow I don't see you as a conservationist. Even if you'd gone and bonded with the wildlife."

"True. But my uncle really made a difference in my cousin's life with that one trip he'd invited us all on."

"There's a point here, right? You want me to go out there and make a difference."

"The point is that my uncle didn't care that only one of us took him up on his offer. He put everything into that trip just as if we'd all gone. He didn't hold anything back."

I gazed at her.

"It doesn't matter if there's five girls or fifty, does it?"

"No."

Tracey raised an eyebrow. "Then do your stuff, *chica*."

I laughed. Spanish and Tracey didn't mix. Sounded like she was saying "chick-a."

We both went out there and I told my story. I gave it my all. And at the end, after reliving things I'd give anything to forget, I felt cleansed. Like I was finally able to step outside of myself and use that experience to help others.

Nash had left the room as I went into details of what I'd had to endure. I knew he couldn't handle listening to it. But Tracey sat with her eyes riveted on me.

After I took questions and passed the workshop on to the other speakers, I sat beside Tracey.

"I never knew," she said.

"Now you do."

She nodded. "I'm glad I came on this trip."

I reached for her hand. "I'm glad you did too."

• • •

Will's parents lived in an older home in Carlsbad. They had enormous windows with views of the ocean. His father was a podiatrist, his mother was in real estate.

"Lupe wants to be an architect."

And she's practically dropped out of school. Did he forget that part?

They had a table on the backyard patio. Looked like it came out of a home and garden magazine. It was set with colorfully matched plates and silverware, flowers, a pitcher of water, and glasses for both the water and orange juice.

A Mexican servant brought out a plate of bagels and another with fruit.

"Have a seat, Lupe," Mrs. Preston said.

"Sure."

The maid, or whoever she was, filled my orange juice glass. Hell, I could have done that myself. "*Gracias,*" I said.

She smiled at me and continued filling everyone else's glasses.

Will sat beside me and placed a hand over mine. He winked.

I was nervous, but he made things easier. I wore the old lady top with the fluffed-out sleeves that Tracey had me buy. I figured rich white people would go for that style of clothes.

"Bagel?" he asked.

"Okay."

He lifted the plate and I chose a blueberry bagel. Then I took a few grapes and a couple of strawberries.

"My dad will be here later. He had an early appointment. That's the way it is with him."

"Yes," Mrs. Preston said. "Sometimes he has to work Saturday mornings. Once you get into the medical program, William, it will be like that for you too."

"Uh-oh, I'd better enjoy myself while I have the chance then, huh?" He smiled at me and eased closer, dropping a kiss on my cheek and lingering.

I smiled at him, but eased back, feeling uncomfortable with his closeness when his mother was staring at us.

"Honey, behave. You're embarrassing the poor girl."

"Am I?" he whispered, and kissed me one more time before straightening. "All right, all right." He spread cream cheese over his bagel and began to eat, asking about his sister who had recently married and moved to Arizona.

Mrs. Preston spoke proudly about Will's sister, sharing with me how intelligent her daughter was and how her new husband was some kind of scientific genius.

"He's a nerd," Will threw in.

But Mrs. Preston defended her new son-in-law.

We spent the longest hour and a half of my life having breakfast. Then his father got home around noon. We chatted for a short while, then Will took me to his bedroom.

"I got you something," he said.

"It's not an engagement ring, is it?"

He got this look on his face like my cousin Rico got when he was hoping to get chosen as a goalie on his soccer team and they picked someone else. Like a big chance had been swept out from under him.

"Is it?" I asked, feeling like an idiot for opening my big mouth.

Will burst out laughing. "Got you."

I smiled and shook my head. "Yes, you did."

"No, nothing that dramatic." He offered me a bag decorated with colorful spring flowers.

I took it and looked inside, and pulled out a black and gold bikini. "Thank you." I eyed him and smiled. I wouldn't be able to wear this very often. Didn't have a pool and didn't know how to swim. But the thought was nice.

"Will you put it on?"

"Now?"

"Yeah. Then we can hang out in my parents' pool and sit in the Jacuzzi." He gave me a sly look. "I know you like Jacuzzis."

He pulled me into his arms and we kissed. But he wasn't stopping at one kiss. His hands roamed my body, possessively.

I pulled back. "Come on. Stop. Your parents are out there."

"Lupe, I'm twenty-two. They know I have sex."

"I know, but . . ."

"Just a quickie. Please."

I didn't feel like it. "Do you have to have sex every goddamn day? I swear, I think that's the only thing you want from me."

My outburst apparently shocked him. "That's not all I want, but . . . forget it."

"I'm sorry."

"I thought you liked it."

"I do. Don't make a big deal about this. It doesn't feel right at your parents' house, that's all."

"Okay. I understand."

He understood.

He kissed me softly, and I melted against him, because he was so wonderful.

"Can I at least watch you get into that bikini?"

"You got it." I stripped as playfully as I could and he watched, touching occasionally when he couldn't control himself, and a couple of times, I almost changed my mind about not wanting to have sex with him. But we finished getting our swimsuits on and hurried out to jump into the cool pool water.

His parents occupied themselves inside and we were left outside alone to play and splash and kiss.

Lunch was served by their servant an hour later. I endured more questions from his parents about my family, my goals, how Will and I met, where I lived.

"You realize Will won't have much time for dating and women when he goes into medical school," his father said. This would be next year.

"I'll always have time for Lupe."

"Any woman that dates you has to be realistic about your goals and time constraints."

Will rolled his eyes.

"It's going to be intense, William. You'll have no time to waste on frivolous activities."

Such as? I wanted to ask. Poor guy. No wonder he wanted to have as much sex as he could now. His family planned to tie him to a desk piled with medical books for the next four or five years.

Maybe I wasn't the only one who was being pushed to "succeed."

"I'll be around whenever Will has time or wants to see me," I said. *I'll service him between study breaks,* I thought mischievously to myself. If only I had the nerve to say it out loud and see the looks on their proper faces. "But I won't get in his way," I said instead. "After all, I have my own plans."

They seemed pleased with my response, and later, when his parents went inside, I pulled Will to the side and reached into his swimming trunks. "Let's be realistic about your goals," I said. "You're going to have to schedule some time to relieve a little stress when you enter medical school."

He laughed and guided me to his bedroom. "Want to head over to the downtown San Diego condo? I'm already feeling the pressure of medical school."

"Yes I do. I want you to enjoy as much frivolous pleasure as you can before your life is over."

A few hours later, while I was making love to Will, I forgot about wanting to break things off with him. I forgot that I wanted Nash instead. And I ignored his sweet words of love. Next year, he'd go away to medical school and it would be over between us. I didn't have to rush things. So I lay in his arms and denied any feelings that hinted I might miss being with him one day when he was gone.

Even if I did have an uneasy feeling in the pit of my stomach. Even if I knew that feeling well. It was one that screamed stop, turn around, don't do it, trouble ahead. But it was my style to charge right into disaster.

On the beach, we drank coffee and took a break from the physical for a little while. I brought my notebook and wrote. I wrote all the time now. The book was starting to come together.

"You need a laptop," he said.

"Hmm?"

"A laptop. You need one."

"Probably."

"I'm going to buy you one."

"No," I said.

"Yes."

"If you do, I'll be angry."

"Lupe, you're my girl. I love you. Stop telling me I can't buy you things. I'm going to, and you're going to accept the gift graciously."

I looked up from my notebook. Will was not an assertive guy. And he didn't tell me what to do. "Do you have me confused with someone else? I said I didn't want anything from you, and I meant it."

His jaw tightened. "Why are you so stubborn?"

"Because I am. I do things on my own. That's the way I like it."

"Of course that's the way you like it. That way you don't have to risk trusting or depending on anyone else. I get it, but—"

"You don't get a damn thing. Don't act like you know me, because you don't."

"You won't let me. I'm trying."

"Who asked you to? Who asked you to butt into my life and start demanding things from me?" I slammed my notebook down on the blanket. "Who I live with, who I go out with, what I write with. Damn it, I don't need any of this."

Startled by my outburst, he'd jumped back when the notebook slapped the blanket, and now he only stared at me with his lips set in an angry line.

"I don't need anyone," I said more quietly, all my annoyance carried away with the gentle breeze that blew wisps of hair across my face. "I like being alone."

"If you like being on your own that much then maybe we should arrange for you to do more of that." His tone was cold and hard.

I zeroed in my gaze. There was my opening. But I couldn't get any words out. They were on the tip of my tongue. Just one smart-ass response. One "great, that's exactly what I need." Except, I got a sick feeling inside at the thought of him not being around. I could *not* dump him.

He swallowed but held his frown. "I'm going for a swim. So you get your wish. Be alone."

I thought about going after him and apologizing. Wrapping my arms around him and telling him how much I loved spending my days with him and how happy I felt each time he looked at me. Sinking into the surf and making love to him out here under the warm sun on the cool sand. I thought of a million things I *could* do, but . . . I went back to work—writing and thinking of a thesis that didn't matter much to me at all at that moment.

Will came back about an hour later, dry like he hadn't gone swimming at all. Maybe he just walked around to get away from me. He sat beside me, and when I didn't acknowledge him, he dropped his head on my lap, right on top of my notebook. Forcing me to notice him and letting me know he wasn't going to let my stupid attempt to push him away work.

"Hi," he said.

I smiled. "Hi."

"How's the book?"

"Coming together."

"I'd like to write a book too."

"Why don't you?"

"Someday. What I'd really like is to be a journalist. You know, a serious news journalist."

I ran my fingers through his short hair and gazed down at him. "You should. All the suggestions you've given me on my book have been right on."

He chuckled. "I can't pursue something like that."

"Sure you can. Why not?"

"Lupe, I'm going to be a doctor. Didn't you hear my parents?"

"You don't have to be."

He grabbed my wrist and pulled me down. "Kiss me."

I kissed him.

"I love you."

"Stop saying that."

"No."

"Your dad's right. When you go away, this thing between us will be over."

He frowned. "You're crazy."

"I'm being realistic."

"I *will* become a doctor, just like I'm supposed to. But I will *never* give you up."

"Come on, Will. You'll marry some well-off white chick and I'll be a memory of the time you went slumming."

He shot up off my lap and frowned as if he were too appalled to speak. But then he did. "Sometimes the poor little Mexican girl routine you play is cute. And sometimes it's just plain stupid. Let's go."

Yes, I was stunned. And yes, what I said was stupid. And yes, I should've apologized. But no, I did not.

Eighteen

While becoming Americana is a worthwhile goal, you have to be careful not to step on those you love to achieve your dream.

LUPE PEREZ

Before Will, my last teenage sexual experience, at the age of fifteen—the one in my garage with Victor—left me mentally numb for hours afterward. I went home and climbed into bed and fell asleep. The next morning I got up, showered, had a bowl of cereal, and walked to the bus stop to catch a bus that drove one and a half hours to the Palisades through crazy bumper-to-bumper traffic.

I got through two periods of classes before I freaked out. I had some kind of anxiety attack, I don't know. I couldn't breathe. I was burning up and itching and felt like I wanted to crawl out of my skin.

The teacher sent me to the nurse's office, where I think I scared the crap out of the woman.

"I'll call your mother," she said.

"No. Call Marcela."

Marcela was my emergency contact and she was paying for my education—an agreement she and my mother came to after I was released from juvenile camp.

At that moment, I knew Marcela was the one person in the world I could count on. When she showed up, I threw my arms around her and clung like a baby chimp to its mother. She signed me out of school for the day and I sat trembling in her car.

"What's wrong?" she kept asking.

"I don't know."

"Did someone do something to you?"

"No."

"Did you take something?"

She meant drugs, and for a split second I was angry. "No!"

"Okay. Okay." She buckled me in and took me to the apartment she owned back then.

As soon as I walked inside I began to feel better. The feeling was similar to how your body starts to warm after you come out of an air-conditioned building and you stand in the hot, hot sun—comforting and warm and like you're coming back to life.

Marcela brought me a glass of water.

"I fucked Victor yesterday," I said.

She cringed. She knew I was sexually active. "Congratulations. Maybe you'll win the Nobel Peace Prize for being the one female to bring comfort to the most boys in one neighborhood. He is from your neighborhood, isn't he? Or have you moved on to the adjoining area of L.A. County?"

Tears ran down my face. "He didn't use a condom or anything. What if I get pregnant or catch some disease?"

Her expression softened. "A little late to think about that now."

"I know." I continued to let the tears fall and didn't even attempt to stop them.

"I'll take you to a doctor. We'll have you checked out," she said. "And whatever happens, we'll deal with it."

I nodded. We spent the rest of the afternoon watching TV and eating fattening chips and dip. I don't remember what we watched. All I remember thinking the whole time was that it was over. For the longest time I'd thought that screwing whomever I wanted made me powerful—showed the world that being raped by my brother didn't hurt me in the least. But it did. And I continued to hurt myself by having indiscriminate sex. But I was done.

I never told Marcela how much it meant to me that she stood by my side no matter what stupid thing I did. But she probably always knew.

I got the call as I was leaving my apartment to meet Will for a date that night. Katie, Marcela's sister, called from the hospital.

"She was working late in the props department," Katie explained. "Her cramps were so sharp that she couldn't walk to her office. The guys working with her helped to carry her to her office and called the ambulance, but it was too late."

"She lost the baby?"

Katie sniffed, and I didn't have to be in the same room with her to know she was crying. "Thought you might want to know."

"I'm on my way." I hung up and grabbed my purse and keys.

"Marcela lost the baby," I said to Nash, who was working out with his weights. "I'm going to the hospital."

"Oh, no." He stood. "She okay?"

"I think so. Katie didn't mention that Marcela was in any danger, and I think she would have if she was. I'll call you at home later."

"I should go with you, but damn it, I have that initial interview with the stupid network. I'm supposed to walk them through The Vibe."

"No big deal. I'll let you know what's up."

"Okay, drive safely."

I gave him my "yeah right" look and hurried out to my bike.

Without being reckless, I raced to the hospital. Marcela's entire family was there. Her sisters, grandmother, a few cousins, people from work, and a few of her friends. I found Marta, who immediately pulled me into a sad embrace.

"Oh, *mi'ja*," Marta said. "Thank you for coming. Marcela will want to see you."

"How is she?"

"Physically okay, but she's devastated."

"Can I see her yet?"

"George is in with her now. Sit with me."

I hugged Katie and Anna, and sat with the family to wait. After her mother and sisters and grandmother got their ten minutes with Marcela, I was allowed to go in. She looked like death.

When I walked in, she closed her eyes as if to shut away having to retell what had happened to yet another person. I sat beside her bed and placed a hand on her arm. She moved her hand and gripped mine. For a few minutes, we didn't speak.

"My grandmother tells me I'll have others," she said, her voice devoid of emotions. "My mom and sisters keep saying how sorry they are and how it's all for the best because there was probably something wrong with the baby. And George blames me because I wouldn't rest. If you've got some goddamn words of wisdom to try to make me feel better, do me a favor and save it."

I tried to keep from crying. "Hell no. You know me better than that. I think this is fucked up and nothing is going to make you feel better right now."

Marcela closed her eyes in sort of a long blink. Tears ran down her cheeks. "I didn't want the damn baby."

I flinched. "What?"

"This *is* my fault. I didn't want to be pregnant and this is the universe getting back at me."

"That's crazy talk, Marcela. You can't believe that."

She began to cry and pulled on my arm.

I stood and hugged her. "This isn't your fault. Come on. And George can't possibly believe that."

"He does," she wailed. "He didn't say so, but I saw it in his eyes."

"That's just your guilt talking. But I'll kick his ass if he even hints that it's your fault."

She laughed in between her sobs. "I feel like shit, Lupe. I've felt like shit for months, but right now, I feel like I lost part of myself."

"You did, dude."

She cried harder and I decided I should keep my mouth shut. But I tried again.

"And you should grieve, right? But I know you'll get past this. That's what life's about, you know? Shitty things happen and every time you deal with one more piece of crap, you get stronger."

She nodded.

I eased away from her. "I better let you rest. I'll stop by your place and see you in a day or two."

Again, she nodded.

"And I *am* sorry."

"I know."

I left her room, grabbed George by his shirt, and pulled him aside. "Did you tell her this is her fault?"

He looked horrified. "No."

"She thinks that's what you think."

George's jaw tightened and his eyes went sort of blank. "She wouldn't slow down. Just kept pushing herself. Even on days that she wasn't feeling well. I just wish . . ." He dropped his head back and stared at the ceiling.

"So you are a little pissed at her."

"No." He sounded defeated. "I was angry about what happened, but not at her. I've hated to see her so sick and frail lately. I'm just glad she's okay and this is over."

I touched his arm, and he looked at me. Awkwardly, he took a step forward, and not knowing what to do, I gave him a hug. "You've got to make it clear to her that it's not her fault."

"I will."

"And I'm sorry about this, George." I stepped back. "Next time, I'll be there every day to help her out. We'll baby the shit out of her. All of us."

"There isn't going to be a next time. I'm not going to make her go through this again."

"You'll change your mind. She'll be fine and—"

"No. She never wanted any damn kids anyway. She was doing it for me. Listen, I'm going to go sit with her."

"Good. Go."

I went back and said good-bye to the family, then left. Once I was far away from everyone, I stopped against a wall and drew a breath. Tears moistened my eyes and then suddenly I was crying. Damn it. Why did this happen to them? Marcela didn't deserve this type of pain. Damn it.

When I got back to Nash's place, he was there waiting to find out about Marcela's condition. He clicked off the computer and asked how she was.

"Not good."

"What happened? How did she lose the baby?" He stretched back in the computer chair.

I shrugged. "Who the fuck knows? Because life sucks, that's why." I felt tears threaten again, but I didn't want to cry in front of Nash. "I'm going to bed."

"Wait." He grabbed my arm and stopped me. "What can I do?"

"Nothing."

"Lupe. Where are you going, sweetheart?" He pulled me close and my tears came full force. I held on to his shirt and cried.

He kissed the top of my head and wiped my eyes and made soothing sounds.

Comforted by his arms and feeling less alone, I turned my face up to tell him I was fine and our lips touched. An accident. A mistake. An opportunity that neither of us shrank away from—not even Nash. He kissed me and I parted my lips to invite him inside.

I clung to him as his hands roamed my back. I needed this closeness so badly. Just one relationship with someone that I loved had to go right. I pulled him toward the couch and he eased me down.

But he must have had a moment of clearheadedness, because he stopped.

I sighed. "Are you going to tell me how this is wrong and how we shouldn't be doing this? How we're going to burn in hell for even thinking of each other this way?"

Nash smiled softly and ran his fingertips along my face. "You're an angel in disguise, you know that? You're so *good* inside, Lupe."

I shook my head.

"Yes. You are. You give and you give of yourself until you're totally drained."

"So do you."

"No. I'm much more selfish."

I frowned. He was crazy. There was nothing selfish about him.

"Except when it comes to you. I refuse to think of myself and what I want."

"Then think of me."

"I am." He slid beside me rather than on top. "I'm also thinking of someone else you seem to have forgotten."

I frowned.

"Will called when you didn't make your date," he said. "I told him you had a family emergency. Maybe you should call him."

Maybe I should. Maybe I should get up before I make a huge mistake. But I shook my head. "Will is wonderful—too good. I'm beyond lucky to have him. But, I'm yours, Ryan. No one knows me better than you. I don't belong with Will. You know that." *You're just scared*, a voice inside my head said. *Because you could really love Will. Nash is safe.*

For long tortuous moments, he stared at me, then took my lips in a sweet tender kiss that could never be described as passionate or sexual even though it was on the lips. His hand caressed the back of my head. "Lupe, I do love you, you know?" he said. "And I do realize that you're not a little girl anymore—to others. But to me . . . you are."

"But I need you to get past that."

"You need a friend who isn't going to take advantage of a mixed-up girl."

"I'm not mixed-up."

"You are and you're looking for comfort in totally the wrong arms."

I felt like he slapped me. "You're an idiot."

"Probably."

"You really think I don't know what I want?"

"I really think that ten years from now, if this happens, you're going to be asking, 'how could he have ruined my life, the selfish bastard?' Yes, I think you're going to regret it."

I pulled him close and crushed my lips to his. He kissed me back just as heatedly, though probably with more devotion than attraction, and that pissed me off because I felt like he was placating me, allowing me to take out my frustrations while he remained nothing but the cool target. *He'll do anything for you. Don't make him do anything wrong*. Marcela's voice came back to haunt me. Then I ripped our kiss apart and drew a breath to the side. "You don't know me at all if you think I'd ever regret choosing you." He stared at me, drawing in deep breaths of his own. "And you're lying to me and yourself, because you want this as much as I do," I said trying to convince myself as much as him.

The doorbell rang and Nash cursed. "Don't move."

Will stood on the other side of the door. "Hey," he said to Nash.

Nash stepped aside and sighed. "Hey, hi Will. Come in."

I sat up.

Will came to my side. He crouched down and looked at me. "What's going on?"

He was the last person I wanted to see. I felt like a traitor. Guilty as charged. "Nothing. My friend just lost her baby today, and . . . you should go home. I'm not in the mood to talk to anyone."

"I'm not just anyone. I'm your boyfriend." He reached across and touched my swollen lips, then looked up at Nash, figuring out how my lips had gotten that way.

He stood. "I'm a fucking idiot. Are you sleeping with him?" he pointed to Nash.

"No."

"Don't lie to me." His voice was loud and accusing and felt like he'd physically shaken me.

I couldn't deal with him right now. "Will, please. Let it go."

"Let it go? Look at me and tell me what the hell is going on between you before—"

"Nothing, I—"

"I want the truth, Lupe. Now."

I glared up at him. "What do you want to hear, that I fuck him every night? Fine. Now you know the truth."

Nash started to shake his head as Will turned to him. "She's upset. It's not true."

But Will threw a punch and hit Nash in the jaw. "Asshole."

Nash didn't fight back, and Will turned to me. He reached for my chin and forced me to look at him. "I trusted you, and I *loved* you."

"Will . . ." Shit. What could I say? "I'm sorry."

"You're sorry? Don't be. You did me a favor." He pulled his hand away. "I might have done something really stupid and asked you to marry me one day. Think of what a fucking ass you would have made of me then."

He was tearing my heart out and I started to cry.

"And save the tears. You're working on becoming a cold-hearted American, remember? Congratulations. You can start waving the flag now." And he left.

"That was smart," Nash said. "Brilliant." He rubbed his chin.

I wiped my eyes and drew a breath, knowing the hole in my heart would fill back up. I didn't care. I couldn't. "He had a good ride. Now it's over. He's right, I did him a favor."

"Shit, Lupe. You're impossible."

"What am I supposed to do, keep dating him when I'm still in love with you? I want *you*, Ryan. Don't you get it?" I sniffled. "Do you want me or not?"

He rubbed a hand across the top of his head. "Oh, man."

"If you don't, I'm moving out. You won't see me again. I can't take this anymore."

"Once you're feeling better, we'll talk about this."

"No." I shot to my feet, my emotions raw and on the edge. "You either love me or you don't. You want me or you don't."

"Damn it," he yelled. "I love you. And because of that I just might not want you."

I didn't understand. I'd never understand him.

"Let's sit with this a few days. Just a few days. Okay? Give me that. You can't go anywhere right now anyway."

"Okay. Fine. Whatever. Maybe I'm better off without either of you."

"Don't be childish."

"Go to hell, Nash. I'm tired of you playing games with me. You're the one who needs to decide what you want."

In my bedroom, I curled into my blankets. But I didn't sleep.

For a long time as I tossed and turned, I couldn't figure out why I wasn't sleeping. I was exhausted. Then it hit me. It was Will and the look in his eyes. Pain. *I trusted you, and I loved you* he'd said.

But I hadn't trusted and loved him. Not like I should have. I managed to pull myself emotionally out of every sexual encounter we'd had. I felt the physical pleasure, but none of the emotional—and I was good at that, an expert.

I kept my heart closed, knowing that one day it would be over anyway, because I didn't deserve a guy like Will. Who was I kidding? Not myself.

But I never intended to hurt Will, who has shown me nothing but kindness from day one. I curled into a ball in my bed and hurt all over. I was wracked with guilt. Even more than guilt, I felt regret. And knew that no matter what happened between me and Nash now, I had to go back to Will and make things right. Somehow.

Marcela was released from the hospital within two days. George begged her to take a leave of absence from work, but she told me she was going back next week.

"If he was as mean as I am, he wouldn't be talking to me right now. I can see it in his eyes, that he's furious. But he won't show me. He agrees with everything I say, and does anything I ask," she said.

We sat in her backyard and stared out at the ocean. Her infinity pool rolled off the edge of the slope, and when you gazed at it, it appeared to connect with the ocean. The illusion was awesome. And Marcela loved illusions. I turned to her and didn't see any of the enthusiasm for life she usually had. And for some reason, that scared me. Marcela was my rock. She was my role model.

But role models need a kick in the ass every once in a while and I decided to give it to her. "Of course he does. Because he feels guilty for what happened. He doesn't blame you, like you said. He blames himself for putting you through the pregnancy."

Tears touched her eyes. "He just doesn't get it that I don't want children."

I believed her and George believed her. The difference was that he thought she'd change her mind. "Why?" I asked.

"Why what?"

"Why don't you want kids?"

"I just don't."

"Why?" I knew why. It was one more commitment to George. One more unbreakable bond to her husband. To her, children meant she'd be stuck forever to one man, like her mother had been "stuck" with her father when Marcela had been born.

"I don't have time for children. My job is too important."

I nodded. "Right. The movie business wouldn't be the same without you."

"Don't start with me, please."

I reached across a small glass table where our iced teas in sweaty crystal tumblers lay untouched. "I'm not going to, but Marcela, let me say just one thing."

She turned to gaze at me with a mixture of hostility and fear and pain. "Talk."

"You create cartoons. You're a big kid yourself. You'd be a great mom."

She drew a breath and started to tune me out, but I squeezed her arm. "I don't believe you don't like kids. I don't."

"I didn't say I didn't *like* them. I just don't want any."

"Of course not. Because then you and George would be a real family. You wouldn't be able to pretend that your job is the most important thing in your life, and that George is a close second."

"What are you talking about? I *love* George. He *is* the most important thing in my life."

"Really? Dude, I've watched you lead him around like a puppy on a chain for years now. But every time he asks you to take a small step toward being a real family, you freak."

She closed her eyes and rested her head on the cushion of her chair. "You don't know what you're talking about."

"First just getting you to set the wedding date—"

"Shut up, Lupe." She shook her arm loose from my hold.

"Look at when you decided to buy this house. He practically had to get on his knees and kiss your toes before you'd agreed to buy it."

"I said, shut up."

"As long as you stayed in that little apartment of yours, you could pretend you were still dating. But buying a house together was huge deal, wasn't it? It was a commitment."

"I said, shut the fuck up!" Her eyes were open now and she was sitting straight up and stiff as a surfboard.

"You've been married five years and he hasn't had all of you yet!" I shouted back.

"What would you know about giving of yourself?"

Everything, because with me, what you saw was what you got. I didn't play games. *What about with Will?* asked a voice in my head.

"I give it all," I said, ignoring the voice. "I get kicked in the teeth all the time, but I don't hide from anything." I stood. "And damn, Marcela. You're the one who taught me that."

She gazed up at me. "I'm going to tell you something. Just this once and you have to promise never to tell anyone. Ever. And never bring it up again."

I shrugged. "Okay."

"I'm scared shitless."

"I know."

"No. You don't know. I'm afraid that once I have kids, I'll love them so much I won't care about my career anymore. I won't care about anything or anyone but my child. I'm afraid I'd love George so much more than I already do, and that from that moment forward, he could destroy me as easily as if I were a paper-thin wafer cookie. I'm scared of losing who I am."

Interesting. Because I thought the opposite. I thought that one day, if I married Nash and had lots of children, I'd find myself. I'd be whole. I'd be worth something, because others would need me and want me.

We both sat quietly, gazing at each other, and I frowned. Were we both absolutely wrong?

"Marcela," I said softly, not even realizing that I was speaking until the words sort of spilled out of me, "maybe you wouldn't be losing who you are. Maybe you'd be becoming more of who you are. And maybe if you never take that chance and embrace motherhood, you won't need George to destroy you—because you'll be doing it all on your own. Just maybe."

"Having kids won't make me more. Not everyone has to have kids."

"That's true. But if you're afraid to have them because you're afraid to love . . . you said you're afraid you'd love them too much, that you'd love George too much. If that's true, then you're not whole anyway. You're only a fraction of what you could be. I mean, hell, Marcela, loving other people is what it's all about. Or else, I don't know . . . why are we here? What are we going through all the day-to-day bullshit for?"

"I'm afraid of losing myself, Lupe. That's the sad truth."

"You can never do that, girl. You're too busy being hung up on yourself."

For once, she seemed speechless. She looked out at the ocean. She pulled her legs up and hugged her arms around her knees. "How did you get so smart?"

I shrugged and sat back down. I placed my elbows on my knees and rested my chin on my upturned hands. "I've had great role models."

She chuckled. "Do you realize you're the only one I've ever given to and loved unconditionally? Why is that?"

I turned to her. "Because I needed you so badly."

She nodded. "And I didn't lose a bit of myself in the process. That's what you were thinking, right?"

I shook my head. "Nope." I smiled. "But I'm glad you realized that all on your own."

We sat back and enjoyed our teas the rest of the afternoon. We watched the tide change as evening approached. And there was a cosmic click in the universe. For whatever reason the two of us were thrown together in life, today, this moment, completed a natural cycle. Something changed. Something closed. Something was . . . completed.

Nineteen

Just because you become Americana doesn't mean you can have it all. That's only a myth!

LUPE PEREZ

I didn't want to face him, but I knew I had to. After two weeks of spending every afternoon after work with Marcela, I called Will and asked him to meet me at school. Marcela was okay now and agreed to take a whole month off work. To reconnect and reaffirm their love, she and George were going to vacation in Mexico. I figured I needed to do a little reconnecting myself.

He waited for me under a tree by the science building where we've shared lunches many times. As soon as he saw me, he motioned that we walk. "What's up," he said. "I have lots of studying to do. Finals are going to be a bitch. And I got offers from three universities. The medical schools are all great, so it just depends on where I want to live for the next few years. I think I need to schedule a trip to each place and see what strikes me as—"

"I'm sorry," I said. "And if you'll shut up for just a second, I'll beg and plead for your forgiveness until you feel your ass has been royally kissed."

He paused and glared at me. "I don't want your apology. Doesn't do a damn bit of good. Doesn't erase anything."

"I know. It doesn't erase the fact that I love Nash."

His jaw tightened. "What do you want, Lupe?"

"But I'm not sleeping with him. Not yet."

"What the hell does that mean? What am I supposed to do or say to that?"

"Nothing. If you'll just listen."

He continued to look at me like he wanted to slap me. But he listened, didn't talk.

"We, you and I, just happened. I didn't expect it to, but it did, and maybe there's a chance for us. Maybe my feelings for Nash will go away with time. If—"

"If what? If I keep you totally focused on me? If I love you enough?"

"No, but—"

"I will *not* play second string to any guy, do you hear me?"

I nodded.

He sighed. "I love you. But . . . you have to love me back. Do you?"

Oh shit. Why did he have to ask me that? Why couldn't we just keep dating and forget that I'd screwed up? "I don't know. I want to."

"But do you?"

Yes. "No." I shook my head regretfully. "I don't."

He nodded and swallowed. "Then I wish you luck, Lupe. Go to Nash. Have a good life."

He turned to leave, but I reached out and grabbed his arm. Because I cared about him and I liked him and I didn't want things to end this way. "Wait. Please."

"For what?"

I blinked away tears. "Don't . . . just wait . . . I can learn to love you."

He moved closer and tipped my chin back. "Do you want to do something for me?"

I nodded. "Sure. Anything."

"Get whatever you need to get out of your system. Sleep with him. Marry him. Have kids with him. Do what you need to do. But don't ask me to take scraps. I'd rather lose you than know I've got only a piece of your heart."

I pulled him close and kissed him. He was so much wiser and kinder than me.

He kissed me back. Hard and passionately.

My tears mingled in with our wet lips. My body went up in flames the second his body came into contact with mine. I wanted to connect with him, to feel him inside me, to feel loved and wanted. Everything about him screamed that he was the right guy. Not to lose him.

"I don't want to let you go," I whispered when he pulled back.

"You can't have us both." His voice was thick and hoarse.

"I know. Not fair."

He managed a chuckle. Then he stepped back, but his hand still caressed the back of my head. "You'll be fine. Go get what you want."

Then he turned away and almost ran, leaving me confused because something told me that what I wanted was impossible. Because I *did* want them both.

The next morning, I beat Nash to the center. I went through the usual routine: turned on computers, started a pot of coffee, put out some Mexican pastries. Then I welcomed the early risers who usually showed up before, or instead of, going to school.

Nash got after them for skipping class. I didn't bother. I knew that if I harassed them they'd just go cause trouble in the streets. At least here they were safe, and I usually got them involved in something valuable. Besides, it was never far from my mind that I wasn't much older than the teens who hung out here—I wasn't exactly looked at as an authority figure.

I grabbed a bottle of Windex and a rag and began cleaning the mirrored door to our supply cabinet. Girls loved this door because they could stand in front of it for hours and check themselves out. But somehow, there were always smudges of lipstick on the glass. Which made me wonder—how close did their faces get the mirror? Jeesh.

"How's that article coming along?" I asked Samuel as he helped himself to a pastry.

"You know," Samuel muttered, barely awake.

I tried to make some sense of his response. "Someone should make it public about the mold in your building. I really liked your idea about publishing an article on the dilapidated buildings in L.A. and tying it in to how they take advantage of illegals who are too afraid to complain." I stopped scrubbing and moved in closer to him. "You could be like one of these undercover reporters, you know?" Heck, *I* was getting excited about this.

He nodded.

Yep, excitement just poured out of this kid's pores. Ah huh. I tried one more time. "Really, I'm serious. You should do it. It would be an eye-opener to so many people who don't live in the barrios. They don't know what we go through, right?"

He met my eyes and we connected. Yes!

"I've started," he said. "But I don't have the words."

I offered an encouraging pat on his shoulder. "Write with your soul, the words will come. Trust me, Sam." I needed to take my own advice. My thesis was bogged down again after the fiasco with Marcela and Will. I wasn't sure how to go about putting all my ideas together now that I'd written them down.

I saw a hint of a smile, and took that as a positive sign. I left him in peace to eat his breakfast and contemplate his article. Even if nothing ever came of it, he would at least have done more writing than he probably did at school.

I went back to the glass door.

Vicki strolled in, picked up a magazine, and went to the filing cabinet to get the fashion forms she'd designed and filled out religiously. "Damn, it's off its track again, Lupe," she said as the file drawer got stuck coming out.

I watched her yank the drawer in frustration. "Ricky, can you fix the filing cabinet for Vicki?"

"You need to buy a new one. *Shee-it.*" But he got up from the computer where he was doing a word search and headed to the cabinet.

"Thanks, bud."

He patted my ass as he passed by me.

"Hey, hands off the help." Nash walked in like a tornado and gave Ricky a warning look before I could get a word out of my mouth.

Ricky grinned. "Lupe knows I don't mean anything."

I rolled my eyes. Sixteen-year-old guys were walking hormones. Come to think of it, all guys were.

I followed Nash to his office. "Coffee?"

"What are you doing here?"

"My boss needs me to work late tonight, so I'm going in after one."

"Yeah? So what are you doing *here*?"

"I miss being here."

The coffeepot had stopped hissing and popping and fragrant steam came out of it as I filled his cup. I used to love to start my day looking at and talking to Nash. I placed his cup on his desk and sat across from him, pulling my legs up on the chair.

"You'll be happy to know I got my first belt in my self-defense class last night," Nash said.

"Great. How is that going?"

"The female instructor flipped me twice and pinned me against the wall once. Then she almost tore my fingers off in a painful arm lock."

"Sounds like you're learning a lot," I said.

"Yeah. That if anyone attacks me, I'm screwed."

I laughed and got up, figuring I'd better get back to the kids.

"Maybe you want to go with me next time?"

I wrinkled my nose. "I don't think so. I can already fight."

"You can defensive-girl-claw some poor unsuspecting fool. I'm talking sport here. I'm talking graceful self-defense. I'm talking going with me so you can protect me from the instructor."

Shaking my head at him, I turned away, a smile still on my lips. "You're a big boy. You can handle it alone."

"Seriously. Think about it—it would be good for you."

Yeah right. "Good for me how?"

"Good for your spirit. Will help you focus."

"I'm focused. Right now, I'm going back out there to focus on our members who are probably plotting one brilliantly devious scheme or another."

"Hey," Nash said.

"What?"

"You've been avoiding me lately. What's up?"

"Nothing. And I haven't been avoiding you." Though I had been afraid of what his response would be. I made sure not to be home when he was and to be already in bed when he got home from work. "I've been working and spending time with Marcela. Might have been nice if you had stopped in to see her."

"I did."

"Once."

"You're changing the subject."

"Do you really think this is a good place to talk about . . . things?"

He lifted his hands up in the air. "Sure. Let's talk."

"I'm going back out there."

"I'm too old for you. We have sort of a teacher/pupil history together that's difficult to shove away. And I'll never be able to offer you the kind of life you deserve; I'll be poor forever and I don't care."

"You think I do?"

"I want you to care. I want you to be something," Nash said.

"I *am* something."

"That's not what I mean."

"Then what the fuck do you mean?" I raised my voice even though I knew the kids in the other room could hear me. "I'm so damn tired of hearing about this, this woman you're trying to make me into. Can't you just take me as I am, and love me?"

He stood. "I do love you. Calm down."

"Do you? Do you love me, really?"

"Yes," he whispered. "Yes, I love you more than anything, Lupe. But . . . not that way."

I looked away from him. Not romantically. Not like I loved him. Or *did* I love him that way? Did I simply idolize him and want him because he has been my safety net?

"I tried. I've told myself again and again that you're right. That you're grown now and that you're not *really* my sister, and—"

"Forget it." I needed to get away from him.

"Wait." He hurried around the desk and took my arm. "Because I love you and want to give you whatever you want—whatever I can—I'd like nothing better than to give you this, Lupe. But every time I touch you . . . sexually," he sighed, "it feels wrong."

Wonderful. Just what I wanted to hear. Now that I was completely mortified, I could go out to the alley and hope to get hit by a flying bullet or maybe a diaper full of shit. "Fine, I told my boss I might need a place to stay. He offered to give me a raise I don't deserve so I can cover my own rent."

His eyes actually filled with tears. "Oh baby."

"It's okay."

He tipped my chin. "It's not okay. I don't want you to move out. I like having you with me and knowing you're safe every night."

"But I can't have you taking care of me anymore. That's part of the problem. How can you see me as a woman when I'm still dependent on you?"

"Maybe," he said just above a whisper, "I don't want to see you as a woman. Maybe I like our relationship the way it is. You're the only family I have. I don't want to fuck that up."

With a growing frown of understanding, I stared at him.

"If we did this, if we became a couple, it could ruin everything. You understand that?"

Yes, actually, I did. But it didn't make it hurt any less to know I'd never have the fairy-tale dream I'd always wanted, with him. "I guess . . . I was willing to risk it."

He closed his eyes. "I never want to hurt you."

"Then don't."

He drew a breath and pinned me with a look. "If we got involved, I couldn't promise you that. I spent years trying to build you up, and a relationship with me could destroy it all."

"You make yourself sound like a monster."

"Women don't come first in my life. And you know it."

But I would. I always had. "Don't you ever want to get married and have kids and—"

"Hell no. I don't want kids."

"But you love kids."

"I don't want my own. I'd be a worse parent than mine were to me. I'm too absorbed by my work. Besides, the last thing the world needs is more kids."

His revelation left me speechless. I'd pictured us with a house full of kids. "I didn't know," I said.

How ironic that the two people I loved most in the world—Nash and Marcela—both argued the importance of work over family. Two people who worked for the benefit of kids, yet didn't want any of their own. I didn't get it. It struck me as cowardly to hide behind a job, to refuse to put your heart on the line. Both urged me to "get a life," but what about them?

Releasing my arm and urging me closer as he closed the office door, he said, "It's not a big deal."

What was he talking about? It was a huge deal.

"Look, let's take the rest of the afternoon off together. We can talk about what you need from me. I don't want you to move out."

But a knock at the door interrupted before I could answer. A minicrisis; Nash was needed.

"Sure, I'll be right there," he said, then looked at me like he'd just remembered I was still in his office. "I'm sorry, Lupe. You don't mind, do you?"

"No," I said. He was always walking away from me lately.

"We'll talk tonight," he promised.

I nodded, though I was talked out. What else was there to say?

The reason I had to work late was because I was traveling with my boss to Santa Barbara. We were putting together a big campaign for a business out there, and would need to be at their offices first thing in the morning. We drove about three hours and checked into a hotel.

"I want to be there at five in the morning, so I'm going to schedule a wake-up call for about four," he said as he dropped me off in my room. "Enough time for you to get ready?"

"Yes."

"Get to bed early," he called as he left me. I had a great room with a view of the ocean. The only thing that would have made it better would have been if I hadn't been alone. Resigned to the fact that I was, I pulled out my company-issued laptop. I looked over our proposal and worked on it a bit. Then switched gears and moved on to my thesis. The quarter would be over by next month and I'd take my finals. I hadn't decided if I was going to continue next quarter. Part of me wanted to get my degree and part of me didn't.

I could live the rest of my life working for this company and helping Nash out at the center. I'd have a good life. And maybe "a good life" was good enough.

I reached for the phone and called him. "I probably never got around to telling you that I wouldn't be home tonight." I told him about the morning meeting.

"Well, I'm going to miss you."

Why didn't I believe him? "Did you eat?"

"Yep. A sandwich."

"No wonder you're missing me."

"Yes, you're spoiling me with all those home-cooked meals."

Since we never made it a habit to chat on the phone, there was a moment of silence and I thought, *We don't have anything left to say.* I thought of Will and all the sweet nonsensical calls we made to each other and I suddenly wanted to end my call to Nash. "I better get to sleep. Burton's making me wake up at four a.m."

"Thanks for calling."

I wondered if he would have called *me* when he realized I wasn't coming home tonight. Or was he so busy and involved at The Vibe that he would barely have had a moment to realize I was gone? "Good night."

"Hugs, kiddo."

I hung up and tried not to let it bother me that neither of us said, "I love you."

The next morning, Burton, another PR person, and I toured the offices of the New Age company, which produced things like little rock fountains and Japanese bonsai plants in decorative pots. They had been successfully selling to customers in the form of catalogs and had a couple of the large chain department stores carrying a few of their products, but they wanted to expand and create franchises throughout America, starting with California.

Just like I did for Fish Net, Inc., I'd spent hours studying their company and products and had created a PowerPoint presentation to show them what I thought their website should look like.

Burton did his pitch first, then passed the technology stuff to me. We worked well together.

Afterward, he took me to the hotel bar and ordered drinks for both of us. "You looked fantastic today. Confident, enthusiastic, and gorgeous. Good for you, Lupe. You're working out great."

"Thanks."

"You keep this up and you'll be moving up quickly in this company."

I nodded. "I'd like that."

He pointed to my drink. "Not what you wanted?"

I hadn't touched it. "I'm underage, remember?" Not that a sip or two would kill me, but I wasn't in the mood.

He shrugged. "In Europe kids are adults at eighteen. I don't worry too much about age." He raised an arm to call the waiter and ordered a Coke. "But we don't want to break the law, do we?"

"Not me."

He grinned. Burton was aware of my past and I had been honest about my previous arrests. He'd taken it all in, questioned me to death, but in the end had laughed and said, "I like girls who can kick a little ass."

And that had been the end of it.

"You planning on finishing your degree, Lupe?" he asked as he scanned the room. The man was a ball of energy who was never still for long.

"I'd like to."

"You should. Whenever you need time off for classes, just take it. As long as you get the work done, I don't care what hours you put in. I'm going to approve you for educational reimbursement. We have a program."

That was great—unbelievable. "Thanks, Mr. Burton. That's really nice."

He finished his drink and let his gaze finally land on me for more than two seconds. "Has nothing to do with nice. I'd like to keep you around. You're a good worker."

"Thank you. I'm trying." But I didn't believe him. Probably because of Tracey, he was being more than generous to me.

"And you're great to look at."

I didn't have a reply for that.

"And I like to look." He sighed. "You probably think I'm a dirty old man."

"No, sir." Tracey's uncle *was* a dirty old man. But I liked him. He was a great boss. And now that I seemed to have mastered the whole clothes, hair, and makeup thing, I was okay with people looking. In fact, I was starting to like it a little.

"Let's get on the road. What do you say?"

"I'm ready."

• • •

I got home to a vase full of flowers and dinner cooked for me for a change. Nash and I sat in the tiny kitchen to eat and talk about our days.

Afterward, we cleaned up together. We stood so close to each other we were almost touching, but neither of us reacted to that.

Finally, I reached for the elastic band on his hair and loosened his short ponytail. His hair fell to his shoulders.

He smiled and kissed the side of my face.

Wanting to test this once and for all, I dropped my sponge and turned, wrapping my arms around his neck. "Put your hands on my breasts."

"Lupe, come on—"

"Do it. Touch me."

He sighed. "Our hands are wet. We're in the kitchen."

"Would you prefer the bathroom?"

He smiled despite his obvious discomfort, then placed his hands on my bare hips. My low-slung jeans and cropped top left my whole midriff exposed.

"Is this really that hard for you?"

He frowned and his hands traveled up my body and his thumbs played with the undersides of my breasts. "Is this really that easy for you?" His hands moved higher and now his thumbs rubbed the hardened tip of my nipples through my shirt and bra.

Our eyes locked. Damn. Yes, it was easy. Because I could detach. I didn't have to think about what was happening. I could just let it take place.

He backed me against the refrigerator, his moist thumbs rubbing a wet spot on my top, creating little thrilling electrical tremors that ran from my breasts down the center of my body.

"It's just sex," I said.

He flinched. "Is it?"

"Sure."

"No," he said. "Look at me."

"I am."

"Look at *me*."

I stared at him for a long time, and I realized what he was saying. This stupid act would take him off the pedestal. Maybe I wanted him off. Maybe I needed him off.

"You've put all your trust into me," he said. "And you're asking me to betray it."

Why did I have to love a psychologist? I pushed his hands off me and intended to leave the kitchen.

But he blocked me in with one hand above each of my shoulders. "This is my fault because I've let it go on for too long."

"Get out of my way."

"I didn't want to hurt you or destroy your illusion. I thought you'd outgrow it. But when you didn't, I thought I could participate in it. For you. But I can't. I won't. Even if you leave here tonight and never return, at least I'll know I did the right thing."

I pushed him away and stormed into my room to pack.

He watched me. "I want you to know that there was at least one guy in your life that you could trust."

I had collected so many clothes in the last few months that I couldn't fit them all in my duffel bag. "Shit," I yelled when things tumbled out. I'd just have to come back for them when he wasn't here.

Leaving everything behind, I reached for the keys to my bike.

"Hey," he reached for my arm, but I swatted it away. "You don't have to leave. You can be angry and stay."

I stopped, tamping down on my rage. "Why did you ever tell me you loved me?"

"Because I do."

"No! Don't say that anymore. Just don't."

"Okay."

"I did and I do trust you, and I know you think you're doing the right thing—"

"I am."

"And because of that I'll forgive you one day for being so damned blind that you can't see how good we could have been together."

For the first time during this exchange, he looked angry. "I'll do the same. I'll forgive you for not seeing how good we *are* together—as friends."

I left. Alone again. Not sure where I'd go.

Twenty

No one can tell you what becoming Americana really means. It's something you have to figure out on your own.

LUPE PEREZ

Since it was so close to Christmas, I moved in with Marta and Juan until after the holidays. They had Marcela's and Anna's old bedrooms free, so I took Marcela's. Since I'd already signed up for traffic school on the day before Christmas Eve, I decided to go. Didn't feel like it.

In fact, I flopped in my seat like some of the kids at the center who don't want to listen to anything we have to say.

An officer walked up and down the aisle, passing out a stapled handout. I took it and paged through it.

"Hey," he said. "Don't I know you?"

I glanced up at him. "Probably. I'm well-known in the industry."

"That's it." He snapped his fingers. "The UCLA job fair."

"Oh, yes." I smiled despite the attitude I was trying hard to project. "You get around."

"I do a lot of promotional outreach things with the community. This isn't my normal duty, though. I'm filling in for a buddy."

"What a pal."

He grinned. "So, did you think any more about joining the force?"

Of course not. "I'm usually on the wrong side of the law. In case you haven't noticed, I'm sitting in traffic school."

"I noticed." He finished passing out his handouts. "What was your name again?"

"Lupe Perez."

"Lupe, that's right. I actually ran a check on you when I got back to the station."

"Uh oh."

"Yes. You had a pretty violent crime on your record."

"I slashed a police officer's face open with my knife."

He flinched. "Looks like I won't be recruiting you after all."

"Sorry."

"So am I. I think you'd make a fine officer."

"Really? Why?"

"I read the article on you in your school paper."

I groaned. Had anyone missed that article?

"You've turned yourself around, and you're helping others avoid what you went through. Serving and helping is what we're all about."

I nodded. "I have a love/hate relationship with that uniform you're wearing. But mostly a lot of respect. I'm sorry for the things I've done."

His gaze touched me deep inside, and for a moment, I could totally see myself doing what he does. I was disappointed that I'd blown the chance to be part of a system that helps others. Especially when I realized that more than anything, it was what I enjoyed doing most. Not computer design. Not preparing to enter the business world. But helping kids at The Vibe.

"You think . . . you think I might be able to contact the officer I attacked, and . . . say how sorry I am?"

He shook his head sadly. "I can't give you personal information about one of your victims."

Boy that was harsh. I had left behind "victims." A reality for which I'd never forgive myself.

"But I'll pass along your words and sentiments."

He moved to the front and started class.

I got through the eight-hour class and at the end received my certificate to prove I'd endured.

"You'll slow down from now on, huh Lupe?" the officer said.

"I'll try," I said. "Thanks." I'd more than try. No more speeding. No more breaking the law in any way.

After helping me find an apartment in Santa Monica, Tracey and Madison took me away for a weekend of pampering and relaxation before finals. We went to a day spa/fitness retreat combination. Like schizophrenics, we attended these intense aerobics and Pilates classes where I was left aching and exhausted, then flopped onto a massage table or into a hot spa where every tiny fiber in my body relaxed. Back and forth all weekend. By Sunday night, I wasn't sure who I was anymore. We went out to a fancy dinner on Sunset Boulevard. They ordered a bottle of wine, and no one carded us. I guess when you pay in the three figures for a bottle of wine, no one cares how old you are.

My hair, makeup, and nails had been done by experts at the spa, so I probably looked older. I was proud that I paid for the spa retreat on my own. But Tracey insisted that the makeover and dinner were on her. Now that I knew her and saw how she throws money away, it didn't bother me quite as much, so I let her.

Madison held up her wine goblet. "To us and our bright futures."

I allowed myself a glass of wine. After the onslaught of endorphins that our physical trainers said we'd released, I already felt higher than a kite.

We touched glasses.

"So," Tracey said. "Tell us about breaking Will's heart. We haven't asked and you're obviously not going to share on your own."

I took a sip of wine. "Just didn't work out."

"He said you were cheating on him with your roommate."

"I wasn't."

Madison gave one of her sexy, naughty smiles. "Come on, Lupe. It's just us girls. You can admit the truth to us."

"Oh, yeah," I said. "I can trust you two, all right."

"Her roommate is totally hot," Tracey said. "He also works with her at The Vibe."

"Really?" Madison looked interested.

Tracey nodded. "Looks like one of those gritty home improvement guys they put on the sexiest-men-alive calendars."

Madison sipped her wine and eyed me curiously. "You only pretend to be uninterested in guys. Apparently, you know how to pick them and you've got your own private stud at home."

"Nash is totally hot," I admitted. "But to me, I don't see that. I see my friend and the guy I'm meant to spend the rest of my life with even if he doesn't see it that way. I just love him and I always will. I didn't mean to hurt Will."

Madison reached across. "Let me give you some advice. Have your fun with your stud, but don't let Will go. He's good for you."

"Nash was good for me too, but that's over. He doesn't want me."

"Girl, a guy that works in East L.A. with gang members is not good for you."

"And Will will take you back," Tracey said with certainty.

I drank more wine. My head was pounding.

"Besides, I thought you were really into Will."

"I am. I mean, I was." I looked around the fancy restaurant, like the one Will promised to take me to and never did. "Do we get to eat here, or are we just going to drink this fucking wine?"

Tracey lifted an elegant hand to let our waiter know we were ready. Then she dropped her hand onto mine. "Fuck men," she said, using a vulgarity she rarely had before. When I gazed at her in surprise, she winked. "Literally. Fuck them all, and then go on with your life. Who needs them?"

I smiled. I decided they were both crazy, but fun to be around.

Madison shrugged. "I still say she should take Will, but it's her life. More wine?"

"Why the hell not?" I said.

My boss was kind enough to give me finals week off. In the library, I crammed last-minute information into my head, then rushed to each class and took the test.

I arrived only a couple of minutes early to my cultural ethics class. Will leaned against the wall reading his book. *If he doesn't look up, I can pretend I don't see him*, I told myself. But of course, he closed his book, and he saw me, and everything I'd been telling myself for the past month about this having been just a little college crush, something I'd forget, a rebound affair, crumbled in front of me.

I'd missed him.

Though he didn't take his eyes off me, he also didn't encourage me to come any closer. No smile. No wave. I looked away.

Within a minute, our instructor arrived and we were led inside. I took my seat, and he returned to his previous seat, about three rows above. I put him out of my mind and focused on the test. The multiple-choice exam was simple enough. An hour and thirteen minutes later, I was finished.

I turned in the exam and, unable to help myself, took one last look up and found Will gazing right back at me. *I'm so sorry*, I said inside my head. He looked back down at his desk and I left.

But as I walked out of the building, I heard him calling after me. I turned around and waited as he ran up to me. "Wait," he said.

"Hi, Will."

"Where are you going?"

"Home, I guess. I'm done for today. Tomorrow I've got an economics final, so I'm going to go study for that."

He shifted a backpack on his shoulder. "Let's go somewhere."

"Will . . ." I shook my head. "No."

"The beach. On your bike. You promised to teach me how to ride."

"Why are you doing this? Why today?"

"Because this has been hell for me. Just seeing you again is sending me into a tailspin and I don't want to walk away from you. I can't."

"But you did. You told me to make a life with Nash. And I . . . chose to." Because I could have chosen not to listen to him and instead pleaded with him to forgive me.

He narrowed his eyes. "Just like that?"

"No, not just like that." My heart was splitting. "All my life I thought he would be the one. And then you came along and . . . I'm miserable because I miss you so badly. Half the time I think I'm crazy."

"If he's who you've always wanted then you *should* be with him. I want you to be."

I shook my head. "Man, Will, I feel so bad about this."

"Don't feel bad for me."

"I feel bad for us, because I . . ." What? Did I love him? Maybe I did. Not the way I loved Nash. But, yes, I loved Will. And I ached for him physically.

But, I couldn't say it. That would be unfair to him.

He touched my face. "You know, Lupe, I look at you and I feel like I've drunk some kind of voodoo potion or something. Things start to tingle and sparkle inside me. It's insane. I've never felt like that with anyone before."

"I'm sorry." I didn't know what else to say. I didn't know what to do.

"Can I ask you for something?"

"Anything." And I meant it. I needed to do something to make things up to him. He could write about me in the paper again. He could write I was a total bitch. I didn't care.

"One more day. Give me one more day. Take me for a ride on your bike."

I wasn't sure what that would accomplish, but I agreed.

Twenty-one

If you're not careful, it can all fall apart right before your eyes.

LUPE PEREZ

I took him to Venice Beach, where we found a stretch of parking lot not commonly used during the week, and I gave him a tutorial on motorcycles.

He took control of the handlebars and I sat behind him, holding on to his waist with one arm and instructing with the other.

He glanced over his shoulder. "Feels great having you pressed against me while I take control. We should have done this a long time ago."

"Do you plan to listen and pay attention?"

He chuckled. "Yes, I insert the key, pull the choke, turn the ignition to the on position, and make sure the kill switch is set to run. Got it. Next?"

He was a quick learner when he took his focus off me and paid attention. I showed him how to shift gears. "Make sure the gear shifter is set to neutral."

"Okay."

"Squeeze the clutch lever with your left hand all the way to the grip."

"Like this?"

"Right. Now, press the start button with your right thumb." I pointed. My breasts were pressed tight against his back and I had to shake myself mentally not to react.

"Is the motorcycle going to go when I do that?"

"No, it won't move. But keep your thumb on the button until the engine fires, okay?"

"Okay."

He followed my instructions exactly, and when the motorcycle started, he turned around and gave me an adorable smile.

"Good, Will. Now gradually push the choke in."

We were ready to go. But he needed to practice starting the bike a few more times, so I showed him how to turn it off. "Now do it again."

"All right." He performed each step perfectly.

"Turn it off and do it again."

"No, I got it. Let's go."

"One more time, Will. Turn it off."

He groaned. Then he lifted an eyebrow as he looked over his shoulder at me. "You're a slave driver. Of course, the fact that you're willing to do it again and again is one of the things I like most about you."

"All right, get off." I kicked my leg around and slid down out of the seat.

"Hey." He grabbed my arm. "What's wrong?"

"Fuck you. This isn't a game. I don't want you flirting with me or teasing me or making fun of me or whatever you're doing."

He gave me a cold stare followed by a nod. "I'm just trying to have a little fun."

"This isn't fun for me." I pulled my arm loose. "Breaking up with you hurt, and being here with you again is making me bleed inside all over again."

"Then why did you agree to come out here? You must know I only wanted to feel close to you again."

Hell, I didn't have the slightest idea why I was there, maybe because I felt I owed him for the way I treated him. "I . . . I guess I miss spending time with you, and I know you want to learn this." I sighed. "So do you want to try again and quit with the personal comments?"

He nodded again. "Let me try this one more time."

"Go for it," I said, waving for him to do his thing. "I'll watch from here."

Again, he started the bike easily. Now it was time to get back on and let him ride. I climbed back onboard and again wrapped an arm around him. "A motorcycle is heavy, but it's like riding a bicycle. It's about balance."

"Balance. Okay."

I showed him how to use the gearshift with his foot again, and how to hold the brake with his right hand so we wouldn't lurch forward.

"Ready to move?"

He nodded. But we both had our helmets on and I wanted to hear verbal confirmation.

"Ready, Will?"

"Ready."

"Okay, simultaneously, you're going to release the clutch and twist the throttle."

He did, but twisted too hard and we took off. I clamped on tightly to his middle. "Release the throttle! Now!"

We slowed. "Shit," he said and laughed.

"Let's try it again." I drew a deep breath.

"Whoo, this is great!"

I laughed. I loved his childish enthusiasm. And his smile. And, damn, so many things about him.

After a couple of hours of scaring me half to death, he got the hang of coordinating gearshifting with the throttle and brake, and he took me for a longer ride.

We rode up the Pacific Coast Highway, the salt air blowing on our faces. Will stopped in Santa Monica and we walked up the pier. He bought hot dogs and we sat on the bench to eat them.

"That was awesome."

"Glad you enjoyed it."

"So where did you learn to ride?"

"Sort of on my own, but I took an MSF course before I got my license."

"What's MSF?"

"Motorcycle Safety Foundation course."

"Hmm. You know what?"

"What?"

"I'm going to buy a bike."

"Really?"

"Yep. And sign up for that course."

"Good idea. You'll learn everything there. They were great."

"Yeah, that sounds perfect. I'll buy a bike, load it onto my truck for the big move, and then I'll have both."

"Big move?"

"I'm going to Stanford, you know?"

"No, I didn't know."

"Yep. Leave in a month."

And why did that depress me?

We ate silently.

"Next time you see me, I'll be a doctor."

Would there be a next time? And what would *I* be? A mother? An architect? "Is that what you really want to be?"

"What do you mean?" He crumpled up the paper wrapper.

"I don't know. You've told me a million times how much you enjoy writing for the paper and how you would love to be a journalist."

He laughed. "I'm not going to be a journalist. I'm going to be a doctor."

"Why?"

"Because that's what I'm supposed to be."

"Says who?"

"Well . . . it's just . . . what I've always known I was going to be."

"Now you're lying."

"Let me rephrase that: what I've always known I was supposed to be. I guess it's what my parents expect."

I took his hand. "But is that going to make you happy?"

He shrugged. "Probably not. Just like being an architect isn't going to make you happy."

He was right. That was Marcela's dream, and Nash's desire, for me to be wealthy and successful. But did I ever stop to analyze if I wanted any of that? No.

"So," I said. "Here we are, on the brink of jumping off into the future that's probably not what either of us wants. Are we going to do it anyway?"

We sat there silently, knowing that if we didn't change our minds right now, right this second, we would take a bend in a road and never be able to return here.

Finally, he smiled. "You can't even imagine the feelings you stir up inside me, can you?" He threaded his fingers through my long hair.

I watched him, unable to respond.

"You'll follow your heart. You'll do exactly what you're meant to do. I'll do what's expected."

My heart sank. I don't know what I had hoped or expected him to say, but that wasn't it. Whatever had been between us was over. "Thanks for always accepting me the way I am, Will."

"I love you the way you are."

"I wish you'd accept yourself the way you are too. You're a great writer. You should do what you love."

"Now, I'm a great writer. You can't seem to make up your mind."

Maybe I couldn't, because right now, I wished I could turn back time and go back to when he and I were dating.

He leaned forward and kissed me. I placed an arm around his neck and kissed him back. A long, drawn-out kiss that touched my heart and my soul. For once, with Will, there was no sexual longing; instead I felt like the gates of my heart were opening.

"Make love to me," he said against my lips.

"I can't."

"You can and you want to. Make love to me just one more time."

"I can't." How could I make love to him knowing it would be the last time? That he was going away and I'd never see him again? That would be like taking a knife to what was left of my heart. "Let's go."

He sighed. "I guess it would be stupid."

"Yes." Yes, yes, yes.

"Don't expect me to ever get over you."

"You will. You have to."

We walked back to the bike. "I know I have to, but I don't see how I can. Even knowing you were sleeping with your room—"

"I wasn't, I told you. And I'm not."

That seemed to please him. His shoulders straightened. "Really? You're not lying?"

"I've never lied to you. Well, maybe when I told you that I *was* sleeping with Nash. I wasn't. But I wanted to. And that's just as bad, right?"

Will nodded, almost in slow motion.

"It wasn't sex I wanted. I wanted him. I was with you, but I wanted Nash. And you were right to get rid of me, Will. You deserve better than that. I'm sorry."

"Yeah. Me too." He pulled the keys out his pocket. "Let's get back to UCLA."

"I'll take the keys."

"Can't I drive back to school?"

"It's a long way. I better do it."

"Come on. I can handle it. I'll be careful. Besides, I love to have your arms around me. And this will probably be the last time."

I sighed, and against my better judgment, I nodded. He didn't have a license. Had only been practicing a couple of hours. There were lots of reasons why this was a bad idea, but I couldn't deny him anything else. Not after denying him the love he deserved from me. Besides, Westwood wasn't really all that far from Santa Monica. Just a straight shot down Santa Monica Boulevard.

He did well. So well that I had him pull into a gas station on Sepulveda. He got gas and I went to the restroom.

Out of the corner of my eye, I recognized one of my brother's friends—the fat one that had tried to make a play for me on my porch a few months ago. He recognized me too.

Without acknowledging him, I went back to Will and the bike. "Done?"

"Yeah. This is easy on gas too. I'm definitely getting one."

"You're going to spend thousands to save a few dollars on gas?"

"Well," he admitted with a shy shrug, "the excuse works for me."

We climbed back on and Will pulled back onto Santa Monica Boulevard. All he had to do was hang a left on Westwood and ride it in. "You're doing awesome," I yelled in his ear under the helmet.

He nodded.

As he was approaching the intersection, I noticed an old car sort of like Nash's riding too close to us on the right. But inside was my brother's friend. He'd followed us. As Will turned on the blinker to get in the left turn lane, the car swerved into us.

I yelled for Will to punch the throttle or move quickly to the left, but there was no way Will had enough control of the bike to maneuver away from a car that had purposely bumped us and taken off.

He lost control and the bike headed into oncoming traffic. I reached forward to help him, but it was impossible for someone my size sitting behind the driver to reach the handlebars.

Will jerked the handlebar to the right when he realized we'd crossed over the double yellow line. This caused him to lose his balance and total control of the bike. As if in slow motion, the bike began its descent onto its side. Luckily, as it fell it slid back on the right side of the lane and spun into the intersection. We hit pavement, and I felt the entire right side of my body explode in pain.

Twenty-two

Becoming Americana involves breaking the unwritten family code of "family first." The new mantra becomes "me first."

LUPE PEREZ

People surrounded me and Will immediately and helped us get to our feet. Will cried out in pain and I figured his leg must be broken because he couldn't stand.

I was scratched up and my heart wouldn't slow down, but I was okay.

Cops showed up, then an ambulance. They put Will on a stretcher. "I'll call you later," I promised him.

"I'm sorry, Lupe."

"Not your fault. Don't worry."

I stayed to give the police report and to be treated by paramedics. I didn't need to be taken to the hospital. In fact, I wanted to go to the police station to talk to Captain Martinez.

A tow truck took my bike away, and I rode in the back of the police car to the station. For the first time, I went willingly.

When I got to the station and Captain Martinez sat me down in his office, I relaxed. "That bastard tried to hurt me on purpose. Followed me from the gas station."

"You think your brother is behind this?"

"I don't know. Maybe not. He could have just been pissed because I turned down his sexual advances or because they think I blew the drug deal for Carlos. Either way, Carlos is hiding out in the neighborhood. Why can't you guys find and arrest him?"

"Because he's hiding."

"Great, you and George Bush have the same answer for everything."

Martinez cracked a smile. "I just don't have the manpower to track down one guy. He'll mess up again and we'll get him."

"What if I helped you?"

He eyed me suspiciously. "Helped me how?"

"I can find him." And turn him over.

"Lupe, stay out of it. Stay away from him."

"I want him caught. I want him put away forever. His stupid friend could have killed me tonight. If I hadn't been riding since I was sixteen and learned how to take a fall and roll away from the bike, I'd be in the hospital with Will."

"This might not be Carlos's fault this time. Did you give a description of the car and driver?"

"Yes."

"Go home. Leave the police work to me then."

I stared at him. I'd find Carlos on my own and figure out what he was up to. And if he had anything to do with tonight's accident . . . either the cops would take care of it, or I would. "I'll be in touch. I'm counting on you to help me."

He shook his head. "I'll try, Lupe. I'll try."

That night I didn't return to my empty apartment. I went home to Nash, who had dismantled my bed and moved the computer back into the spare room. He was arranging cinder blocks and wooden boards to make shelves for books when I gazed into the room.

"Lupe?" he said, looking surprised to see me. Coming to his feet, he noticed my shredded clothes and the blood stains from my scraped arm and leg. "What the hell happened?"

"I got in an accident on the bike."

"Shit. Are you okay?"

I nodded.

"I don't like you driving that stupid motorcycle."

"Well, it'll probably cost more to fix it than it's worth, so I don't think you'll have to worry about that anymore."

"We'll get you a car. I have money saved up."

I hated the idea of being cooped up in a car. But it was time to make the switch. "Okay. I'll pay you back."

"No, you won't. I'm doing this for you. And for me. I want you around." He gently wrapped an arm around my waist and held me. "Thanks for coming home."

I relaxed against him, feeling nothing but tired. He placed his lips to my ears. "Let's get your clothes off."

I followed him into the bathroom, where he filled the tub with warm water. "Get in and soak for a while."

"Okay."

Like a toy puppet, I followed his instructions. I lay in the water sort of in a daze, hearing a faint ringing in my ears. Between spending the afternoon with Will, and the accident, and wanting to find my brother to get rid of him once and for all, I was numb.

Nash knocked. "How are you doing?" he asked from the other side of the door.

I closed my eyes. What was I doing back here leaning on him? Who could blame him for thinking of me as a child when I ran to him every time life got hard? "I'll be out in few minutes."

I gently soaped up a sponge and washed off the caked-on blood.

It stung where layers of skin had been torn off. I moaned. "That son of a bitch," I said.

"You say something?"

The water in the tub was red.

"I'm coming in," Nash called and stepped inside with a large towel, looking away. "Here."

I took the towel and stepped out of the tub. "You can look now."

But what he saw was the water. "Oh my God. Are you still bleeding?"

"A little."

"You should go see a doctor."

"In the morning."

"Are you sure? I could take you right now."

"No." I gazed at him. What would I do without him? "Thanks, Ryan."

He nodded. "You look beat."

"I am."

He stepped out of the bathroom so I could walk out. "I just took your bed apart. You can have mine tonight. I'll sleep on the couch."

I could sleep on the couch too. I could sleep standing up. "Do you have a pair of sweats and a T-shirt?"

"Oh, sure. Sorry."

He hurried to his room, then stuck his head out. "Come on in."

I followed him into his bedroom.

"You're going to get lost in these." He handed me the clothes.

"I don't care. It's just until morning."

"Man, Lupe, you could have really been seriously hurt."

I didn't tell him the accident had been intentional or that I was with Will. I would in the morning. Right now, I didn't have the emotional energy. "See you in the morning, okay?"

He stepped to the door, but held back. I could see and hear all he wasn't saying. Blaming himself for letting me go. Trying to figure out how to make things better. Worried that I was going to ruin my life now that I wasn't under his direct supervision.

"Go on," I said. "I'm dropping this towel in five seconds whether you're here or not."

Shaking his head, he stepped out.

I changed and stepped up onto his bed and was asleep the second my head touched the mattress.

In the morning, I called Burton and told him about my accident. He had a rental car sent out to me within an hour so I could get to the university for my final.

"But you need to see a doctor," Nash protested.

"Later. I've got to go to the hospital anyway, so I'll have someone check my scrapes then."

"You going to see Will?"

"How did you know Will was in the hospital?" I frowned.

"He called last night to tell you he's fine. Broken leg."

My stomach dipped. "When did he call?"

"When you were in the tub. Tried your cell phone first, he said, but you weren't answering."

So Nash had known I had been with Will. "I was going to tell you I was with him."

Nash shrugged. "None of my business."

"I was just too tired to go into it last night."

"There's something to go into?"

"Not really, I guess. I taught him to ride. We were going back to school when one of my brother's jerk friends bumped us."

"Someone intentionally ran into you?"

"Shocking huh? Welcome to Carlos's world."

"Did you get his license number . . .?"

"Police have all I can remember. The key is to find Carlos. As long as he's in our neighborhood, we're going to continue to have problems."

"Why don't I like the look on your face and the way you're saying that?"

I avoided his gaze and headed to the door. "Because you're paranoid."

"I don't think so." He opened the front door for me. "Go somewhere far away. Don't come back. I mean it. Stay away from The Vibe, from me, from all of us. Do this for me."

I nodded. "Soon."

"Now."

"I can't. Not yet. Besides, you need me at The Vibe for the TLC taping."

And I could see he still intended for me to help him out with the interviews. He didn't argue. "Promise you won't do anything reckless."

I knew he wouldn't approve of my plan to set up Carlos, but I had to do it whether he wanted me to or not. "I promise," I said, and I hurried out of his apartment.

After my economics exam, I drove out to Carlsbad. Will had gone home to recuperate and he asked me to go see him.

His mother greeted me coolly, but she was polite and invited me into her home. "He's been sleeping most of the day."

"I won't tire him out."

But the second I walked into his bedroom, he perked up and waved me over.

"You weren't sleeping?" I said, as I took a seat across from him in the little retreat he had beside his bed. He sat in a chair watching

TV. All bedrooms in this house were suites with their own bathrooms, sitting areas, and walk-in closets. Awesome.

"I've been going in and out. The damn painkillers they gave me knock me out. You're okay, huh?"

"Yeah, it all happened so fast. But I managed to pull my leg up before we hit the ground. I think I actually jumped off."

"Good. I was worried about you."

Hell, he didn't need to be worried about me. "I'm sorry you got hurt, Will."

"I'm the one who's sorry. I'll replace your bike."

"No, I'm going to get a car."

"Fine, I'll buy you a car."

"I've got it covered. You don't have to do a thing for me."

We stared at each other. "Lupe—"

"Don't."

His jaw tightened and then he nodded. "Wanna watch TV with me?"

Not really. I just wanted to hug him and be with him. "For a little while, but then I need get home."

He scooted to the side and placed his leg on the coffee table.

Sitting side by side, we watched TV together. He fell asleep after a while. I watched him with a lump in my throat. When I made a move to get up, his eyes flickered open. Before I got too far away from him, he reached for me and pulled me back, his lips crashing into mine possessively. Without hesitating, I kissed him back like I'd wanted to do from the moment I set foot in his room. We melted into each other, drinking in every bittersweet emotion sitting on the surface, until I realized that tears were spilling from my eyes. I pulled back and stood, wiping my face.

"Good luck, Will."

He cursed. "Stay with me. Come to Stanford." He tried to get up and almost fell over.

I reached for him to hold him up and he clamped onto me, his chest pressed tight against mine. "I'm not stupid. I understand what you feel about Nash. But I know you love me too. I know it."

"Sit down, Will," I said, my heart going out to him.

Awkwardly, he backed me toward his bed. "And you're going to make love to me now and tell me how much you love me. Then we're going to figure out how to fix things."

I helped him guide the two of us onto his bed. "You *are* stupid. I feel guilty for what happened to you and for the way I've acted. So, I could tell you I loved you and have sex with you and not mean any of it. Just to ease my guilt."

He lay back on his bed, dragging and lifting his leg up, grimacing at the pain. "No you couldn't. You're not a liar."

Gently, I stretched out beside him. Although the muscles of my face felt strained, I smiled. "You are in no condition to have sex."

"You'll just have to do all the work."

I reached for his face, placing my hand against his cheek. "Will . . . we're nothing alike. This could never work long term."

"But do you love me?"

I leaned over him and touched my lips to his in a feather-light kiss.

"Do you?" His eyes were intense as they searched mine too intimately. "Because if you do, we'll make it work. I promise you."

In that instant, I realized Will would completely alter his future for me. I had the power to derail all his plans, everything his parents wanted for him. All I had to do was tell him I loved him and he wouldn't make a move without me.

I pulled away from him, shook my head, and ran out. See, he was wrong. I *was* a good liar.

Marcela was back from Mexico. She looked healthy and happy, and she announced to all, "I'm pregnant."

And as if Marta had soaked every piece of food with hot chiles, everyone at the table did some version of coughing, reaching for their water glass, or simply stopping eating altogether. George tossed his fork on the table and stalked away without a word.

"We agreed to wait, but I couldn't. George needs this," she said.

"Marcela, you don't make a decision like that on your own," Marta said.

"I thought he'd be happy."

I began to pick at my rice. What the hell was she doing now?

"So, isn't anyone going to congratulate me?"

Her father got up and kissed her and pulled her into his arms. Her sisters followed. Marta didn't move. Marcela gazed at me.

"Thought you didn't want this," I said.

She shrugged and looked more at peace than the last time we spoke. "Hell." She smiled. "I need someone to watch cartoons with me in the morning."

I shook my head.

"For once, you were right," she said. "Enjoy it, it probably won't happen again for ten years."

"George didn't look happy."

"He's afraid. And he *did* blame himself for what I went through the last time. I'll go talk to him."

"Good idea. Do it now," Marta said.

Marcela stood. "You love him more than you do me, *Mami*. Jeeze."

"Well, of course," Marta said. "He's a good boy."

"Yes, he is." She gazed at his back with love and tears. "And there's nothing I want more than to have his baby, and prove again and again how much I love him."

"There's nothing a man values more than his children," Juan said. "Except his wife." He reached across and put his arm around Marta and squeezed her shoulder. "He doesn't want to lose you, *mi'ja*."

Marcela kissed her father. "Oh, believe me, he never will. But I know what you mean. This time I'm going to take extra-good care of myself. I'll be fine." Marcela glanced at me and winked. My mentor was back, and I was proud of her.

Nash, who had practically ignored me the entire day, leaned over and whispered in my ear, "This is what you want one day, isn't it? A family like this."

I cut into my barbecued chicken. "I love kids."

He smiled. "You'll have everything you want."

I wasn't so sure about that anymore. "Just not with you." Or with Will. I rolled up a tortilla and met his gaze.

"No."

I nodded and took the chicken off my fork and followed it up with a bite of tortilla.

"You don't need me anymore. You're ready to handle things on your own," he said, pride in his voice.

He was right, of course, I didn't *need* him. Not for survival. I didn't need him or Marcela or my parents. I could survive on my own now.

"Friends, though?" he asked.

I winked at him. "Always."

He kissed me on the cheek. "Thanks for not hating me, kid."

"I love you, you idiot."

I turned twenty on a rainy Sunday afternoon in February. Marcela invited Nash and I out to dinner on Rodeo Drive. The place reeked of money, and after the third course, I was ready to go home. I remembered what Will had said about how ridiculous a seven-course meal was. But remembering Will was a mistake, because it made me wonder what he was doing. If he'd gone off to med school. If he was moved in and settled and happy.

"So what is it?" George asked.

"What's what?"

"Your birthday wish," Marcela said. "Weren't you listening?"

"I've already got everything I want."

"Ah, come on," Nash insisted.

Wasn't exactly true, but I had nothing to complain about. Good friends, nice new apartment, a job that paid well. I was still lonely, but I couldn't have everything. "I wish," I said to Marcela, "that you have an easy, healthy pregnancy."

Her smile slipped. "Oh."

"That's a beautiful wish," George said.

Marcela nodded. "It is. Thank you."

Nash slid a box about the size of a coffee mug across the table until it touched my plate. "We thought there might be one more thing you might want."

I gazed up at him.

"Open it, it's your gift from the three of us."

"And my parents too," Marcela said. "But they couldn't be here tonight."

The little box, wrapped in balloon paper and dwarfed by colorful ribbons, seemed to smile at me. I touched it with my index finger and thumb.

"Well? Open it."

I lifted the box and shook it. "Wow, thanks guys."

"You can't thank us until you open it." Marcela sipped from her glass of water. "Might not be your style."

"My style?"

"And you might hate the color. I still think the color is wrong for her," she said to George.

"Shh, you're going to spoil the surprise."

She flung an arm around his shoulder and leaned close to him, but her eyes were on me. "Come *on*," she said.

Curiosity finally got to me and I tore through the paper. The box had a lid that fell off once the wrapping that held it together dropped. With the lid, a key chain with three keys dropped as well. I frowned.

Nash placed a hand on the back of my chair. "Now you have to promise to go slow. No speeding. Okay?"

Speeding? I turned to him, then to Marcela and George. "I don't understand."

Marcela rolled her eyes. "*Mensa*. We got you a car."

"A *car*?"

"Let's go see it," Nash said with a big grin.

"It's *here*?"

"George drove it here. That way you can take it home tonight."

I was stunned. A car. "Oh my God," I whispered. Then I jumped out of my seat. "Yes, I want to see it!"

George asked the waiter to hold dessert for a few minutes and we all walked outside. A brand new, shiny fire-red Mustang convertible was parked beside Nash's old clunker. A silver bow decorated the convertible. I walked over to it and ran my hands over the cool, shiny metal. "You guys wouldn't be playing with my heart would you?"

"You have to be super careful with it," Nash warned.

"I liked the black better," Marcela said. "What do you think?"

I smiled and looked at her. "I think it's perfect and I'm going to get a million tickets with it."

"No!" Nash said.

"It's a V6." Marcela walked beside me, a mischievous grin on her face. "Are you sure you wouldn't prefer black? I see you in black."

"You would."

I walked around it one more time then screamed and wrapped my arms around Marcela. "Thank you!"

Then I ran to Nash and did the same. "I can't believe you let her pick out a convertible."

"I know you hate to feel boxed in. But promise you'll be—"

"It's red, I'm young, every cop in L.A. is going to stop me. But I don't care. I love it. Thank you!"

George tapped my shoulder. "Where's my hug? I picked out the color."

I threw myself at him. "You are the perfect man."

He grinned and patted my back. "Tell my wife that."

Marcela shoved me out of the way. "Your wife knows that, so you can stop feeling up my friend."

I jumped up and down. "All right, all right, all right! I'm going for a drive. Who's going with me?"

All three suddenly looked way too serious.

"Ah, she's pregnant and I've got work to do, so we should be going," George said.

"Right," Marcela agreed.

"Yeah, I've got to get back to The Vibe. My boss makes me work these long hours and if I don't get back soon, she's going to fire me."

"Right," Marcela said again.

"I don't believe this. You all are afraid to drive with me?"

"No." They all shook their heads.

"I'm a great driver," I argued.

But they didn't look convinced.

"Fine." I kissed each of them one more time. "Thank you. I love you all, but I'm going to go play."

I opened the car door and the smell of new car enveloped me. "Ah." Then I looked over the ragtop. "It's really mine?"

"All yours, kid," Nash said.

"You're the best friends in the whole world. How did I ever get so lucky?"

"Go on," Marcela said with a look of pure sisterly love. "You're going to be putting in major babysitting time, so go have fun while you still can."

As I got into the car, I heard Nash.

"She's going to kill herself in that."

"You didn't see me rush to get in with her," Marcela answered.

"Wonderful."

"Let her go, Nash. It's way past time," Marcela said.

"I know."

And with a lump in my throat from the myriad of emotions, I started the car and left.

Twenty-three

In the end, becoming Americana means being true to yourself. What makes America great is that it is able to absorb so many "individuals."

LUPE PEREZ

Mari had recovered, but had not stopped using drugs. I went to see her.

"You shouldn't be here, Lupe."

"I guess I'm still hoping you'll realize that you're killing yourself."

"I know. But I'm off the downers."

Minor improvement. "I want to find Carlos."

First disbelief, then suspicion flashed in her eyes. "Why?"

"I want to make things right."

"I don't know, Lupe."

"One of his friends ran his car into my bike last month. I need to know if it was his idea."

Her eyes shifted around. Then she walked outside to her backyard that overlooked a liquor store. "He's been going back and forth to Mexico. I doubt he had anything to do with your accident."

"Attack, you mean."

"But if you really want to talk to him . . ." She pointed to the fence. "His customers drive behind the liquor store. Carlos meets them on this side."

"Tonight?"

"Your guess is as good as mine. But his stash is here."

Great. Just what Mari needed. Easy access to all the drugs she wanted. Not that Carlos would put up with her taking his merchandise without his permission. She'd only do that once.

"Thanks, Mari. I'll be back."

That evening I stopped by the police station with the information on where to find Carlos. Proud of myself for coming up with his whereabouts, I strolled inside and asked to see Captain Martinez.

He sat behind his desk with his feet up, eating a submarine sandwich in an unusual moment of calm at the station.

"Good?" I asked.

"Mmm, pastrami, lots of mustard. Want some?" He pointed to the other half on his desk and lowered his feet.

I shook my head. "I came to tell you where to find Carlos."

"*What*? Damn it, Lupe." He wiped his lips with a paper napkin. "Didn't I tell you to stay the hell away from him?"

"I haven't seen him. But I know where *you* can. You can catch him dealing and—"

"You," he started, trying to talk and chew and swallow at the same time, "don't get it. There are hundreds of small-time dealers out there and it doesn't mean a goddamn thing to put one away—"

"But one more away means one less place for kids to get drugs."

"So they'll get it from someone else!"

"What does that mean? You just let them go, then? You let them win and refuse to do your job?"

"No!" As if suddenly drained, he shook his head and leaned back in his seat. "No. We chase these guys down every day, and make arrests. A few days later they're back on the street or their replacement is. It's damned frustrating."

I nodded.

"We rely on the narcotic divisions to bust the real traffickers. At least then, we have some hope of curbing the flow into the area, and we can put them away for more than a few years."

"Mari said Carlos has been going back and forth to Mexico, so you've got to assume he's buying in huge quantities for resale."

Martinez studied me and began to jiggle in his seat. "And where do you think I'd find him?"

"Behind JJ's Liquor. Mari's house sits behind it and Carlos works from her side of the fence."

Martinez reached for his sandwich. "I'll see what I can do about checking out this 'lead.' But don't get your hopes up. More than likely, Carlos isn't sticking around one place. And don't get involved."

"I'm already involved."

"If I have to arrest you again, I will, and this time I won't lift a finger to get you off, got it?"

"Got it," I said and headed to the door. But I was going to see Carlos. If I had to get my own evidence against him, I would. If I had to take him down myself, I'd do that too. I wanted him out of my neighborhood—out of my life. For good.

The Learning Channel crew set up shop at The Vibe. Initially, Nash directed the tour through the center. He was fabulous, his charismatic personality wooing the producer, who made sure the cameras followed Nash from all angles.

I did my part, going over the birth of The Vibe and the security it had provided me every day after I got out of school. I emphasized the leadership skills I'd learned by taking on more and more responsibilities through the years, and how today I was able to complete the circle by giving back.

They filmed the everyday classes we offered at The Vibe and the rhythm of our days while they interviewed some of the kids. After a half day of that, they assigned a cameraman to follow each of us.

Having someone tape my every move from when I got up in the morning to my work at the ad agency to wrapping up my thesis at the university gave me a déjà vu feeling of being under surveillance. Not since my days at juvenile camp had I been shadowed this way.

At one point, I escaped into the bathroom at work just to be alone for a few moments. I washed my hands, checked my hair and makeup, and finally decided I had no alternative but to go back out there.

The cameraman, of course, was waiting with the darn thing pointed at me as I took my seat behind my desk.

"Are you really going to use all this?"

"No, not even a small fraction. Most of it will be cut in the editing process."

"Good, because watching me work on the computer is pretty boring."

"But your responses to my questions are not."

He was continually talking to me, which made it even more difficult for me to get anything done. I talked about my life and Nash and my neighborhood. He asked me if I thought The Vibe offered the kids a solution to their street problems. I told him that it was more of a sanctuary. I wasn't sure what real solutions would involve, especially in light of my discussion with Captain Martinez.

"It seems to have been the solution to your problems. Why do you think that was?"

Questions like this interrupted me throughout the day and

made me actually consider questions I never thought of before. "Well, I don't know. I felt cared for. I saw that other possibilities existed outside my immediate environment. I knew others would help me and I wasn't alone." But The Vibe wasn't the only thing that made something in my mind click. It was Marcela and her family, and it was my desire not to die in the streets. "Maybe it was because I became involved in the success of The Vibe," I said. "The center can't take all the credit. Those kids are making positive choices and we're there to support them."

We continued to chat, me and the man behind the camera.

The entire taping took about two days. When they finally wrapped up, they bought pizza and soda for everyone and the kids loved it.

I delayed the encounter with Carlos until all this was over. With cameras shadowing me around everywhere, meeting with my drug-dealing brother wouldn't have been . . . sensible.

But the night after the party, when it was just us again, I told Nash I had things to do and left The Vibe. I didn't want to take my new Mustang into the neighborhood, so I walked. In about twenty-five minutes I arrived at Mari's house. I knocked, but heard nothing. Scoping out the place and seeing nothing, I knocked again. This time, Mari's father opened the door.

His eyes narrowed. "Lupe?"

"Yeah, hi. I'm looking for Mari."

"She's on the back patio, hanging out with friends."

"I'm supposed to join them."

He jerked his head. "Go on."

Like most of our parents, they assumed we were just kids doing kid things. Drug or gang involvement didn't stress them out much, it was just the way things were done and basically we were "just kids."

When Mari saw me walk outside, she froze and paled. Carlos however, stood, placing his beer bottle on a glass table.

He strolled toward me and circled behind me—then he took my arm and led me toward the side of the house where a single-car garage was located. Once we were out of sight of the others, he slammed me against the garage wall. "Tell me you have a great reason to be here or you're going to pay the hospital a visit tonight before going home."

He'd knocked the wind out of my lungs, but I met his eyes. "You didn't hear I got run off the road by one of your friends?"

He frowned. "What are you talking about?"

"I was on my bike. He ran right into me."

"Who?"

"The fat guy that used to sit on the porch with you."

"Gabriel?"

"I don't know his name."

"Why the hell would he do that? You're full of shit, Lupe."

"I'm not full of shit. He recognized me and I recognized him. And he came after me on purpose. Maybe because you told him to."

He scowled and let my arm go. "Why would I tell him to do a thing like that?"

"Why do you do any of the things you do to me? Because you're an asshole."

His grin grew slowly. "No, it's because I own you, bitch. You never have understood that, have you?"

"Nobody owns me."

"You walked the streets safe because of me." He jabbed at his chest. "You had food to eat because of me. You owed me and I took what was mine."

Incredulous, I stared wide-eyed at him. He still believed he'd done nothing wrong. But even more astounding, he believed he'd made some kind of sacrifice for his family. "I *owed* you?" I really wanted to kill him.

"I took the risks, it's always been on my back. You bet you owed me. You still owe me."

In a crazy kind of way, what he said made sense. Had I been safe all these years because I was his sister? Did I owe him my loyalty? "I was a child, and you . . ." I looked away. The kind of payback I owed him would leave him a eunuch. But I buried all that hatred, because I had come here to make him believe I was on his side. "As long as you keep your hands to yourself, I'm willing to put the past behind us."

"You're the one holding on to the past, not me."

"Good. Then we can start fresh."

"What are you talking about? What do you want?"

"Protection."

His eyes scanned down my body in disgust. "I'll take care of Gabriel. Now go."

"And in return, I can help you out. You're right. I owe you." Saying those three words made me want to vomit.

Turning away from me, he shook his head. "Forget it."

I reached for his arm and he turned around and gripped my face painfully.

"*Mira*, I said forget it. Get out of the neighborhood. It's what you've always wanted, *no es sierto*?"

I pulled at his arm and drew my head back to free myself, showing him I was no longer afraid of him—that I was willing to stand my ground. "I work here. I still live here."

His face came nose-to-nose with mine. "Leave. Get out. *Mami* wants that for you." He stood tall and dismissed me again. "So, let's make a deal." He pulled out a pack of cigarettes, shook one out, and lit it. "This will be the one thing we do for her. You get out. Understand?"

"I don't want out completely. I like working at The Vibe."

He laughed and blew smoke my way. "We have the same clients, don't we? Who do you think is more successful, you or me?"

"You're only more successful if you chase off people like me and Nash. If the kids think they have no alternatives then—"

"Give it up. You might 'save' five, ten, twenty in your lifetime? How many others live by the laws of the street?"

To me even one saved was worth it, but how could he understand? "Right. The rules of the street. They've gotten you far, haven't they?"

"You know it. I found my family out there. People who have done things for me my real *familia* didn't and couldn't. And now it's my turn to rule. No more small-time stuff for me, *mi'jita*. Just stay out of my way. Because though I didn't tell Gabriel to run you down, and he's going to pay for touching my sister without my permission, I won't hesitate to take you out myself if you interfere."

As if he couldn't be bothered to talk to me anymore, he swaggered away. Flashing lights on the other side of the wooden fence caught his attention—some kind of code that a customer waited on the other side.

I started to follow him, when my arm was restrained again. I turned around to get whomever it was acquainted with my fist, when my gaze locked with Nash's.

"What, how—?" I stammered. He was the last person in the world I expected to see here.

"I knew you were lying to me," he said.

"Nash." I was confused. "Did you follow me?"

"When you didn't take your car, I figured you were up to something."

"Look, I'm not lying and I'm not up to anything. I'm taking care of the past once and for all."

"You're flirting with disaster. The past is over and you're hanging on to it because you need help."

What in the world was he talking about? He needed to leave before he ruined everything. "Go back to The Vibe, Nash." I pulled my arm free. "I'll explain what I'm doing later."

Carlos was conducting his deal over a cutout in the fence, and I made my way closer to him. I was pretty sure now that he wasn't behind Gabriel's attack, and he'd promised to take care of that problem for me. He even gave his blessing, in his own way, for me to go on and make a success of my life.

I could ride off into the Hollywood sunset and put all this behind me. But not until I took care of this problem. Carlos had to be put away. After he finished his deal, I would approach him. Warn him that the cops knew where he was—for family and blood and to get him to trust me. But then I had to make sure the L.A.P.D.'s narcotics division knew exactly what he was doing—and I would be the inside snitch.

Then I could live the life Nash and Marcela and everyone wanted me to live. Walk away from all of this. Even The Vibe.

I'd made a deal with Burton to be his indentured servant for the next four years—though admittedly, no servant ever had it so good. I'd work for him and get the perks of educational benefits, and money enough to pay for and furnish my Santa Monica apartment. Away from all this.

Behind me I heard lots of commotion. Loud voices inside the house, followed by screams on the porch. I'd turned to see what the problem was when Nash approached me again, begging for me to get out of the yard and away from my brother. But I heard clicks and I saw weapons drawn. I saw the flash of badges, and the echoes of warnings in authoritative voices.

My brother yelled something in Spanish, and all of a sudden shots were fired from the other side of the fence. These were returned by the police on our side. I covered my ears and dove to the ground. The squeal of tires behind the fence signaled an end to the battle.

My brother had also ducked for cover or had been hit, I wasn't sure as I got to my feet. Everything appeared to move in slow motion, and then I froze completely when I turned and saw Nash on the ground covered in blood.

I dropped to my knees instantly and reached for him. I tried to breathe, to speak, to make my heart beat, but everything ceased to move.

All except for my body, which allowed my arms to lift him and check for the wounds. He had two, one in his chest, one in his stomach.

He lifted a hand to my face. "Cops called to say they were on their way. I called—" He winced, then his lids started to close as blood poured out of him and onto my lap.

"Ryan," I gasped. "No, no, Ryan."

His arm fell away from my face, and I shook my head desperately. "No!" I shouted again. My eyes stung with tears and my throat ached from dryness. In disbelief, I kept shaking my head and staring at him, lying there, gone.

"Miss," an officer touched my shoulder, but nothing seemed real. I felt like I was floating out of my body, watching both me and Nash on a patch of dirt in the middle of a neglected backyard. But that couldn't be us. This wasn't part of the plan. This was never part of the plan. The plan I kept refusing to follow.

Then as if suddenly coming back to life, I looked up at the officer, pushed his hand away. I ran to where my brother lay on the ground and picked up the gun he held loosely in his hand. I aimed the gun at his head and stood there with cops behind me warning me to put the gun down.

Carlos had been hit too and he lay there trying to breathe.

"This is your fault!" I shouted. "All your fault."

But it was my fault too. Mostly my fault. I never should have come back here.

Carlos looked weak, like he wouldn't make it if I didn't let the paramedics through. All I had to do was stand there long enough and I wouldn't have to shoot him. He'd be dead anyway.

"Lupe." I heard my name being called behind me. Captain Martinez.

"Not worth it, *mi'ja*. Put the gun down."

I looked over my shoulder. Without Nash my life was over anyway. So what if I went to jail? At least when I got out, Carlos would be gone too.

"Lupe," he said gently and walked up beside me. "You can't do this."

I met his eyes and then gazed at the gun in my hands. "I know. I can't do anything. Nothing that I'm supposed to do."

"This isn't what you're supposed to do."

No it wasn't. My hand shook. I couldn't shoot anyone, even a bastard like Carlos. "I won't kill him."

"Then give it to me."

I glazed at Carlos one more time and shook my head, then passed the gun to Captain Martinez, who took me in his arms. I stood there for a long time, letting him hold me. A cry started somewhere deep inside me. It grew like a great wave, like a tidal wave, picking up speed and energy and power with each second. When it finally came crashing out of me, the scream went on indefinitely, and was so loud that everyone stopped what they were doing to observe what true heartache and grief and loss look like. After the sob drained every ounce of strength from my body, I collapsed. My fight was over.

My world went dark.

Epilogue

Seven Years Later

Checking out the fish tank and kid-sized furniture with cartoon character images on them, I walked into the office of the new pediatrician and held Marcela's six-year-old son's small hand.

"Are you sure he's going to be nice?"

"I'm sure."

"How are you sure?" Juan asked.

"*Mi'jo*, the doctor used to be a friend of mine. We're just going to say hi."

"I'm not going to get a shot?"

"No."

"Are you sure?"

He drove me nuts with all his questions and some days I wanted to stick peanut butter in his mouth to give him something else to occupy his tongue with. "*Callate, ya.*"

"I don't like being quiet. It's boring."

I gave him a warning look.

"If he even comes close to me with a needle, I'm running out."

"You'll be polite," I said, wishing he didn't have his mother's mouth.

He raised an eyebrow, challenging me, and I had to resist the urge to smile. I loved having him once a month when Marcela and George dropped him off at my place and allowed me to babysit while they spent a night alone in a hotel.

The nurse called us in and then kept Juan busy weighing him and talking to him.

"Dr. Preston will be right with you."

I nodded. Juan began to play with all the instruments.

A few minutes later, Will walked in, taking my breath away.

He smiled at Juan, then briefly gazed up at me before opening the chart. He froze and jerked his head back up. "Oh my God."

"Did you really used to know my aunt?" Juan asked.

"Ah, yes," Will said, looking from me to Juan. "Yes, I did."

"Are you going to give me a shot?"

"I don't think so."

"My aunt promised you wouldn't."

"Then I won't."

Juan nodded. "Okay, then you want to listen to my heart?"

Will smiled. "Sure."

Juan climbed onto the table and waited. Will stared at me the entire time he told Juan when and how to breathe.

"Aunt?" he asked, clearly confused.

"He's Marcela's little angel." And that he was. She was so in love with this kid that they were inseparable. George had to drag her to work in the mornings after they dropped Juan off at Grandma and Grandpa's house, and she often took extended lunches to be with him. Though Grandpa would usually shoo her away. After raising three daughters, finally having a boy in the family was like giving Juan Sr. a second chance at parenthood.

Will checked Juan's eyes and nose and throat. "Really? I remember Marcela," he said. "I called her often when you wouldn't see me."

"Not wouldn't. Couldn't." After Nash died, I spent two weeks locked up in his apartment. Me and the tequila bottle and my hallucinations of Nash and happily ever after. I refused to see Marcela or Tracey or anyone. Finally Will came by, knocked the door in, and pulled me out, checking me into a hospital where they pumped IV fluid into me for three days.

When I came out of it, I asked Marcela for a huge loan, which she gave me, and I disappeared. I went away to finish my degree in the desert of Arizona. I went to school full time and finished my degree in three years then jumped into a master's program.

Will smiled at Marcela's child. "You look just fine to me, pal. Would you like to go pick out some stickers while I talk to your aunt?"

Juan looked questioningly at me. He was a good boy and was loved by so many aunts and uncles. We never let him out of our sight unless he was with family, because we all knew what he meant to Marcela. I nodded to let him know he'd be safe, and he smiled. "Okay."

Will instructed the nurse to keep Juan busy and happy, then he closed the door, crossed his arms, and leaned against it. "Well?"

"Heard you graduated and opened a clinic, and I was afraid you wouldn't have any patients being such a new doctor and all, so I brought you one. Marcela doesn't know. She already has a pediatrician, but I figured two is better than one."

He stared at me, almost in disbelief. "Just like that, you think you're going to walk back into my life again?"

"Chill, I'm not walking into your life. Just your office."

He smiled, then shook his head like he couldn't grasp that he was looking at me. "How *are* you?"

"I'm good."

Seconds passed and neither of us said a word. For a moment we went back in time—at least I did. And I relived everything that had gone so tragically wrong. "I'm actually here because I have to say something that I've wanted to say for a long time and . . . well, couldn't."

He nodded, encouraging me to go ahead.

"First, I'm sorry. And second, thank you, Will."

"For what?"

"You know for what."

"That was ages ago."

"I know, but it's bothered me for ages. You were there for me when I needed you most. And I ran away from you twice."

"All in the past." He shrugged.

"I know."

"So now you're back in town?"

"Sort of. I got a job as a lecturer at the University of San Diego in the Latino Studies Department."

"Did you ever finish your thesis?"

"Of course. I mailed it to Professor Reyes, but he told me to turn it in to Arizona State. It was published."

"Great."

I nodded. "Yes."

"So you did it." He pushed away from the door. "Look at you."

"Look at you. A doctor. Wow."

"This was easy for me. But for you, it must have been hard. Going through everything alone."

It had been unbelievably hard. I blamed myself for Nash's death. How could I not? And so many nights I'd wanted to die too. Moisture returned to my eyes. "I always thought Nash made me strong, you know? He was everything. His dreams were mine. His vision of The Vibe was mine. I . . . was so wrapped up . . . you know . . . in him."

Will nodded his understanding and moved just a tiny bit closer. He watched me, pain in his eyes—maybe his own, or maybe from seeing me struggle with this explanation.

I smiled and shrugged. "It was hard to start thinking for myself, without Nash, without Marcela, without anyone."

He reached across and touched the side of my face with his fingertips. "I guess you needed to do it all by yourself."

I nodded. "When I heard you'd opened up the clinic, I couldn't stay away. I owe you so much that—"

"You don't owe me a thing."

"A thank-you and an I'm sorry, yes, I do."

His gaze connected with mine.

"And probably a lot more, but that's the best I can do for now." I moved toward the door but he didn't move aside.

"Lupe, can I ask you something?"

"Sure."

"Did you ever love me?"

Oh, man. I drew a breath. I still loved him when I thought back to the young boy who had been devoted to me enough to give his heart so unconditionally. "Would you really believe me if I said yes?"

He nodded slowly.

"But I made a choice, and it wasn't you." I chose Nash's dream, to become exactly what he'd wanted me to be. I ran. Even though Will had been there to pick up the pieces. To nurse me back to health, to watch me cry over another man. I'd still turned away from him and left.

"You chose to heal the only way you knew how—alone."

We stared at each other in the cold, sterile room.

"Are you going to make that choice again?"

"What do you mean?" I frowned.

"I mean, here we are, both finished with school. Doing what everyone expected us to do. I'm done pleasing others. How about you?"

I had left The Vibe and never returned. I had done exactly what Nash wanted me to do, turning my back on my past and never looking back. And now, I only agreed to take this position in San Diego because it was far enough away from L.A. that I didn't have to drive by any of my old haunts. If it weren't for Marcela and little Juan, I'd never step foot in that county again. "I think . . . I'm ready to please myself, but I'm not sure what I want anymore."

Something like relief crossed his face. "Maybe I can help you."

"How?"

"Since I knew you when, I can remind you about some of the things you wanted. To help others. To make a difference. To—"

"I've been to a shrink since then, and I don't want those things anymore."

"I can't believe that."

"It's true. I only wanted to be this savior because by helping other kids, I was attempting to make my own childhood right. Nash had the same issues. It's a reliving and correcting of the past. But I can't correct any of it, all I can do is move forward. Which is what I'm doing."

"Funny, I thought you did those things because you were kind and didn't want others to go through what you did. You cared and that made you special, not sick."

"I guess we were both wrong."

"Maybe your shrink was wrong, and she and Nash and all

your well-intentioned friends simply buried what was so amazingly you."

"Look, I didn't come here to argue with you, or for a lecture, I—"

"Came to see me because you still think about me."

I stared at him with my mouth open, searching for a response. Yes, I thought of him.

"It's okay, you can say it." He stepped back and leaned on the patient table with a soft smile. "I think of you too."

"Will—"

"I've had a total of three semicommitted relationships since you, and a string of meaningless flings where I acted like a heartless bastard. All to prove . . . I don't know what." He angled his head. "Maybe that I hadn't lost my heart to a tough Latina chick back in college who would never love me like I loved her."

I flinched. "Can you stick the knife in a little deeper? I don't think you've punctured my heart clear to the other side yet."

"Come on." He reached for my hand and surprised me when he pulled me out of the room. He signaled for the nurse to keep Juan busy just one more second.

He pulled me into what seemed to be his office and pointed to a picture of the two of us on his bookcase. One that Tracey had taken at lunch one day. He had other pictures as well—of his family, some with friends at the beach or at parties. But not of other girls. Just me.

Then he pulled the blinds open and pointed outside.

Curious, I moved to the window and peeked through it, noticing right away the sweetest motorcycle I'd seen in a long time. From the corner of my eye I saw him watching, waiting for my reaction. I turned to him with a growing smile. "You crazy fool. You learned to ride after all."

"Still chasing the thrill."

I laughed.

"So . . . ," he said. "Why did you come to see me? Really. To torture me some more? To show me how much more beautiful you've become and how you still plan to lead your life without me?"

"Without you?"

"Or will you finally choose me?" He smiled.

I stared at him. He still wanted me after all these years? "We're not kids anymore."

"No, I'll be thirty next month. And you're twenty-six, twenty-seven? And we both have careers and life is never going to be perfect. Who the hell cares anymore?"

Tears touched my eyes. I couldn't be this lucky. He couldn't still be interested in me. With a watery smile, I said, "If you want a date, all you have to do is ask. You can cut all the drama."

He frowned, then burst out laughing. "Yeah, I want a date."

"Okay." I nodded. "Okay."

"Okay," he said.

Unable to stop myself, I reached for him and pulled him into an embrace. He held me tight against him. His arms felt like home. "Thank you," I whispered, then I pulled away.

"For what?"

I repeated what I said earlier: "You know for what." I opened the door.

"Hey, Lupe," he said.

"Yeah?"

"You're welcome."

I smiled. Juan came to pull at my hand and with one last glance at Will, I left with the only guy since Will and Nash that I'd opened my heart to.

Seeing Will again was the right thing to do. Even back in college I knew he was the right one. This was a mature, equal love that could grow and thrive. Nash had been right to reject me like he had. I had loved him, yes, but I'd been more in love with what he represented: goodness, trust, safety, and love itself.

He saved me and he died for me. Something that would weigh heavy on my soul forever.

I could never fix what happened, but I'd accomplished what Nash wanted me to, which was the very least I could do. *I did it, Nash. I got out.*

Hell, I'm so far removed from where I came from that sometimes it seems like none of it ever happened. I still long to go back sometimes. To my *barrio.* Will was right; no matter what the psychologist said, when I worked at The Vibe I felt alive, and when I helped others by Nash's side, I knew I was doing what I was meant to do in life.

The Vibe was taken over by a corporation. After the piece came out on TV about youth empowerment centers and the tragic death of its charismatic manager, calls poured in to Marcela offering money and buyouts. She picked a buyer after making sure that was okay with me. She said she started that place because of me and now she felt she needed to sell it, also for me.

I agreed. I couldn't even think of returning to The Vibe back then. But I'm through running. On my back, below my left shoulder, I decided to get a new tattoo last month. I chose an Aztec tribal design similar to the one I'd rejected when Tracey and I got our first tattoos together. I love it.

One day, when the money really starts coming in, and I pay everyone back who has helped me, I will go back to my neighborhood.

I'll rescue one person at a time. Somehow, I think Nash will understand . . . he'll know that I've become the best person I could. I've become a real Americana by keeping the best part of my Mexican self and sharing it with others. I've merged my worlds, and that's what becoming Americana is really about.

Thesis Complete

or

The End